TO KILL A SAINT

MICHAEL SWIGER

To my daughter Audrey,
I love you more than you will ever know.

1

Saturday, October 14
Clifton Park, 6 miles west of Cleveland
Lakewood, Ohio
2:04 A.M.

Cuyahoga County Prosecutor, Peter Saul, fumbled for the phone on the nightstand beside his bed.

"Who is this?"

"April Denholm. Sorry to wake you, sir, but we've stumbled onto a pretty gruesome scene a few blocks from your house."

Peter Saul looked over at his sleeping wife, Marilyn, her red hair draped across her face. He spoke in a hushed whisper.

"What'd you find?"

"A women called the station a few hours ago to report a peeping Tom over at St. Andrew's Church. We didn't get here until a few minutes ago."

"Why the delay?"

"She's notorious for false alarms, so the local police didn't take her seriously."

"Go on."

"When the patrolmen arrived, the front door was open, so they walked in and found a corpse stabbed to death on the altar. It's pretty messy."

"Did you call Jimmy Graham?"

"He's already here snapping pictures."

"I'll be right over."

1

"There's more."

"What?"

"The pastor is all scratched up, and he isn't talking."

"I'll be there in ten minutes."

Saul hung up the phone then turned on the lamp on the nightstand. He slung his legs over the side of the bed and fished his feet around for his slippers. He shuffled over to the closet and pulled a pair of jeans over his pajama bottoms. He tugged on an Ohio State sweatshirt, a pair of wingtips, and grabbed his tan overcoat. He walked around the other side of the bed, leaned over, then kissed his wife on the cheek. She opened her eyes.

"What time is it?"

"It's very late."

"Where are you going?"

"They found someone murdered over at St. Andrew's."

"That's just down the street."

"Don't worry, everything is fine."

"Check on Jason before you go."

"I'm sure he's okay."

"Just look in on him."

"I will. Go back to sleep."

He kissed her on the forehead; she closed her eyes. He walked down the hall and noticed light reflecting on the hardwood floor under his stepson's bedroom door.

That kid will be the ruin of me.

He trudged down the arched stairway, across the great room with its vaulted ceiling, and into the attached garage. A few minutes later he parked his black BMW on the street outside St. Andrew's Church. Yellow police tape, strung from tree to tree, fluttered in the breeze and surrounded the white-sided building. The steeple's silhouette reached into the moonlit sky. Lights blazed through the windows. Saul walked up the uneven sidewalk and nodded to the uniformed patrolman standing near the front door.

Lieutenant April Denholm met him inside the vestibule, her bright blue eyes looking surprisingly alert for this time of the night. Wheat-gold ringlets dangled around her oval face and partially covered her milk-white neck and narrow shoulders.

"Give me the scoop," Saul said.

"The deceased is a blonde female approximately 25 years old. No ID. She was stabbed repeatedly, dozens of times actually."

"Does the pastor know her?" Saul asked.

"If he does, he's not saying. You want to talk to him? We've got him in the office."

"Not yet, I want to look around first."

They walked down the center aisle; the sound of their shoes echoed through the cavernous room and mingled with the rapid clicking of a camera shutter. As they approached the sanctuary, a sickish-sweet scent of blood mingled with a tinge of sage permeated the air. The victim came into full view, tied to the altar. She lay with her arms and head hanging off one end of the altar, her blonde hair spilling back toward the floor. The pink blouse was ripped open and saturated with blood. Her bra was hiked up around her throat. Ample breasts were cut to ribbons. Punctures and slashes riddled a taut abdomen. White lace panties hung from her left ankle. Coagulated blood blanketed the stone altar, and puddled on the floor in an irregular, black pool. A gray skirt lay crumpled on the floor.

Jimmy Graham stopped snapping close-ups and turned toward Saul.

"Howdy, Pete. How's this for a little late-night excitement?"

"I could do without it, Jimmy. What's your take?"

"Well, it looks to me like one of the first blows must've hit a lung. You see how this fine mist of blood covers everything like red spray paint?"

"Uh huh."

"If you look close you can see it emanates from this one diagonal wound here to the right of her sternum, right here, between the ribs." He pointed with his finger. "Blood in the lung must've mixed with air and sprayed everywhere."

"You're a regular Sherlock Holmes," Denholm said.

"You got any better explanations?"

"Lose the attitude people," Saul said. "We all have a long night ahead of us. Jimmy, I want pictures of everything."

"I'm on it."

"Any sign of rape?"

"It's hard to tell."

"We'll probably have to wait on the autopsy for that one."

Saul turned toward Lt. Denholm. "What about this peeping Tom?"

"Detective Myles is talking to the neighbor right now."

"Good."

"We found some footprints near that window over there."

"What?" Saul's eyes flew open wide. "What are you talking about?"

"We found footprints."

"Why didn't you say so?"

"We found them since I called you."

Saul's forehead wrinkled. "Let's go have a look."

They walked toward the side door to the right of the sanctuary. A uniformed officer stood in the doorway, his crystal blue eyes blazing; he stepped aside. Around the side of the building, two lights mounted on tripods illuminated a large patch of ground.

"What did you find?" Saul asked.

"We've got a pretty good set of impressions," Lt. Denholm said. "They look fresh but a little indistinct."

"What do you mean, indistinct?"

"Whoever stood here didn't stand still, almost like he was dancing in place."

"Can you lift the impressions?"

"I'll be able to get a couple good casts. There may be more footprints around here. I'm keeping everyone off the grounds until daylight."

"Good, good."

"You think the perp staked out the scene before he went in and took care of his business?" Graham asked.

"Maybe."

"Or a lookout," Denholm said.

"Or maybe a witness." Saul patted her on the back. "Take your time, these prints are critical."

"Now do you want to see the good pastor?"

"Yeah, I guess it's time."

The group walked back around the church. Crickets chirped in the cool air.

"You know," Saul said, "it's been my experience that most homicides that get solved are done so within the first 48 hours."

"Why's that?" Denholm asked.

"Any witnesses who haven't stepped forward within the first couple days probably won't appear at all. And usually new clues don't surface after the initial investigation."

"That makes sense."

"So, we need to take our time and make these first hours count. The Chinese general Sun Tzu says, 'That which depends on me, I can do; that which depends on the enemy cannot be certain.'"

"That's interesting."

"What's this guy's name?"

"Jamison. Pastor Howard Jamison."

They walked back in the side door then crossed the front of the church. A uniformed officer tied a plastic bag over the victim's left hand. On the left-hand side of the sanctuary two uniformed officers stood with their backs against a door; they stepped aside. Saul and Denholm walked in and closed the door behind them. Off in the corner of the small, rectangular office sat a chubby, bloody, middle-aged man with his face buried in his hands. Thin hair lay plastered to his balding scalp by a layer of sweat, like strands of brown seaweed. He wore a light blue shirt with the sleeves rolled up to the elbows and a pair of pleated, tan Dockers.

"Pastor... Jamison," Saul said.

The man looked up. Three deep gouges ran from the center of his high forehead and down his left cheek. Dry, crusted blood ringed the nostrils of his beak-like nose. His puckered eyelids quivered as a pair of vacant gray eyes darted around the room.

"Pastor Jamison." Saul threw a leg over the edge of the desk and bumped a book – a Satanic Bible. "I need you to tell me what happened."

Jamison started to say something, checked himself, then dropped his head.

"What did you do?"

Silence.

"Pastor Jamison, it would really be helpful to tell us what happened here tonight."

No response.

"Do you know who that girl is?"

Jamison looked up; his face went white to the lips.

"Pastor, it's quite late," Saul said, his voice rising at each word. "And there's a dead girl in that room over there, on the altar for Christ's sake, and I want to know how she ended up with a chest full of holes."

Tears welled up in Jamison's eyes, brimmed over his lashes, then ran down his cheeks. His thin lips trembled; he spoke in a breaking voice.

"I'd like to talk to an attorney."

Saul didn't speak for a long moment, then a wolfish smile spread across his face.

"In that case, you have the right to remain silent..."

2

Hunter St. James jolted awake from the sound of a slamming door. He stared at the ornate-plaster ceiling for a moment then looked over at the empty half of his king sized bed.

"I wonder where she—"

He heard bottles clanking in the bathroom sink, followed by a shrill string of obscenities he didn't think Pamela Marsh knew. When the sound of her approaching footsteps reached his ears, he covered his head with the pillow and braced himself.

"I'm late!" she yelled.

He peeked an apprehensive eye at the clock from under his feathery shield.

"No you're not. It's only seven."

"Not that kind of late."

"How many kinds of late are there?

"My period."

"Oh." He raised his eyebrows. "How late?"

"Eight days."

"But you're on the pill."

"Yes, I know, but I'm still late."

"What do you want to do?"

"I want my period."

"I want you to have it too."

"I want it now."

"Did you try clicking your heels together three times?"

"I could scratch your eyes out when you say stupid stuff like that."

"What?"

"This isn't something you can joke away."

Hunter sat up and rubbed the sleep from his eyes. Pamela Marsh stood in front of the alcove of windows beside the bed with her hands on her hips. Her golden blonde hair touched her shoulders in gentle waves. Half-squinted blue-gray eyes bored into the side of his face. The nostrils of her aquiline nose flared in and out with each breath. Her dark red lips were stretched as thin as threads.

"All right," he said. "I'll buy one of those pregnancy tests on the way home from work."

"And then what?"

"Then we'll deal with it."

"I'm not having a baby."

"Why not?"

"I'm telling you, I'm not."

"Go to work. We'll deal with this later."

"Fine."

She turned abruptly, sending her hair out in a defiant fan, then stormed from the room leaving a faint floral scent. He heard her high heels tapping down the hardwood steps then out the door.

"Unbelievable."

He sat up in bed for a few moments, staring at the copy of Jean-Paul Sartre's *No Exit* sitting on the nightstand beside the clock.

"Maybe old Jean-Paul had it right."

He strolled over to the bathroom and looked at the wake of destruction Pamela left behind.

"How come she never throws a tantrum at her parents' house where the maid can clean up the mess?"

8

He picked up the bottles of Tylenol and Vitamin C from the sink and put them back in the medicine cabinet. He closed the mirrored door and looked at his face. Bristles of brown hair stood on end. He leaned forward to get a closer look at the ever-increasing crop of gray hair popping up. He examined the beginning of a blemish on the bridge of his long Roman nose. He splashed some hot water on his face, lathered up, then shaved. When he finished, dribbles of blood appeared along the ridge of his square jaw, including a pretty nice gash beside the mole on the right side of his chin.

A few minutes later he drove his midnight-blue Jaguar down Euclid Avenue, past Severance Hall - the home of the Cleveland Symphony Orchestra and Concertmaster Pamela Marsh. Fifteen minutes later he parked on Superior Avenue across from the Rockefeller Building. He took the elevator to the top floor office suite of Owens, Ryder and Scott. He hurried past the young receptionist with the lush application of rouge; she hung up the phone and called after him.

"Mr. Scott's waiting for you in your office."

"It's Saturday. What's he want?"

"I don't know, but he looked mad."

"Wonderful." He started toward his office door.

"Hunter."

"Yeah."

"You've got something stuck to your face." She pointed to her chin.

"Oh, that." He peeled off the blood-encrusted toilet paper. "I lost a fight with my razor this morning."

"Good luck with Mr. Scott."

"Thanks."

He walked toward his office, reached for the brass doorknob, and took a deep breath. *This can't be good, Old Boy.* He shoved open the door to find Scott reclining with his feet propped up on the desk and his hands laced together behind his head. In spite of his 70 years, he still looked vigorous. His hair was iron gray and thick. A network of lines seamed his face, but his brown eyes were clear and luminous. He spoke with a considerable sense of his own worth.

"Morning, Hunter."

"Good morning, Mr. Scott. What brings you here on a Saturday morning?"

"Sit down, I want to talk to you."

Hunter obeyed, perching himself on the leather couch next to his desk.

"I got a call from Mr. Basik over at Cleveland Metal Products last night, and he told me a curious thing that I couldn't believe. He said you advised him not to sue the *Cleveland Plain Dealer*."

"Well... yes... I..."

"Why in the world would you do that?"

"He had no basis for a claim."

"What's your point?"

"I thought I—"

"Mr. St. James, we are a law firm, and a law firm is a business. The purpose of a business is to make money. You do understand that, don't you?"

"Yes, of course, but I—"

"We make money by charging clients for our services; we charge them a lot of money, and they're happy to pay."

"I thought I owed him the truth."

"Our clients don't want the truth. Our clients want to sue people either to get money for nothing or to piss somebody off. It makes them feel better."

"I'm sorry."

"You're sorry?" Scott spoke like a lecturer coming down to the level of a child. "I'm sorry Mr. Basik took his $20,000 retainer over to Rose and Rose. I'm sorry he'll be paying them $300 an hour instead of us, that's what I'm sorry about. The next time you get a twinge of idealism, recuse yourself from the case before you turn away a paying client." He stood and made his way toward the door. "And keep this in mind, all associates here serve at the pleasure of the partners. Which means you can be dismissed at any time. Is that clear?"

"Crystal, sir."

"Good."

Scott walked out and slammed the door.

"What a day."

Hunter walked around behind his desk and wiped the shoeprints off his leather ink blotter. He plopped down in his chair, feeling like a teenager who had just been grounded. He'd been chewed out before, but this was the first time he ever remembered being bawled out for doing the right thing, for actually being ethical. He shook his head and looked out the window at the panoramic view of the Cleveland skyline and Lake Erie beyond. He thought about how the coveted office came open in the first place when the last boy wonder blew the McPherson case; a week later he was on the street.

He set to work on the pile of depositions stacked neatly on the desk, but his mind drifted back to Jean-Paul Sartre's contention that after death there is nothing. The theory seemed to make sense and affirmed Hunter's atheistic beliefs, but he couldn't seem to wrap his mind around nothingness. It didn't feel right in the pit of his stomach. Then this morning's argument with Pamela popped into his mind. The idea of her being pregnant actually made the hair stand up on the back of his neck; she really didn't seem like the motherly type. He considered driving down to Severance and catching her during a break in rehearsal, but then again, this wasn't the sort of thing best discussed in public.

He grabbed the stack of depositions and jammed them into his briefcase. It was impossible to focus with this pregnancy thing hanging over him. He picked up the phone and pressed the intercom button.

"Jill, has Mr. Prescott come in yet?"

"No, but he called from One to One and said he'd meet you there at noon."

"Cool. Anything else?"

"Actually, I've got a couple of messages for you."

"Fire away."

"Ms. Marsh called while you were meeting with Mr. Scott."

"What did she want?"

"She said to tell you not to come to the concert tonight, that her sister was in town, and afterward they were going to New York. She said she'd call you from there."

"Wonderful. Anything else?"

"One last thing. The Court Administrator called and said something about you being assigned a pro bono client."

"What did I get, a drug case?"

"First degree murder."

"What?!" His voice cracked. "You can't be serious."

"As a heart attack. The arraignment is on Monday."

He shook his head. "Wonderful."

3

One to One Fitness Center
University Circle
Cleveland, Ohio
12:20 P.M.

Faith McGuire leaned forward on the exercise bike and picked up her bottle of water. Sweat ran down her face and dripped on the electronic speedometer. She took a sip, put down the bottle, then chugged away at the pedals with added determination. The stationary bikes faced a glass wall overlooking the gym's weight room. She glanced over at her friend, Monica Frisk, a full-figured woman in pink leotards, pedaling halfheartedly and stretching her neck toward a couple of men working out on the Nautilus bench press machine below.

"Blue Eyes is down there with Gargoyle."

"I see him," Faith said.

"Why don't you go down there and introduce yourself?"

"Yeah, right."

"Why not? It's better than stalking him."

"I'm not stalking him."

"What do you call this?"

"I happen to prefer cycling in the same spot."

"At precisely the same time he works out on..."

"Tuesdays, Thursdays and Saturdays."

"I rest my case."

"All right," Faith said, wiping her brow with the back of her hand, "so maybe I'm interested."

"Go down and meet him."

"He's probably got a perfect girlfriend who's ten thousand times prettier than me."

"Are you nuts? Women kill to look like you. I'd kill to look like you."

"Give me a break."

"Well, if you don't go down there, I will." A playful line showed in Monica's smile. "His friend is starting to grow on me."

"Now I know you're crazy."

"He's sort of cute."

"You call him the Gargoyle."

"Some gargoyles are cute."

"No they're not."

"I'm going down there."

"You do and I'm outta here."

"Do you plan on staying single the rest of your life?"

"I'm not ready to start dating again." Faith thought about her ex-husband, and those raw emotions came flooding back. The infidelity stung her heart, but the abandonment hurt worse. "Besides, as soon as a man sees Jeremy, he's going to run the other way."

"You just have to find the right one."

"And Blue Eyes is the right one?"

"You'll never know from up here."

"Then I guess I'll never know."

12:27 P.M.

Hunter St. James effortlessly pressed the entire stack, some 320 pounds for ten repetitions. He sat up on the end of the bench and took a deep breath.

"I wonder who's going to get the La Salle case," Gordon Prescott said, stepping forward for his turn at the machine. Prescott stood almost 6 feet tall and was muscular but not well defined. His broad face was riddled with pockmarks, and he could not see without his thick glasses. His wide and irregular mouth sat atop a large, square chin. Hunter always thought he looked like a character out of Dante's *Inferno*.

"Not me," Hunter said, rising from the bench. "I'm in the doghouse."

"From what Jill said, you're under the doghouse. What were you thinking?"

"I felt sorry for the old guy. He didn't have a snowball's chance in hell to win."

"But he has deep pockets." Prescott laid down and struggled under the weight. "You must be some kind of freak of nature. Lighten that up a little."

"Even if I wasn't on the hit list, I still couldn't have taken it." Hunter bent over and moved the pin about halfway up the stack. "I've got a pro bono case in Cleveland."

"You? You're a contract lawyer."

"Who are you telling?"

"What are you going to do?"

"Get out of it. So where were you last night?"

"*Templetons* meeting."

"Again? How often do you guys get together?"

"Depends, usually once a week."

"What do you talk about?"

"Stuff."

"What kind of stuff?"

"I can't say."

"You've known me since we were kids, and you can't say."

"You'd lose respect for me if I broke my vow of secrecy."

"I already don't respect you."

"Funny, funny."

"Why don't you talk to them about me?" The two men traded places. Hunter put the pin at the bottom of the stack then pressed out ten reps with little effort.

"I did."

"Well?"

"No can do."

"Why not?"

"Your dad."

The answer struck Hunter like a blow. His father had been arrested for embezzlement and fraud, accused of swindling his elderly clients out of their life savings. He maintained his innocence throughout the trial, but the jury convicted him in less than two hours of deliberation. The judge sentenced him to ten years, but he never served a day; they found him hanging from the air vent in his cell the morning after sentencing. Hunter spent his entire life with the shameful specter of his father's legacy haunting him. He always felt like he had to be twice as good as the next man just to stay even. No matter how well he did at Ohio University or later at Case Western Reserve University School of Law, he couldn't escape the stigma. He discovered that the social stains don't wear off in some circles. Redemption was impossible.

"Are you going to see Pamela perform tonight?" Prescott asked.

"Naw."

"Why not?"

"Her sister's in town and taking her to New York. They're leaving after the concert."

"Shopping?"

"Among other things I'm sure."

"Old money sure is nice."

"You're from old money."

"That's what I said, old money sure is nice."

Prescott laid down and began benching. About halfway through his set, Hunter said, "Pamela thinks she's pregnant."

"What?!" The weights slammed to the deck. "What?!"

"She missed her period."

"You've got to be kidding."

"I wish."

"Good God. I hope snobbery isn't inheritable."

"I'm not in the mood."

"What are you going to do if she is pregnant?"

"Slit my wrists."

4

Monday, October 16
Lakewood, Ohio
7:45 A.M.

Peter Saul sat down at the kitchen table and inhaled the delectable scent of bacon frying on the stove. He opened the morning edition of *The Plain Dealer* to see a picture of himself standing on the courthouse steps; the headline read, "Justice Will Prevail". The article detailed the grisly discovery of the mutilated woman found in the sanctuary of St. Andrew's Church and discussed the upcoming arraignment of Pastor Howard Jamison.

"Did you see this, honey?" he asked his wife, working over the stove.

"What?"

"This." He held up the paper.

"That's a nice picture of you."

Marilyn walked over and placed a steaming plate of scrambled eggs and bacon on the kitchen table in front of him. She draped her arms around his neck and kissed his cheek. "That's my man."

"This case is going to be a media extravaganza."

The sound of footsteps thumping down the stairs caused the couple to swivel their heads toward the living room in time to see Jason Saul emerge. The tall, lanky teenager schlepped into the kitchen with his shoulders slouched forward. He tucked his angular head against his chest so that his spiked black hair drove his body like a prickly hood ornament. Three silver rings pierced each eyebrow and dangled over his pale blue eyes. Black lipstick accentuated his ashen face. His unlaced jackboots clopped across the tile floor. He refused to make eye contact with his stepfather.

"What do you want for breakfast, dear?" Marilyn asked.

"Nada, I'm outie."

"What does that mean?" Saul asked. "I told you about using slang in this house."

"No, mother, I would not like to indulge in the morning eating ritual. I'm now going to my institution of learning." He slammed the door behind him.

"I'm worried about him," Marilyn said. "He hasn't said two sentences to me since Friday."

"The boy is a disgrace."

"What do you think about sending him to see a counselor?"

"A psychiatrist is more like it."

"Do you know anyone in Cleveland?"

"Oh no. The last thing I need is for your embarrassment of a son to be associated with me. Find someone in the Yellow Pages."

"Do you think he'll go?"

"He'll go all right, he'll go, or he'll move out."

"He is just going through a phase."

"I'm telling you, Marilyn, that boy is tap dancing on my last nerve."

Cleveland, Ohio
8:25 A.M.

Hunter St. James parked his car in the lot across the street from the Cleveland Justice Center. He thought back to the only case he tried in Cuyahoga County, shortly after graduating from law school. He couldn't remember his client's name, but he did recall the overpowering stench of sweat and smoke and despair the first time he walked into the attorney visiting room. What a fiasco that case turned out to be.

His client had been charged with one count of drug possession and faced a jail term of six months. But the man had an alibi; he and his girlfriend had made an amateur pornography video, with the time on the tape coinciding with the exact time the crime supposedly occurred. Hunter put the woman on the stand, only to discover she was only 16. Instead of six months for the drug charge, his client ended up receiving five years for statutory rape.

Initially, Hunter thought practicing law in the same building his father did was an ingenious way to stick his thumb in the eyes of all those who smirked over his father's ruination; now it seemed foolhardy.

He grabbed his briefcase and walked inside the front door of the dual-tower facility. Twenty minutes later he found himself sitting in a tiny visiting cube waiting for his newest and soon-to-be-former client. The door opened and in walked a rather overweight man stuffed in a blaze orange jumpsuit. His comb-over barely covered his bald head. Scabs crusted the three welt-like scratches running down his forehead and across his cheek. Dark circles encompassed his eyes, but an odd smile curled up the corners of his thin lips.

"My name is Hunter St. James, and I'll be representing you this morning."

"Howard Jamison, pleased to meet you."

The two men shook hands then sat across the small square table from one another.

"Allow me to explain what's going to happen this morning," Hunter said. "In about a half-hour you and I will be standing in front of a judge for an arraignment hearing. The prosecutor will formally state the charges pending against you, then you will enter your plea. I'm assuming you intend to plead—"

"Not guilty."

"That's what I thought. Now let me give you the real deal. From what I can tell, you're in for a world of hurt, and I'm not the man for the job. I specialize in contract law."

"Contract law? Then why are you assigned to my case?"

"Luck of the draw, or in your case, bad luck of the draw. So after the hearing I'm going to recuse myself from the case. The judge will ask if you wish to dismiss me, and as soon as you assent, he'll appoint another lawyer, hopefully more qualified than me. Sound good to you?"

"I guess so."

"Good. I'll do all of the talking, and this hearing will be less painful than a trip to the dentist."

"I hate the dentist."

"Bad analogy."

"What about bond? Won't they give me bond?"

"Once you enter your plea the judge will set bail. But my guess is he will set it way beyond what you can afford; they always do in high publicity cases. So, you might as well get comfortable, you're not going anywhere for a while."

"Great." He leaned back, his body rigid. "What do you think my chances are?"

"Like I said, I'm a contract lawyer, but I'd say you're hit. As soon as the press plasters your scratched-up face across every newspaper in the country, you'll be pretty much screwed."

"But I didn't do it."

"Save it for your next lawyer. I really don't care whether you did it or not."

"God will see me through th—"

"Whoa there, big fella. Now you're really barking up the wrong tree. I don't believe in God, and to be perfectly honest with you, I don't trust anybody who makes his living off the superstitions of others."

"I'm sorry you feel that way. You'll never find peace, holding onto that kind of belief."

"Peace! You've got to be kidding me." Hunter stood up; the idiocy of the notion jarred him. "I'm not the one facing lethal injection."

"But I'm the one with peace."

"Then you obviously have mental problems."

A knock at the door.

"What is it?!" Hunter shouted.

"They're ready for you upstairs."

"Let's go," Hunter said. "Peace my—"

The deputy led them down a narrow hall with cameras mounted near the ceiling every few feet. They took the elevator to the 7th floor. The doors opened, and an explosion of flash bulbs blinded them. Reporters shouted questions and thrust microphones in their faces. Hunter followed the deputy, blazing a path through the throng.

The courtroom looked surprisingly Spartan, small with only a few rows of seats for spectators. An elderly man in a black robe hunched over a plain-looking bench with a pair of round-lens reading glasses perched on the end of his nose. A man about 6 feet tall stood behind the prosecutor's table wearing a navy blue suit. His salt and pepper hair was combed neatly to the side. Hunter took his place behind the defense table with Jamison standing to his right. The judge banged his gavel.

"Come to order. Is the State prepared to proceed with the arraignment of Mr. Jamison?"

"We are, Your Honor."

"Very well, Mr. Saul, proceed."

"Thank you. It is the contention of the State of Ohio that on Friday, October 13th, the defendant, Mr. Howard Jamison, did kill by stabbing Ms. Lucy Evans. The defendant is hereby charged with one count of Aggravated Murder, a violation of Ohio Revised Code section 2903.01, to wit, no person shall purposely, and with prior calculation and design, cause the death of another. Further, the defendant is charged with one count of Kidnapping, a violation of Revised Code section 2905.01, to wit, no person, by force, threat, or deception, by any means, shall remove another from the place where the other person is found or restrain the liberty of the other person to terrorize or to inflict serious physical harm. Your Honor, further charges may be forthcoming as the investigation continues."

"Mr. Jamison, do you understand the nature of the charges

pending against you?"

"I do, Your Honor," Jamison said in a faint voice.

"How do you plead?"

"Not guilty, Your Honor."

"Very well, your plea of Not Guilty has been heard and accepted. I bind this case over to the Grand Jury. Bond is set at one million dollars. Court is adjourned." He rapped the gavel.

"There's one more thing, Your Honor," Hunter said, holding up his index finger.

"What is it?"

"I'd like to recuse myself from this case. My client is not confident in my ability to defend him."

"Is that true, Mr. Jamison?"

Jamison bowed his head and mumbled something under his breath.

"Mr. Jamison?"

"No, Your Honor, I've changed my mind. I'd like to keep Mr. St. James."

5

Cleveland Justice Center
10:25 A.M.

Peter Saul walked into the 3rd floor conference room with a cup of coffee in his hand. He looked around the long, rectangular table and recognized almost everyone present. April Denholm whispered to Detective Kathy Myles. At the far end of the table, forensic expert Jimmy Graham flipped through a stack of photos then handed one to County Coroner Russell Mansfield. Two uniformed patrolmen rounded out the assembly.

"I see the gang's all here," Saul said as he took his seat. "All right, Lt. Denholm, give us the overview, then we'll go around the room and compare notes."

"The victim is a 24-year-old woman named Lucy Evans. According to Jamison's secretary, the victim had been coming to see Jamison regularly for counseling."

"What kind of counseling?"

"She didn't know."

"Continue."

"The victim is a Lakewood native. That's about all we know about her so far."

"What about Jamison?"

"He's originally from Sanford, North Carolina."

"What's he doing here?"

"The secretary said the denomination rotates their pastors every couple years, said Jamison has only been at St. Andrew's for a few months. According to her, he wasn't really popular with the congregation, said he was some sort of fundamentalist zealot or something. We're still digging."

"Dig. I want everything. Who was first on the scene?"

"That would be us, sir," the tall uniformed patrolman said. "Dalton and West."

"According to the arrest report, you didn't request a search warrant before you entered the church. Why not?"

"We had probable cause," Dalton said, cocking his head and lifting an eyebrow. "The front door was open. The body was in view."

"It's a question that's going to be asked somewhere down the road. You gave the right answer. What did you do next?"

"We searched the place."

"Did you split up?"

"No."

"Good, go on."

"Like I said, the girl was in view, so we checked for a pulse."

"She was dead as a doornail," West chimed in.

"Then we went room by room until we found Jamison balled up in the corner of his office with his hands covered in blood."

"Did he say anything?"

"Nope, so we called for backup. I stayed with Jamison while West went and cordoned off the area with police tape to preserve the integrity of the crime scene."

"Very good. Did you ever leave Jamison alone?"

"Nope. I stayed with him until the Lieutenant arrived and sent me next door to get the facts off the neighbor who called in the complaint."

"Did you interview the neighbor?"

"Nope. Just got her name and address then turned them over to Detective Myles."

Saul looked over at the dark-haired detective with almond-shaped brown eyes and dimples.

"Ms. Myles, if my memory serves me correctly, you were interviewing the neighbor when I arrived on the scene."

"That's correct, Maria D'Ogastino, sir. A crazy old Italian woman."

"Crazy?"

"You know, nuts."

"What did she say?"

"She could barely speak English."

"Just because the woman's an immigrant doesn't make her crazy," Denholm said.

"I know how to do my job."

"You could have fooled me."

"Bite me."

"Eat a bug."

"Ladies, please," Saul said.

"What's 'eat a bug'?" Myles asked under her breath.

"Focus please. What did the old woman say?"

"She said the place is haunted."

"Her house is haunted?"

"No, the church is haunted. She said she hears strange noises over there at odd hours; people coming and going day and night. We've got a file an inch thick of false alarms she reported."

"Obviously, this wasn't a false alarm. What made her call this time?"

"She said she was washing the dishes – her kitchen window faces the church – and she saw someone snooping around the corner of the building, peeking in the window, so she called 911. She heard a scream, looked out the window, and the figure was gone."

"What time did this take place?"

"Around midnight."

"Did she see anyone leaving the scene?"

"No."

"So, you are telling me our only witness so far thinks the place is haunted. She'll be a peach on the witness stand. What about you, Lt. Denholm? Tell me about the footprints."

"We got a good set, sir. Before I made the casts, I set up the camera on the frame and got some excellent shots. The footprints couldn't have been more than a couple hours old by the time I got there. The moulages came out perfect, size 11 tennis shoes of some sort. I made copies and sent them off to BCI for identification."

"Good work. Keep me informed."

"Will do."

"All right, Jimmy, give us the nitty gritty."

Jimmy Graham looked to be about 45 with a wild mop of salt and pepper hair. He stroked his neatly manicured mustache as he began to speak.

"I spent the whole weekend in that church, and we're still not finished. I got pictures of everything. These are the prints of the girl." He passed the stack down to Saul. "As you can see, we counted over 30 entry wounds. Looks like Jamison was awfully pissed off."

"Looks like it."

"There was so much blood, her clothes didn't dry until Saturday night. The altar is still drying. Anyway, we went over the place with tweezers and collected 50-some envelopes of fibers, soil, hair, and we even found a pretty sizeable emerald."

"An emerald?" Saul's forehead wrinkled up. "Are you sure it was an emerald?"

"It could be costume, but it looked real to me. And as far as we can tell, it didn't come from jewelry on the victim; she wasn't wearing any."

"It's probably been on the floor for years," Saul said.

"Probably. Then we divided off the church into grids and went over each section with the evidence vacuum."

"Have you sprayed the place with Luminol?"

"We haven't finished vacuuming yet."

"What's the holdup?"

"You saw the place, Pete, it's huge. Besides, it's a painstaking process to catalog each section. We can't start lifting prints until the vacuuming is complete, or the powder will contaminate the sweepings. We'll be ready for the Luminol tomorrow."

"I don't mean to be indelicate, Jimmy, but we arraigned Mr.

Jamison this morning, which means I have to present something to the Grand Jury soon, very soon."

"I'm working on it."

"How long?"

"Two days, give me two days."

"You have till Wednesday at noon."

"I'll be done."

"Mr. Coroner, when's the autopsy?"

"Today at one."

"Good, good. Are we missing anything?" He looked around the table; everyone shook their heads. "All right people, we've got a peeping Tom who just might be the only material witness to this murder. Find him."

6

Cleveland, Ohio
12:45 P.M.

Hunter St. James sat quietly behind his desk listening to Mr. Summit reiterate the facts of his case for the umpteenth time. He tried to focus, occasionally nodding and smiling, but his mind raced between Howard Jamison and Pamela Marsh. *Jamison must be certifiable to pull a stunt like that in open court, but as far as that goes maybe insanity is something to consider. No. There still must be some way to get out of representing a psychotic, murdering pastor. And what was up with the prosecutor looking so familiar? Then there's Pamela. Her call last night couldn't have been phonier. Either her sister was in the room, or she didn't want to talk about the pregnancy thing. Odd, very odd. How did everything change so fast?* During their first six months together, Pamela seemed to be everything he wanted – a bright, beautiful, cultured woman from a respectable family. And then all of a sudden, her temperament changed. Bitter. Bossy. Controlling. She abused everyone in her path.

"So, what do you think, Mr. St. James?"

"I... uh... I've got everything under control, Mr. Summit. I'm expecting them to make us a settlement offer soon. I'll give you a call as soon as I hear anything."

Hunter stood and offered his hand. The old man shook it then turned to leave as Gordon Prescott walked in.

"The big dogs want everyone in the main conference room. It's time for the La Salle announcement."

"Wonderful." Hunter grabbed a legal pad, then the two men hustled shoulder-to-shoulder down the hall.

"How'd it go this morning?" Prescott asked. "Did you get out of it?"

"No. Jamison wouldn't release me."

"You've got to be kidding me."

"I don't know what went wrong. I had him all talked into it, then at the last minute he flipped on me."

"Maybe he's got a death wish."

"There's easier ways to commit suicide."

"Death by *ineffective assistance of counsel* is a new one."

They entered the expansive room and sat next to one another on the side of the mahogany conference table facing the wall of windows. Three life-size portraits of the founding partners hung on the wall at the head of the table. A dozen men in dark suits milled around and exchanged whispers. The room went silent when the three partners made their grand entrance. Ryder, a scrawny man, toothy, with a pipe-like neck, strolled in, followed by Scott with his perpetual scowl. The two men took their seats on opposite sides at the head of the table. A few moments later Albert Owens arrived. The senior partner was a tall and stately man, scrupulously dressed, with a drawn, thin face and long, curved nose.

"This will only take a minute, gentlemen," Owens said, leaning over and bracing himself on the table. "As you know, our firm has landed the La Salle account. I don't need to belabor how much our new multinational client means to this firm and the entire Cleveland area. If they land the new convention center contract, it will mean millions. And because our French client will need skillful representation to maneuver through the international red tape, the partners and I have decided to give this account to our best and brightest young talent, Mr. Gordon Prescott."

The room burst into hypocritical applause.

"People, please, please." Owens motioned with his hands. "I'm authorizing Mr. Prescott to assemble a team to work with him on this project. I expect a list of names on my desk for final approval by 4 o'clock today. That is all."

The suits started filing out of the room.

"Mr. St. James," Owens said in a condescending tone. "Would you please stay behind for a minute?"

Hunter froze in his tracks. *Well, Old Boy, this can't be good.*

The Key Tower Building
Cleveland, Ohio
12:55 P.M.

Faith McGuire flipped through her worn copy of the *Diagnostic and Statistical Manual of Mental Disorders*, waiting for her newest client to arrive. The book had been her prized possession since her first year of graduate school at Purdue, and she handled it with reverential care, the way a pastor holds a Bible. Her office reflected her approach to therapy - informal and homey. The small room looked more like a living room than an office. A floral-pattern couch lined one wall, with a glass coffee table loaded with books and magazines. She loved her work but began feeling hypocritical after her own marriage fell apart.

A knock at the door.

"Come in."

The door crept open and in stepped a petite, middle-aged woman with unkempt locks of red hair dangling over her shoulders. She smiled, and a small vertical line appeared between her brows that gave her face a charming look of concentrated thought.

"Come in, Mrs. Saul, please sit down."

"Thank you. It smells wonderful in here."

"It's the big scented candle. Cinnamon." Faith pointed at the glass-shelved bookcase where a tiny flame flickered atop a thick fuchsia candle. "I find it very relaxing."

"It's delightful."

"Thanks, now what can I do for you?"

"Actually, I'm here to talk about my son Jason."

30

"What about him?"

"Where to begin? There's so much."

"Well, what made you call me?"

"I'm worried about him. I'm afraid he might hurt himself."

"Has he attempted suicide before?"

"No, but he's been very withdrawn lately."

"How long has he been this way?"

"He's always been a troubled boy, but it got much worse when he entered high school and started running with the Gothic crowd."

"Define Gothic for me."

"You know, the kids dressing in black and dyeing their hair black with all the body piercings. I thought it was just a phase, but now I'm getting worried."

"And you say he was a troubled child?"

"He went from being difficult at age 5 to impossible by 12. In junior high he was repeatedly suspended for hitting the other kids and being disrespectful to teachers. The school social worker suggested he get involved in football, thinking a contact sport would be a good outlet for his aggression, but Jason wouldn't follow the coach's rules and got kicked off the team. He once got in trouble for walking down the street with a key in his hand and scratching all the cars at the curb."

"How is his relationship with his father?"

"His real dad or stepdad?"

"You're divorced?"

"Six months after he was born."

"Tell me about his biological father."

"I met Steve when I was 18, and he was 28. My dad said he was a loser, but he was handsome and fun, and I got pregnant."

"So, you got married?"

"Yep. And turned one mistake into two. Steve drank more than he worked and turned out to be a bum."

"How much contact does Jason have with his biological father?"

"Almost none."

"And your new husband?"

"Peter's a saint. He came along after I hit rock bottom. Steve wasn't making his child support payments, Jason was acting up, then Peter stepped in and made everything work. He's my rock."

"How do Jason and Peter get along?"

"At first like peaches and cream. They played ball and read together and went fishing. Everything went pretty smooth until puberty hit, then Jason started acting out."

"Did Jason ever get in trouble with the law?"

"He's never been prosecuted, if that's what you mean."

"Listen, Mrs. Saul, young people try desperately to define themselves and gain an identity. Adolescence is a trying stage, and teenagers can be egocentric and self-absorbed. This may be nothing more than Jason simply trying to figure out who he is, albeit, in a very annoying manner. And to make matters worse, adolescence usually occurs while the parents struggle through midlife issues."

"Do you think you can help him?"

"That will depend on Jason."

"But you are willing to see him?"

"How about Friday at four?"

12:59 P.M.

Hunter St. James fidgeted at the conference table while the partners waited for the room to clear. When the last man left, Ryder closed the door.

"Mr. St James," Owens said. "It was brought to our attention this morning that you've been assigned a pro bono murder case. Is that correct?"

"Ah... yes."

"And when was it that you were going to notify one of us of your obligation?"

"I wasn't going—"

"You weren't going to?" Owens crossed his arms.

"No, you see, I planned on getting out of it, but things didn't turn out that way."

"Mr. St. James, your performance as of late has not been exactly what we envisioned, especially after the strong recommendation we received from Mr. Marsh, one of our oldest and dearest clients."

"I'm sorry about that, sir. I'll do better."

"Now, I don't expect your obligation in this murder case to interfere with your duties here at Owens, Ryder and Scott."

"No, sir."

"And can we expect that you will conduct your affairs in that case with the utmost discretion?"

"Of course."

"Very good. The last thing this firm needs, now that we've taken on La Salle, is bad publicity. Is that clear, Mr. St. James?"

"Yes sir, Mr. Owens."

"Good. That is all."

7

P eter Saul walked into the morgue, and the overpowering stench of death and antiseptic chemicals assaulted his nostrils. Frigid torrents of air poured down through large, overhead vents. The sound of surgical instruments clattering in a stainless steel sink drew his attention to a pathology assistant working nearby. In the center of the room, Dr. Russell Mansfield adjusted the tiny microphone clipped to the front of his green surgical scrubs. Black eyebrows slanted and hooked down over gleaming blue eyes. A thin line started at his right cheekbone and disappeared at the corner of his mouth. The two men made eye contact.

"Mr. Saul, good of you to stop by. Billy, get Mr. Saul a mask and a pair of gloves."

The assistant complied.

"What have you found so far?" Saul asked.

"Come on over, and I'll show you."

Saul took off his coat and draped it over a surgical stool near the door. He put on the mask, strapped on the latex gloves, then walked over to the autopsy table. Bright lights blazed down on the waxy pale, naked body. It was gutted through a massive Y-shaped incision running from shoulder to shoulder, crossing over the breasts to the sternum and tracing down the length of the abdomen to the pelvis. Saul glanced up at the head where a deep slash ran from ear to ear across the top of the skull, the scalp pulled down over the front of the face.

"The body is that of a well-developed, well-nourished, 24-year-old Caucasian female," Dr. Mansfield read from the chart. "Blonde hair, blue eyes. The body is 62 inches long and weighed 118 pounds."

Saul stepped up to the table and looked inside the gaping carcass. The heart, liver, lungs, and all the intestines had been removed; the spine showed through the thin fascia in the back.

"So far, we've found a few things that might interest you."

"Fire away."

"We found skin tissue underneath the fingernails of her right hand."

"Enough for DNA analysis?"

"Plenty."

"Excellent. I'll bet you dollars to doughnuts that skin will match Howard Jamison."

"We measured and cataloged each wound, 32 to be exact, all from a knife approximately 3.5 centimeters wide and 15 centimeters long to the hilt. And I think you'll find this of interest. We found over a thousand cubic centimeters of bloody pleural effusion in the right thorax; the right lung, near the hilum, showed extensive parenchymal hemorrhage and damage. And the inferior branch of the right pulmonary artery was transected."

"How about that in English one time?"

"Sorry, we've been able to determine the initial wound struck the lung and nicked the heart."

Saul startled as the assistant turned on the power saw and touched it to the skull. Saul watched as the assistant removed a wedge-shaped section of bone. He turned off the saw, set it down on the instrument table, then turned and extracted the brain from the skull, placing it on the electronic scale.

"So she died quickly?"

"You would think so, but actually, no. We found the presence of vasovagal."

"And that means what?"

"It's a transient vascular and neurogenic reaction, evoked by great emotional stress usually associated with extreme panic. The large blood vessels in the abdomen dilate and shut off the blood to the major organs. The slowed heart rate coupled with the rapid fall in blood pressure enabled her to survive a prolonged period."

"So, she was alive the whole time?"

"Precisely. There's one other thing of unusual significance. A rectangular strip of skin 13 centimeters by two centimeters was carved from her right breast."

"Carved?"

"It's gone, and the amount of bleeding indicates the flesh was sliced out while she was still alive."

"She was tortured before she was killed."

"Exactly."

"How much longer until you finish?"

"We'll be at it all day."

"And when will your ruling be final?"

"Thursday."

"Good. We'll go the Grand Jury on Thursday."

"Excuse me, Mr. Saul," the assistant said, stepping forward.

Saul shuffled aside and watched the assistant scoop the stomach and intestines into a plastic bag and then drop the package into the empty cavity. Saul turned to walk away as the assistant laid the slab of ribs on top of the opening.

8

Thursday, October 19
Cleveland Justice Center
9:15 A.M.

Hunter St. James rippled his fingertips on the small metal table in the attorney visiting room, waiting for his stubborn client to arrive, feeling like this entire farce was a monumental waste of time. The man was guilty. Case closed. Hunter inhaled through his nose, and the scent of fresh paint reminded him of the weekend he and Pamela painted his kitchen. She looked so cute in her designer overalls. She seemed so eager to please, but that was before his life hit the skids.

He hated his job. Sure, working at a prestigious firm provided respectability, but pushing paper for money brought no satisfaction. During law school he thought the key to happiness was a fat bank account; after all, success was the best revenge. But money didn't bring happiness. The void in the pit of his soul loomed larger with each passing day. He really didn't know what he wanted out of life, but this wasn't it. He felt like a caged rat - no longer interested in the cheese, just wanting out of the trap.

This wave of desperation dredged up terrible memories of difficult days. He first contemplated suicide on his 16th birthday when the pressure of adolescence grew intolerable. Five years later he almost went through with it upon learning his mother finally succeeded in drinking herself to death. Each time, the fear of nothingness pulled him back from the brink.

Pamela left a voicemail message sometime during the night,

saying she would be home a day early and expected the "examination" to be waiting for her when she arrived. So, on the drive over, he stopped by a drug store and bought a home pregnancy test.

The door popped open and Howard Jamison walked in, wearing a blaze orange smock and matching pants with his hands cuffed in front of his waist.

"Good morning, Mr. Jamison."

"Morning, Mr. St. James."

"Please sit. I wanted to touch base with you on a few things before this case progresses any further. But before I do, let me say that I think you made a disastrous mistake on Monday retaining me as your counsel."

"No, I prayed about it, and I'm certain I did the right thing."

"You'll probably live to regret that decision. Be that as it may, I received a notice that your case is going to the Grand Jury today, and there's no doubt in my mind they will return a true bill of indictment, most likely with a death specification attached."

"Which means?"

"The State will seek the death penalty."

"I figured as much. What happens next?"

"Discovery."

"You'll have to excuse my ignorance, Mr. St. James, this is all new to me. What exactly is discovery?"

"The State will give us access to their files, so we can see precisely what kind of evidence they intend to use against you."

"That's nice of them."

"Then the judge will schedule a pretrial hearing, and at that point the State will offer a plea bargain. And I think the best we can hope for is life without parole."

"I'm not taking a plea bargain. I didn't do anything wrong."

"Mr. Jamison, you were found with the victim's blood all over you. If there was ever an open and shut case, this is it."

"But you haven't even heard my side of the story."

"And I don't want to either." Hunter bent to rub a spot off the toe of his shoe. "It's been my experience that clients' stories tend to evolve as the evidence comes in. So, if I don't let you lie to me now, your lie at the end will probably be a lot more believable."

"I'm not going to lie."

"Save it."

"I may not know exactly what's going on, but I have complete faith that God will use this for His glory and my good."

"You're out of your mind."

"I assure you, I'm not."

"Not that crazy is bad; at some point I'll probably have them do a psych evaluation on you. With any luck you won't be competent to stand trial."

"I'm in my right mind."

"Then they'll gladly strap you and your right mind in the electric chair."

"God will not—"

"I told you, Jamison, I'm an atheist. You might as well be appealing to the Loch Ness Monster for divine intervention as far as I'm concerned."

"Why such hostility toward God?"

"I'm not hostile, I'm simply an educated man. The existence of God is nothing more than a grown-up version of Santa Claus. You can defend the myth if you want to, and I admit it gives people comfort, and it may even be socially useful, but I don't need some psychological crutch to get through life."

"My faith is no crutch. My beliefs are based on fact."

"Evolution is fact."

"Evolution is a farce."

Hunter raised an eyebrow. "You mean to tell me you don't believe in science?"

"I have no problem with science. Science is good. The whole creation versus evolution debate has nothing to do with science. It's biblical Christianity versus the man-made religion of naturalism. The only thing in dispute is the interpretation of the facts."

"What kind of verbal gymnastics are you trying to play?"

"I'm not playing any games. Modern science depends on the

assumption that the universe was made by a rational creator."

"It most certainly does not. You and I are nothing more than the leftovers of some cosmic accidents way back at the beginning of time."

"But you agree the universe had a beginning?"

"Yeah, the Big Bang."

"Call it what you will, but the point is that anything that had a beginning must have been caused by something other than itself. God. Something cannot come from nothing."

"You're full of it."

"There's evidence of design all around you. To put it in legal terms, God left His fingerprints all over the evidence." Jamison adjusted the cuffs on his wrists. "Have you ever read anything by William Paley?"

"No."

"Well, suppose you walk out your front door and trip over a rock. You may ask yourself, 'How did the rock come to be here?' A possible answer would be the thing had lain there forever. Wouldn't you agree?"

"What's your point?"

"Now suppose you stumbled over a watch on the ground, would you conclude it had lain there since the beginning of time?"

"No."

"Of course not. Its parts are put together for an intelligent purpose. It has a spring to give it motion. Its gears are made of brass, so they won't rust. The front cover is glass, so you can see through it. All this is evidence of intelligent design."

"So."

"The watch didn't assemble itself over billions of years of time and chance; the watch had a watchmaker."

Hunter shook his head. "I don't have time for this."

"Hear me out," Jamison said. "Your body is made of trillions of cells, and each cell contains a digitally coded database with more information than all 30 volumes of the *Encyclopedia Britannica* combined."

"And your point is?"

"If a watch implies a watchmaker because of its function and design, then a human cell which is a trillion times more complex than a watch surely must be evidence for an intelligent Creator."

"You do realize the State is trying to kill you?"

"Yes."

"I don't think you do. Now can we get back to your case."

"You're the boss."

"Where was I... ah... yeah, you've probably noticed that your case is generating a great deal of publicity. Whatever you do, make no statements to the press, and don't say anything to the other inmates about your case. Look at everyone as a potential witness against you."

"I won't say anything."

"Good."

Jamison leaned back against his chair and winced.

"What's wrong?"

"I don't know. My back has been really sensitive between my shoulders, almost like a burn."

"Let me see."

Jamison turned around, and Hunter lifted the orange smock. Up near the top of his back, directly over his spine, a blackened-reddish spot the size of a quarter oozed a yellow fluid.

"That looks pretty nasty. How'd that happen?"

"I have no idea."

"How long has it been that way?"

"Since the night I got arrested."

9

Faith McGuire pedaled away on the stationary bike, listening to Elvis Presley sing "That's All Right Mama" in her headphones. She stared out over the nearly empty weight room and saw an elderly Christian man, short, bent, with very weak legs, struggling to push a few small plates on the hack squat machine. His gray-haired wife watched with a concerned expression on her face. The couple reminded Faith of her own grandparents. Her maternal grandfather had suffered through a string of physical setbacks, including a stroke and recent heart surgery. It broke her heart to see him so tired and frail. But she found comfort knowing his distress was only temporal; true life and peace and joy waited in Heaven.

Monica Frisk happily skipped into the cycling area, uncharacteristically late, with a silly grin on her face.

"Where've you been?" Faith asked.

"I've been doing a little spying."

"On who?"

"I waited out in the parking lot until our boys arrived."

"You didn't."

"Blue Eyes drives a Jaguar, and the Gargoyle has a Mercedes 600."

"Are you nuts?"

"Don't tell me you weren't curious."

"Not in the least."

"And get this, I waited for them near the door, and by accident I totally overheard them talking."

"By accident?"

"They're lawyers." Monica squealed and clapped her hands. "Lawyers."

"I don't see why you're getting so excited. They don't even know we exist."

"They will in a minute. We're going down there."

"No, we're not."

"Come on, what are you afraid of?"

"I'm not afraid of anything, I'm just not interested."

"You've babbled about Blue Eyes for two months now."

"I'm not going."

"Fine."

"Fine."

"I'm going."

"Suit yourself, just don't mention my name."

"I won't," Monica said.

"Fine."

"Fine."

"Good."

"I'm going."

"Go." Faith made a shooing motion with her hand.

Monica tugged at the V-neck of her pink spandex top, exposing ample cleavage, then pranced away looking eager for the kill.

Hunter St. James felt the strange sensation that someone was watching him – almost déjà vu – as he and Gordon Prescott walked into the weight room. The gym usually got crowded about this time, but today only an elderly couple with a personal trainer worked on the leg machines. The old guy sort of resembled Hunter's great-uncle who had passed away a couple of months earlier. Uncle Ed had been more like a grandfather than uncle, a decorated World War II veteran and the kindest man Hunter had known. Death didn't seem fair. Why would such a good and honorable man have to face the indignity of death like the rest of the rabble polluting the planet? Hunter stopped in front of the shoulder press machine, sat down, and did a light warm-up set.

"I was going to wait until Friday to tell you," Prescott said.

"Tell me what?"

"I got you on the La Salle team."

"Me?" He let the weights slam. "How'd you manage that?"

"I told the partners I've known you all my life, I trusted you, and knew I could work with you on such a complicated matter."

"And they went for it?"

"I'm persuasive."

"I don't know what to say."

"Don't say anything, just make me look good."

They traded places. Prescott did a set; sweat glistened across his receding hairline.

"So, how's your pastor buddy doing?"

"He's guilty as sin," Hunter said with a snarl of contempt. "He had the nerve to debate evolution with me."

"Sounds like a piece of work."

"You don't know the half of it. The man has one of the oddest collections of disagreeable qualities I've ever seen in one individual."

"When will you see him again?"

"Tomorrow after the indictment comes out."

"Dog breeding should shut him up."

"Excuse me?" Hunter said.

"Man, by working with natural selection alone, has produced an enormous variety of dogs from spaniels to Great Danes in the space of a few hundred years. If you extrapolate those same principles over hundreds of millions of years – voila – evolution produces every living thing on the planet."

"Good one."

"I minored in biology."

"Why would you be interested in biology?"

"I considered pre-med."

"I haven't given up hope on getting out of representing him

yet. There's got to be some string I can pull."

"Screw him. Do the bare minimum and let him fry."

"I'd like to have him declared incompetent."

"The electric chair is more like it."

Hunter sat down, dropped the pin down to the bottom of the stack, then pressed out ten reps with military precision.

"When's Pam coming back?" Prescott asked.

"Tonight."

"This should be really interesting. What happens if she is pregnant?"

"She'll probably have an abortion."

"I still don't understand what you saw in her in the first place. I mean, granted, her dad's a millionaire, and she's got a hot body... on second thought, forget I asked."

Prescott sat down, did his set, then dabbed his forehead with a wet towel. A woman in pink tights sashayed through the door one hip at a time, her blonde hair bouncing over her shoulders with each step. Thin black eyebrows arched over doe-brown eyes. She appeared slightly overweight, but the extra pounds only added to her voluptuousness. Her wide, full lips stretched into a coy smile as she walked right to them.

"Excuse me, but I'm new here. Could you show me how to use this?" She bent over the curl machine, and her breasts nearly bubbled out of her top.

"Why certainly," Prescott said, his eyes bulging.

"I'm Monica Frisk."

"Gordon Prescott. And this is Hunter St. James."

"Nice to meet you." She offered Hunter a limp handshake.

Prescott took the girl aside and demonstrated the preacher curl machine, making sure to flex his biceps in an exaggerated manner. She squeezed his muscle and giggled. Hunter saw exactly where this was going; wild gratuitous sex until Prescott moved on to the next bimbo. Hunter could never bring himself to engage in such behavior. The guilt would take all the fun out of it; it seemed guilt was beat into his psyche by his overly superstitious mother. But what did he care? Prescott and this girl were consenting adults. His mind wandered. Poor Lucy Evans obviously didn't consent to being stabbed to death on the church altar. Defending such a hypocritical monster made his skin crawl. The man must be insane to commit such a heinous crime and still think he did nothing wrong.

Prescott and his new friend returned laughing.

"Little Monica here is stronger than she looks."

"The psych test is my out," Hunter said.

"You're going to take a psych test?"

"Not me; Jamison. The man is delusional. All I need to do is find a psychologist who will say he's crazy."

"Hey, my best friend is a psychologist," Monica said. "She's right up there."

She spun around and pointed toward the second-floor glass enclosure. Faith McGuire was gone.

10

P eter Saul sat at the head of the dining room table, staring at the magnificent plate of roast beef, mashed potatoes and gravy, and baby carrots. He bowed his head and took a big whiff.

"You've outdone yourself, honey."

"Thank you," Marilyn said, serving herself a small sliver of beef.

"Aren't you going to compliment your mother, Jason?"

"Grub's good, Ma."

Saul exhaled audibly and shook his head, looking across the length of the table at the spike-haired, facial-pierced excuse for a human being he called his stepson. This certainly didn't turn out to be the *Ozzie and Harriet* family Saul envisioned when he first met Marilyn. But he comforted himself knowing that in two years the kid would go off to college or the Army or Siberia – it really didn't matter where – just as long as he left.

The metallic clink of silverware on china droned on for several minutes without interruption, until Saul stuffed the final bite of beef into his mouth.

"So, is everything set for the psychologist tomorrow?"

Marilyn glanced over at Saul and said in a confidential whisper, "I haven't mentioned it to him yet."

"Haven't mentioned what to me?" Jason said.

"Your mother made you an appointment with a counselor."

"What counselor? For what?"

"She's a real nice lady, dear, you'll like her."

"No I won't, cause I ain't going."

"Oh, you're going all right," Saul said.

"Screw that."

"Jason, dear, watch your language."

"I don't need a counselor."

"Look at you," Saul said in a condescending tone. "You've got more metal stuck in your face than a pin cushion. You're a disgrace."

"Says who?"

"Says me."

"Like I care."

"You'd better start caring. I'm the one paying the bills around here."

"Piss off."

"I'm not going to sit here and listen to this." Saul slammed his fist on the table so hard the plates bounced. "You'll be at the shrink tomorrow, or you'll be out on the street tomorrow night." He stood up and threw his napkin on his plate.

"Where are you going, honey?"

"Over to St. Andrew's. They're running some forensic tests."

"Have a bloody good time," Jason said in a feigned English accent.

Saul's eyes grew wide. "What's that supposed to mean?"

"Nothing, father."

"You're on thin ice, boy." Saul clenched his jaw. "Thin ice."

University Circle
6:50 P.M.

Hunter St. James read the instructions on the back of the home pregnancy test for the hundredth time while pacing back and forth over the hardwood floor in his living room. The local news blared from the TV in the entertainment center beside the gun cabinet on the far wall, but Hunter didn't hear it. He mouthed the words again and again, until he heard the familiar sound of Pamela's Dodge Viper pull up outside. A few moments later the door swung open, and in walked Pamela, looking exquisite with her blonde hair pulled back in a French twist.

"How was New York?"

"Do you have the test?"

"Right here."

"Good." She slammed the door shut.

"How was New York?"

"Let's get this over with. What do I have to do?"

"Pee in the bottle, and I'll do the rest."

"Where's the bottle?"

"Right here, dear." He opened the box and offered the plastic container. She snatched it from his hand.

"How was New York?"

"I don't want to talk about it. You've made me a nervous wreck."

"What did I do?"

She glared at him through lowered eyebrows and stormed off toward the bathroom. Hunter plopped down on the overstuffed, beige couch and emptied the contents of the box on the glass coffee table. He arranged the tiny eyedropper next to the plastic vial, then picked up the small packet of chemicals and flicked it with his index finger. For some inexplicable reason, something deep inside his heart wanted the test to come out positive. He heard the bathroom door open and footsteps. He hesitated before looking up.

"How come you didn't buy one of those stick kinds with the little plus or minus sign?"

"They're only good with the first morning urine. And this particular kit is the most accurate on the market."

"Here." She thrust the container at him. "Now what?"

"We put two eyedroppers full in this vial, add the chemicals, and shake. If it turns red, you're pregnant."

"Well, do it."

He popped the lid off of the container and inserted the eyedropper. His hands trembled as he squeezed the black rubber bulb; it wouldn't draw the yellow fluid.

"Dammit," he said under his breath.

"What?"

"The eyedropper is defective."

"You're probably doing it wrong. Let me try."

"Suit yourself."

He handed her the instrument. After two failed attempts she looked up with a malignant gleam in her eye.

"Leave it to you to buy a broken test."

"How was I supposed to know?"

"Idiot."

"We might be able to salvage this. All we have to do is pour two eyedroppers full into the vial."

"Are you sure?"

"How hard can it be?"

"Don't screw this up."

He picked up the container and carefully tipped it over the tiny vial. A small yellow drop trickled in. Pamela leaned her face closer to get a better look and bumped his elbow with her shoulder, sending a surge of urine into the vial.

"Now look what you did," she said.

"What I did? What you did."

"Whatever. Just add the chemicals and get this over with."

He ripped open the packet and lifted the vial. He mixed the ingredients, snapped on the top, and shook the amalgamation vigorously.

It turned bright red.

"Oh, no," they said in unison.

7:10 P.M.

Peter Saul parked his black BMW on the street in front of St. Andrew's Church. The streetlights cast a pale glow on the courtyard. He walked up the brick footpath then ducked under the yellow police tape, whistling in the stiff breeze, as the smell of rain blew in off the lake. To the left, two uniformed officers stood on ladders and draped a large green tarp over the windows.

Saul entered through the double doors and looked down the long main aisle. Inside the church all the curtains were drawn shut. He spotted Jimmy Graham huddled over some apparatus at the end of the building near the altar, flanked by a couple of female detectives. One of them, Kathy Myles, spotted him and waved. The rest of the group looked up.

"Come on over, boss," Graham said. "We're just about to start."

"What's with the darkness?"

"When you're dealing with Luminol, the darker the better. The chemicals react with the iron in the blood, causing a glowing effect."

"There's probably enough blood in here to light up the city."

"Probably. But the chemicals pick up even faint trace amounts of blood. You'd be amazed at some of the things this stuff has picked up."

"What do you need us to do?"

"Someone's got to hit the lights when I say, then just stand back and follow me."

Lt. April Denholm jogged over to the light switches near the pastor's office door. Graham poured a can of chemicals into the large green sprayer. He mixed it with a wooden stick, screwed the cap on, then picked up the sprayer by the handle.

"All right, Pete, step right up behind me."

Saul complied.

"Hit the lights."

Complete darkness.

"I'm going to start spraying now."

A faint, yellowish-green mist hissed out of the nozzle and alighted on the floor; a bright-yellow phosphorous puddle appeared.

"As you can see, a tremendous amount of blood was spilled

here at the altar."

Graham continued pumping the sprayer and moving to his right. The large bright-yellow puddle gave way to a splattering of drops, then suddenly the shadowy outline of a footprint materialized.

"Do you see that?" Graham asked, focusing the nozzle over the print. "We might be able to lift that one. It looks like the sole of a boot of some kind."

Soon several footprints appeared with the same tread pattern. They traced the path toward the outside door on the left-hand side of the sanctuary, and a second set of prints came into view, clearly on top and criss-crossing the first.

"What do you make of that?" Saul asked.

"The second set is smooth-soled. So, either the pastor stopped to change shoes, or we've got two suspects."

They followed the second set back to the high-concentration area, returned across the end of the sanctuary, and stopped at the pastor's office door.

"The smooth soles must belong to the pastor," Graham said.

They pushed open the door, stepped inside, and followed the trail to the corner of the office.

"That's where Dalton and West said they found him," Saul said.

"I'm about out of Luminol," Graham said. "Someone flip on the lights."

A couple of moments later the lights came on, and the footprints vanished.

"What happened to the trail?" Kathy Myles asked.

"Completely invisible in the presence of light."

"Remarkable," Saul said.

"Are you all right, sir?" Denholm asked. "You just look a little pale."

"My stomach's a little squeamish. I'm not used to this sort of thing."

The group returned to the altar, and watched Graham mix another batch of the concoction.

"So, tell me, Jimmy, how long after a crime will the Luminol be able to detect traces of blood?"

"Years. The iron molecules in the blood are tiny and easily bind with whatever they touch."

"So, it's conceivable that whoever wore those boots is walking around with physical evidence as a part of his wardrobe?"

"You find the boots, and you'll find a suspect."

"Interesting."

"All right, I'm ready," Graham said, picking up the sprayer. "Hit the lights."

Darkness.

The sprayer hissed and soon the group followed a new trail of footprints from the puddle at the altar toward the outside side door.

"It looks like he was wearing boat shoes. So, now we have three suspects! This must have been the third suspect's escape route too," Graham said.

"Here are two more sets," Denholm said. "They look like police issue."

"Officers Dalton and West were the first on the scene," Graham said. "They checked the victim's pulse."

"Will this stuff work outside?" Saul asked.

"Sure," Graham said, opening the door and being pelted with an autumn downpour. "As long as it doesn't rain."

7:25 P.M.

"What are we going to do?" Hunter said.

"Abort it, of course."

"Shouldn't we wait a couple of days and think this through before making a decision?"

"No."

"Once upon a time we talked about getting married."

"You're out of your mind if you think I'm walking down the aisle in a $10,000 Armani gown with my belly sticking out like some hillbilly."

"I was only th—"

"You've done enough."

Hunter dropped his head into his hands and stared at the vial; he noticed the red liquid crested above a thin line etched into the plastic. An idea struck him like a blow.

"Maybe the test is invalid."

"Wishful thinking. I can feel your little demon seed growing inside me."

"No, for real. We probably added too much urine. We should retest."

Her face seemed to brighten a little. "It couldn't hurt."

"I'll be right back." He kissed her on the cheek. "I'm gonna run down to the drug store and buy a couple more tests. If all three come back positive, then we'll have to deal with this."

Hunter grabbed his leather jacket, hanging on the brass coat rack near the door. He jumped in his car and drove a few blocks to the Rite Aid and scoured the shelves for two more boxes of the identical test. He approached the checkout counter, noticed a teenage girl working the cash register, and suddenly felt embarrassed. He needed something to make this appear legitimate. He picked up a box of chocolate-covered cherries then drifted down the card aisle and found a card that read: *For my Wonderful Wife.*

He paid for the items, jogged out to his car, made a mad dash home - and discovered Pamela's Dodge Viper was gone.

11

Hunter St. James brushed a piece of lint off the sleeve of his charcoal-gray suit coat, while waiting for Howard Jamison to arrive. He felt the nauseating sensation that follows a night without sleep. *Still no word from Pamela. Why would she run off like that before we knew for sure? But then again, it really doesn't matter. Her mind was made up; there would be no baby. Odd for a woman to be completely devoid of maternal instincts. Odd for a woman to be so emotionally detached. Odd for me to remain in such a loveless relationship.*

The door buzzed, and Jamison staggered in. His scanty collection of brown hairs, usually arranged in the cheesy combover, stood up on end like an Indian's headdress. A glassy coating covered his bloodshot eyes, and his mouth dropped open at the corners. Thick-crusted scabs covered the three gouges down his cheek. Overall, Hunter thought he looked like a man who had just been choked.

"Morning, Mr. St. James."

"You look like hell. What's your secret?"

"Young kids beating on the walls and rapping all night." Jamison plopped heavily into the plastic chair, banging his handcuffs on the edge of the table. "Apparently, it's a nightly ritual."

"This won't take long, then you can get back to sleep."

"Sleep is the furthest thing from my mind."

"Your case has been assigned to Judge Boone. A trial date has been set for January 20th."

"Is that good or bad?"

"Beats me. I haven't practiced criminal law in over ten years." Hunter dug his hand into his black leather briefcase and pulled out a manila folder. He slid it across the table to Jamison.

"In there you will find a copy of everything that's happened this week pertaining to your case. As expected, the Grand Jury issued an indictment, charging you with Aggravated Murder with the attached death specification, Kidnapping, and Abuse of a Corpse."

"I saw it on the news last night."

"Also, the State has requested a DNA test."

"Why would they do that?"

"If you read the autopsy, I think it will become clear."

"I don't want to see it."

"Then I'll read it to you." Hunter reached over and snagged the coroner's report. "The body is opened by the usual Y incision extending across the chest and continuing ventrally down to the pubis... yada, yada, yada. Over 1000 cc of bloody pleural effusion present in the right thorax. The right lung near the hilum shows extensive parenchymal hemorrhage... and the inferior branch of the right main pulmonary artery is transected... yada, yada, yada." He flipped the page. "Here we go. Foreign material discovered under the fingernails of the right hand containing blood, skin, and clothing fibers." Hunter tossed the report on the table. "I'd say they're betting your DNA matches the stuff from under the victim's nails. What do you think?"

"Uh huh."

"Is it going to be a match?"

Jamison looked at the floor and ran his hand over the rough scabs on his forehead. "It probably will."

"That's what I thought."

"But I didn't kill her."

"Listen, I'm your attorney, and even I don't believe you. I'm going to be blunt here, it will be a complete victory if I can keep you out of the chair."

"At least try to understand where I'm coming from, or it will be impossible for you to defend me."

"I've got news for you, Howard, it's already impossible to defend you."

"That's my point. If I can't convince you, then you won't be able to convince a jury. But I do have a defense, and it will work. It's a matter of perspective."

"And your perspective is?"

"Do you want me to tell you what happened?"

"No."

"Then I don't know what to say other than I know the Bible is true."

"What's that got to do with your skin under her nails?"

"Everything, once I tell you my side of the story."

"Not yet." Hunter held up his hand, then leaned back in his chair. "I've been giving your creation myth some thought. Have you considered the fact that evolution is happening all around us, even as we speak."

"No, it isn't."

"What about dog breeders?"

"What about them?"

"Using nothing more than natural selection, breeders have produced every variety of dog on the planet in just a few hundred years."

Jamison's brows lowered, deep in thought. "There's a couple of things wrong with your argument. First of all, dog breeders start out with a pre-existing dog already containing a complete genetic code. They add intelligence and arrive at the variability God designed into the species in the first place."

"Intelligence only speeds up the process."

"But the breeding doesn't create new genetic material. It only sorts out the characteristics already present in the DNA."

"It's not dog DNA you should be worrying about."

"You think I'm a fool because I believe God created the world."

"I know you are."

"But you believe everything came from nothing – a scientific impossibility. Now who's the bigger fool?"

"You're really starting to piss me off."

"Were you ever on the debate team, Mr. St. James?"

"Sure. So what?"

"Did you ever have to debate a resolution that you disagreed with?"

"Several times."

"That's what you've got to do here. You're bound by law to defend me, but you despise everything I stand for."

"You've got that right."

"Well, you don't have to believe me. Just walk in my shoes, see what I see, and things won't look so absurd. But it takes a little faith."

"Faith?" Hunter sank back in his chair and shook his head. "I don't believe anything my senses can't detect or is not self-evident to my mind."

"Did they teach you that in law school?"

"No. It's my own little philosophy."

"But your philosophy cannot be detected by your senses, and it certainly isn't self-evident. So, if your premise is true, then your philosophy must be false."

"What?"

"Think about it."

"I don't have time for this." Hunter stood and snatched his briefcase.

"Just give me a chance."

12

The Rockefeller Building
Cleveland, Ohio
3:45 P.M.

Hunter St. James knocked on the polished walnut door, then pushed it open to find Gordon Prescott stretched out with his feet propped up on the desk, flipping through an issue of *Popular Science* magazine. Everything in the office exuded organization and elegance, from the brass globe standing on a glass table in the corner, to the assortment of electronic gadgets lined precisely across the oak and marble credenza behind the high-back leather chair.

"You wanted to see me?"

"Come on in," Prescott said, motioning with his hands. "Have a seat."

Hunter closed the door and walked across the spacious office, his black wingtips sinking into the plush, electric-blue carpet. A sulfurous stench assailed his nose when he got within a few feet of the burgundy-leather couch.

"What's that smell? Is that you?"

"Of course it is. You don't think it smells like that in here all the time?"

"Well, open a window or something, please." Hunter sat down, fanning his hand in front of his nose. "What's with all the gizmos?"

"I was browsing through Waldenbooks at the mall a few months ago, picked up a book on electronic devices, and I've been hooked ever since. Take this for example." He spun around and grabbed some kind of radio apparatus. "This universal remote is so powerful, I can start my car from here."

"Impressive."

"The only problem is whenever I use it to turn on my TV, it shuts off my neighbor's home dialysis machine."

"You're not serious?"

"No." He put the appliance back in its place. "The curiosity is killing me, what's up with Pamela? Is she pregnant?"

"We're pretty sure she is."

"It's a yes or no question."

"The test came back positive, but we may have screwed it up. It's a long story."

"What are you going to do?"

"I don't know. I've been calling her for the past 12 hours and keep getting a busy signal." Hunter ran his fingers through his hair. "My life is a mess."

"Well, if it makes you feel any better, I'm taking that girl from the gym out tonight."

"How's that supposed to make me feel better?"

"Beats me, but it makes me feel pretty good."

"You're a pig."

"Yeah, but I have fun. Are you going to call her psychologist friend?"

"When the time comes."

"Did you see your pastor buddy today?"

"Yep."

"Did you drop the dog breeding thing on him?"

"Yeah, he shot it down."

"Impossible."

"No, he really did. He said breeding simply demonstrates the variability already designed into the genetic code and can't account for how DNA got there in the first place."

"He's a murderer."

"Objection, counselor, ad hominem attack."

"No it isn't."

"Whenever you bash the man and not the argument, the other guy's probably right."

"Screw him." Prescott leaned back and steepled his fingers under his chin. "The main reason I asked you up here is to give you this." He picked up a file from the top of the desk.

"What's this?"

"The first round of contracts from France. I need you to dissect them and draw up articles of incorporation for La Salle."

"When do you need them by?"

"We have to submit them to the Secretary of State at Friday's meeting."

"Will do."

"I'm counting on you, buddy."

"I'll take care of it."

"Good. You working out tomorrow?"

"I may go in early. It depends on Pamela."

The Key Tower Building
Cleveland, Ohio
3:55 P.M.

Faith McGuire traced her finger over the golden frame surrounding the photograph taken just hours after her son Jeremy was born - the most joyful and tortuous day of her life. Physically, she couldn't imagine a more excruciating experience - natural childbirth after 12 hours of intense labor. Emotionally, the euphoria of bringing a new life into the world could not be described by mere mortal words. But then the other shoe dropped. The words of her doctor crushed her. *"Your son is..."*

The phone rang.

She picked up the receiver and cradled it on her shoulder.

"Hello."

"Why'd you run out yesterday?"

"Monica?"

"No, the Easter Bunny. Of course it's me. Why'd you leave? There was an opening for you with Blue Eyes."

"I told you I'm not interested."

"His name is Hunter."

"Hum, nice name."

"And guess who I'm going out with tonight?"

"The Gargoyle?"

"His name is Gordon Prescott the Third, thank you very much."

"No way."

"And he's so sweet and a perfect gentleman, and he's a lawyer."

Faith pulled the receiver away from her ear as Monica squealed with delight. "Congratulations."

"I'll give you all the details tomorrow."

"I'm not sure I want them."

"By the way, Hunter is looking to hire a psychologist to evaluate one of his clients."

"Don't give him my name."

"Too late."

"Monica!"

"Relax, I didn't mention you've been stalking him for the past two months."

"Gee thanks." The electronic organizer on Faith's desk chirped its alarm. "I've got to go. My 4 o'clock will be here any minute."

"I'll call you tomorrow."

"See ya."

"Ba-bye."

Faith hung up the phone, picked up the photograph, and pressed it to her breast. She didn't like questioning God; her strict religious upbringing taught her better than that. But why? A perfect little boy would've meant a perfect little family. But Jeremy wasn't perfect, and Tim ran.

She stood, wandered over to the bookshelf, then struck a long wooden match against the side of the box. She watched the flame flicker and dance for a few moments before lighting the candle. It would take a special man to fit into her crazy life, and he'd certainly need more than dreamy blue eyes.

The door opened and in walked a tall, thin teenage boy

with spiky black hair and several silver rings dangling from his eyebrows.

"Come on in," she said. "You must be Jason Saul."

13

Hunter St. James wandered over to the floor-to-ceiling alcove of windows on the side of his bedroom and looked down on the wild patch of overgrown bushes growing beside his neighbor's house. *Surely that eyesore violates some kind of city ordinance.* He made a mental note to have the bushes ripped out. *What a mess.* Then the weekend replayed through his mind. Two straight days of silence from Pamela pushed him to the breaking point. *Where could she be? She might have fled back to New York as she usually does to escape life for a while. But she's due back at the Orchestra on Monday morning, so she couldn't have gone far.*

He tried to rationalize her disrespectful behavior; after all, she could be with child. But this pregnancy thing only served to demonstrate the disparity in their ideology. It didn't make much sense to remain in a relationship that wasn't leading toward marriage. But with so much time invested, it seemed a waste to throw it away over a bump in the road. Maybe if he showed her a little more affection and a little more patience everything would work itself out.

Contemplating the Jamison situation twisted his mind into knots. Just thinking of the guy made his skin crawl. But regardless of how hard he tried, he couldn't get Jamison's words out of his head: *Something cannot come from nothing - a scientific impossibility.*

"Damn that man."

Evolution was a philosophy, a religion really, that Hunter could wrap his mind around; it explained the senseless violence and suffering surrounding his life, and it conveniently allowed his own immoral deeds. As a lawyer he was trained to examine all the evidence before reaching a conclusion. But did evolution line up with the evidence? Did he even look at the evidence? Where to begin?

Ever since Hunter lay in bed as a small boy he wondered about the nature of the universe and how it came to be. As the cruel reality of life on planet Earth beat against his psyche, he came to believe that matter and space began with "the Big Bang." The laws of science behaved completely by accident. By one chance in a trillion something collided with something else and produced the solar system. By another chance in ten trillion a lightning bolt struck a soup of chemicals, and inorganic matter magically became alive. And then by another trillion accidents, the first single-cell life form evolved into humans, complete with consciousness and intelligence and a conscience.

He never completely accepted naturalism's explanation of how mindless forces gave rise to minds. He considered himself a rationalist, and therefore believed that reason and intelligence provide the only valid basis for truth. But how could he accept his own reasoning when naturalism states that even his mind resulted from some cosmic accident long ago? As Jamison pointed out, it's ridiculous to expect one accident to correctly explain all other accidents. In this light Hunter started to see that naturalistic philosophy rested solely upon circular reasoning. If he appealed to a *rational* argument to support naturalism, he first had to cease being a *rationalist.*

The whole thing gave him a headache, and to make matters worse, Hunter's conscience tormented him perpetually, calling to mind the oath he took to zealously represent his clients to the fullest extent of the law. But Jamison wasn't really a client. Hunter didn't want the case and certainly had no intention of representing the lunatic, especially now that Prescott got him on the La Salle team. Finally, a chance to redeem himself in the eyes of the Partners, a chance to advance his career, a chance to exorcise the demons of the past. The last thing Hunter wanted to do was waste his time fooling around with Jamison.

The doorbell rang.

He glanced at the clock. He wasn't expecting anyone this early; he wasn't expecting anyone at all. The clamorous ringing continued as if someone broke the button.

"I'm coming, I'm coming."

He trudged down the steps, wearing only his pajama bottoms, then swung open the door. Pamela stood with a scowl on her delicate face, holding the morning paper.

"Read this." She slapped the paper against his chest.

"Where've you been?"

"Shut up and read the headline."

Pamela pressed past. Hunter unfolded the paper; the headline read: "Son of Disgraced Lawyer Defending Ritual Killer."

"What's this?"

"Read it, it's all there."

Hunter's eyes raced across the page. The article recounted the familiar tale of countless families bilked out of their life's savings by his father, about the conviction, and his subsequent suicide by hanging in the county jail. Hunter's roiling stomach tightened into a knot.

"Think how this will look for my father," Pamela said.

"Your father? What's this got to do with him?"

"This is socially unacceptable."

"What about me?"

"What about you."

"I get slandered, and you're worried about your family's image."

"People talk."

"Who cares?"

"I care."

"And what's with the disappearing act?"

"Don't question me." She crossed her arms and jutted out her bottom lip. "I'll go wherever I like whenever I damn well please. And stop looking at me like that."

"Like what?"

"Like you're mustering up some courage or something."

Rage boiled up inside him; he fought the urge to slap her smug little face.

"What about the baby?" he asked.

"There is no baby."

"How do you know?"

"Believe me, I know."

"How do you know?"

"Because I'm not a moron, that's how."

"You're pushing me too far Pam-a-la."

"I should have known better than to date below my class."

"I'm warning you."

"You're warning me? That's a good one. You've got no spine. You'll end up just like your father."

"We're through." He pointed to the door. "Get out."

She smirked at him with a look of contempt. "No wonder your mother drank herself to death."

Hunter surged at her, clenching his fists. She stumbled back. He shouted directly in her face.

"I said get out!"

14

Peter Saul balanced an empty ceramic mug on a stack of files and backed through the conference room door. He nodded to the group assembled around the table. Jimmy Graham ran his thumb and forefinger through his mustache as he read an official-looking document. Lt. Denholm chatted to Detective Myles in a confidential whisper. At the far end of the long, rectangular conference table, Coroner Russell Mansfield sat with his hands folded across his lap, starting to nod off. Saul set the folders on the table then headed to the coffee maker. He loved the scent of rich, dark coffee. He poured himself a cup and noticed a box of Dunkin' Donuts. He helped himself to a French twist then took his seat at the head of the table.

"All right boys and girls, I trust you all had a refreshing weekend, but it's time to get back to work."

"Did you see yesterday's headlines, chief?" Graham asked.

"Of course I did, who do you think leaked it?"

"You?"

"Sun Tzu says, 'One defends when his strength is inadequate; he attacks when it is abundant.'"

"Sun who?"

"Sun Tzu, of *The Art of War* fame, a tactical military genius."

"How did you know about St. James' father?" Denholm asked.

"I prosecuted him my first year in the office. One doesn't

forget early victories." He sipped his coffee. "Ms. Denholm, tell me about the footprints by the church window."

"Well, BCI gave us some mixed news. They identified the tread on the impressions we sent, a size 11 Nike."

"Very good."

"Not really. It's the same sole used on all Air Jordans. There's only about a billion of them in circulation."

"What about wear pattern?"

"We may have a little break there. Apparently, our boy drags his left foot a bit when he walks, so the heel on that foot shows considerably more wear than the right."

"Did you find any additional impressions on the church grounds?"

"None. We have no idea from which direction he approached the church or which way he left. We're at a dead end."

"No such thing. Someone had to see something."

"I'll keep digging."

"Jimmy, what about the prints in the luminescence stuff."

"You mean the Luminol?"

Saul nodded and took a bite of the pastry.

"BCI made an immediate match of the smooth-sole prints to Jamison, no surprise there. But no such luck on the bootprints, nor on the boat shoes. They sent the photos over to Quantico to see what the FBI can come up with."

"The Feds will take their good sweet time. Did you have any luck going back on Friday night?"

"No. We sprayed everything with the Luminol, but the rain must've washed away all traces of blood."

An odd grin spread across Saul's face then disappeared. "All right, Doc, your turn."

"I've got good news. Jamison's DNA matches the skin found under the victim's fingernails."

"Excellent."

"I thought you'd be pleased."

"We've got him dead to rights."

"A quick question chief," Graham said, raising his index

finger. "Where'd the ritualistic thing come from? In the papers, I mean?"

"Our esteemed coroner here found a... I'm not going to steal your thunder, Doc, you tell them."

"A section of flesh was carved out from the victim's right breast prior to death. Such action usually accompanies an occult killing."

"What did Jamison do with the skin?" Denholm asked. "We didn't find anything."

"More than likely, he ate it."

Moans filled the room.

"No way," Graham said.

"I'm afraid so. I read about a case where strips of flesh were removed from a victim and eaten by members of the group, including family members of the victim. They believed that eating the flesh of young women enabled them to live longer."

"Sir," Denholm said. "We found something at Jamison's house on Saturday that might support your theory."

"What's that?"

"His personal files on the people he counseled, including Ms. Evans."

"Let me see."

She dug through the box at her feet. "Here it is, but we think pages are missing." She passed the bundle down the table. "We also found about a hundred books on demonology, the occult and satanic secret societies."

Saul flipped through the manila file and stopped on the notes from Evans' first session. The handwriting looked neat and precise - it reminded him of Jefferson's in the Declaration of Independence. Lucy Evans claimed involvement with an organization called the Daughters of Sophia and said the group consulted mediums, attended séances and communicated with spirit guides.

"What's it say, Chief?" Graham asked.

"Not much, just some basics. Who else has read this file?"

"Just us," Denholm said, pointing back and forth between

herself and Myles.

"I'll hang onto this for now, there's no need to make it an official part of discovery until I get the chance to look into it further."

"What do you want us to do next?" Myles asked.

"I want to know everything there is to know about Jamison. His background, where he went to school, names of girlfriends, the brand of toilet paper he uses." He pounded his fist on the table. "And I want it all."

8:15 A.M.

Hunter St. James parked his Jaguar on West Sixth Street in front of Johnny's Downtown restaurant. A brisk autumn breeze blew in from Lake Erie. The hostess met him at the door and escorted him down the stairs to the private wine room. Recessed lights showcased the built-in wine racks on both walls. An oriental rug partially covered the blue marble floor. Gordon Prescott stood, and they shook hands. Something in Prescott's wide-set, dark gray eyes instantly put Hunter on the defensive.

"What's with the breakfast meeting?" Hunter asked as he took his seat.

"I wanted to give you the heads-up before you got into the office."

"Heads-up for what?"

"We've been friends a long time, haven't we?"

"Oh no, this can't be good."

"Look, Hunter, the Partners are in an uproar over yesterday's headlines."

"But it's not my fault."

"It doesn't matter. Bad press is bad press."

"How did you find out?"

"About the story?"

"About the Partners."

"Ryder called me last night."

"He called you at home?"

"Uh huh."

"I didn't think the man could speak. He's never said two words to me."

"They're concerned about the firm's reputation, and they're really concerned about La Salle."

"What should I do?"

"Nothing. Keep your chin up and walk on eggshells. You're under the microscope my friend."

"Wonderful."

"This is a big week for us, the La Salle team that is. Did I tell you I'm off to France?"

"No."

"I'll be teleconferencing from there. How are the articles of incorporation coming?"

"Slow. I've been distracted."

"Hey buddy, I know this has been a rough week for you, but I need you to focus."

"You have no idea."

"If you can't hack it right now, just say so, and I'll get someone else."

"I can do it."

"Be ready Friday."

"I'll be ready."

The waiter came over and filled the white china cups with steaming black coffee. He took their orders and hurried away.

"How'd things go with Pam?"

"We broke up."

"No way."

"I couldn't take it anymore."

"*You* broke up with her?"

"Why does that surprise you?"

"No offense, buddy, but she seemed to be wearing the pants."

"I've never hit a woman, but if she didn't leave when she did, I probably would've knocked her out."

"She was a snake."

"Yeah, but she was my snake."

"You need to find you a skank like Monica."

"That's right, you took her out Friday night."

"And all day Saturday."

"What did you do for two straight days?"

"Do you need to ask?"

"You are truly a pig."

"Oink, oink."

The waiter returned with a tray and placed a marvelous plate of crepes in front of Prescott, and Belgian waffles in front of Hunter. The men ate quietly for a few moments. Hunter looked over at the framed silhouette of a mermaid against a yellow background that dominated the stone wall off to the left, and he thought of Pamela and all the nights they spent together at restaurants like this. He wondered if he'd done the right thing.

"What's up with Jamison?" Prescott asked.

"I think he's playing mind games with me."

"Why? Did he confess?"

"No, it's nothing like that. I wouldn't even let him tell me his side of the story. No, he's got me thinking about things I haven't thought about in years."

"Like what?"

"The existence of God."

"You're still on that?"

"I spent about six hours Friday night on the Internet reading physics and astronomy and that kind of stuff."

"I'll tell you who God is, the Big Bang is God."

"But what caused the Big Bang?"

"If I knew that, I'd be God."

"Something can't come from nothing."

"What if the universe has existed forever?"

"According to my new-found knowledge of thermodynamics, the universe is an isolated system, and the amount of usable energy is decreasing."

"So?"

"That means the universe is running down, so it can't be eternal."

"And your point is?"

"The universe had a beginning, and something had to make it begin, that's all I'm saying."

"You have been giving this a lot of thought."

"I can't get it out of my head."

"Well, here's something for you to think about. If God created the universe, then He must be all-powerful, wouldn't you agree?"

"Sure."

"And if He could do anything, then He could make a star so big that He couldn't move it, couldn't He?"

"I suppose so."

"But if God could not move this star, then there would be at least one thing He couldn't do, right?"

"I guess so."

"Well, if there is even one thing God can't do, then He's not all-powerful, and if He's not all-powerful, then He's not God. Therefore, God cannot exist." Prescott laced his fingers together behind his head. "Think about it."

15

Faith McGuire hurried into work 20 minutes late. The elevator seemed to take its own sweet time creeping up the eleven floors. The doors opened, and Faith darted out past the receptionist toward her office, where she found Monica Frisk sitting in the waiting area eating a bagel.

"You're late," Monica said.

"No kidding." Faith rattled her key into the lock. "What are you doing here?"

"I've got a 9 o'clock on the 3rd floor, so I thought I'd stop in and see my best friend. Is that a crime?"

Faith pushed open the door, peeled off her beige overcoat, then hung it on the brass hook behind the door. Monica followed her in and plopped down on the couch.

"Want a bagel?"

"What kind?"

"I've got cinnamon or onion."

"Cinnamon."

Monica handed it to her. "Why are you so late?"

"Jeremy's been rather sick since Friday night. I spent half the weekend in Rainbow's emergency room."

"What's wrong?"

"Some kind of respiratory infection."

"How is he?"

"Fever's gone. I hated to leave him with Sue."

"She'll take good care of him."

"I know, but I still feel guilty." Faith took a bite. "Where've you been all weekend?"

"With Gordon."

"Gordon the Gargoyle?"

"The same."

"And..."

"What's there to tell, he's a dynamo."

"You didn't."

"I couldn't help it. He was awfully persuasive."

"Sounds like the Gargoyle's got some issues. You're not going to see him again are you?"

"No."

"Good."

"Not until he gets back from France."

"Monica!"

The intercom light flashed on the phone console. Faith picked up the receiver.

"What is it, Stacey? Is my 9 o'clock here?"

"No, but there's a gentleman to see you, a Mr. St. James."

"I don't know any St. James."

Monica's eyes flew wide open. She waved her hands and spit out her bite of bagel. Faith put her hand over the mouthpiece.

"That's Gordon's friend from the gym," Monica said.

"Who?"

"Blue Eyes."

"Oh... oh!" She looked frantically at Monica. "What do I do?"

"See him."

"I can't."

"See him."

Faith took a deep breath and removed her hand from the receiver.

"Send him in, Stacey."

16

9:05 A.M.

Hunter St. James hesitated before knocking on the mahogany door and read the brass nameplate: Faith McGuire, Clinical Psychologist, M.A. For some odd reason he felt nervous. He shrugged away the apprehension and knocked.

"Come in," said the reedy, feminine voice.

He pushed open the door and was struck to the bone in a moment of breathless delight. The petite woman sat behind her desk with the early morning sun glimmering through the window, accentuating the gold and red highlights in the long brown hair cascading down her back. Her skin had a milky, porcelain quality, sprinkled with freckles. Thin sable-colored brows arched over almond-shaped, brown eyes so dark they appeared black. Her little button nose looked adorable. Something in the delicate line of her lips, the bottom at least twice as full as the top, made him want to kiss them. His pulse quickened.

"Sorry to drop by unannounced," he said, glancing at Monica. "Your friend here gave me your name."

"Monica was just leaving, weren't you, Monica?"

"No, I wasn't."

"Monica."

"I guess it wouldn't kill me to be a little early for my appointment."

Monica stood, tossed the empty bagel bag in the trashcan next to Faith's desk, then headed for the door. She stopped to shake his hand.

"Nice to see you again," she said. "Tell Gordon I said hello."

"Will do."

She walked out and closed the door.

"Please, have a seat," Faith said.

"No thanks, I'll only need a moment of your time."

"What can I do for you, Mr...."

"St. James."

"What can I do for you, Mr. St. James?"

"I need a clinical psychologist to evaluate a client facing the death penalty."

"What exactly are you looking for in the evaluation?"

"Competency, first of all. But if he stands trial, then I'm looking for any mitigating psychosis."

"I've got to warn you, I'm not one of those experts who invent disorders to justify criminal behavior."

"I don't want you to."

"And you do realize that anything and everything I write down is for the court and will be entered into the legal process, either good or bad."

"That's all I'm asking."

"All right, I'll do it."

"Here's my card."

He offered his card and leaned his face so close to hers that she could see the extraordinary structure of his ocean-blue eyes with their multitude of colored streaks and flecks. Her heart took off at a gallop. These were the eyes that first caught her attention months earlier from across the gym. *Extraordinary.*

He certainly looked handsome in his herringbone suit and red silk tie. His voice sounded a little higher than she expected, but it was nice. Her palms felt clammy, so she rubbed her hands together. *Maybe he will ask me out. That's stupid. Why would he do that? This is a business call.*

"I would be delighted to evaluate your client," she said.

"Wonderful."

"I don't mean to sound crass, but there is the matter of my fee."

"The State's picking up the tab, it's a pro bono case. Just charge your standard fee, and I'll make sure it gets paid."

"When would you like me to see him?"

"Whenever you can fit him in, but the sooner the better."

"Let's see." She flipped through her leather appointment book. "How about Saturday morning at nine?"

"Perfect."

9:35 A.M.

Hunter felt uneasy about returning to the office in light of Prescott's warning. He just wasn't up for all the smirks and smug little highbrow minions looking down their noses at him, so he decided to run over to the Justice Center and see Jamison. As he negotiated the tail end of rush-hour traffic, his mind drifted back to Faith. She was beautiful, distractingly beautiful. But more than that, a sincere, compassionate quality seemed to radiate from her face; a trait he had never seen in Pamela. In fact, the entire rich girl experiment turned out to be one colossal disaster. The idea of marrying well to remove his social stigma was clearly stupid in hindsight. Now more than ever Hunter believed that if he saved the President of the United States, the headlines would read: "Son of Disgraced Lawyer saves President." But then again, what did he care? Public opinion doesn't bring happiness; neither does making a lot of money. He didn't know the road to contentment, but he aimed to find it.

Faith's face popped back into his mind. *Maybe if there is a God, He brought Faith into my life at this moment for a reason. No. I'm on the rebound. Probably any woman whose knuckles don't drag the ground would be a potential soulmate right about now.* But Faith was captivating, probably the most attractive woman he'd ever seen.

Twenty minutes later she still played on his mind when the

door to the tiny visiting room opened, and Howard Jamison walked in without his customary handcuffs.

"Good morning Mr. St. James, what's the good news?"

"There's no good news."

"Oh. You looked pleased for some reason."

"No, I came to tell you I've arranged for a psychologist to give you a psych exam on Saturday morning."

"I'm perfectly sane."

"That's what we're going to find out."

"You're the boss."

"I'll be in the room the entire time, so if she asks you anything off limits, I'll intervene."

"Whatever you say."

"Now, the judge scheduled your first pretrial hearing for next Thursday, so we need to start thinking about what kind of offer we'll accept."

"I already told you, no deals."

"I know, but you seem not to realize the State of Ohio is trying to kill you."

"I'm well aware, but I've got my convictions."

"Regardless, if we're going to use the insanity defense, we have to declare it at that time."

"You know how I feel about that."

"Well, we'll see what happens Saturday."

"Yes, we will."

A few moments of awkward silence ticked by.

"There is something else I'd like to discuss with you," Hunter said.

"Anything but a plea bargain."

"It's not about your case. It's this whole creation thing. I've got a couple of questions."

"Fire away."

"You believe an all-powerful God created the universe, correct?"

"Absolutely."

"Because the Bible says so?"

"Yes, and because the evidence says so."

"What evidence?"

"Well, the Bible claims that God knows everything, which means He's infinitely intelligent, so the place to find evidence of intelligence is in His creation."

"For instance...."

"When scientists find stone tools together with a bunch of old bones, they conclude intelligence was needed to fashion the tools into a useful configuration. In the same way, no one looks at the Great Wall of China and thinks the thing resulted from an explosion in a brick factory. Obviously, the wall demonstrates intelligence and purpose."

"What's your point?"

"Isaac Asimov, an open atheist, once said, 'In man is a 3-pound brain which, as far as we know, is the most complex and orderly arrangement of matter in the universe.' So, if a simple stone tool and a large brick wall are both evidence of intelligent design, then it would be logical to conclude that the human brain, the most complex arrangement of matter in the universe, is also evidence of intelligent design."

Hunter thought about the argument for a moment; he really couldn't find a basis for objection, so he thought he'd use Prescott's latest ploy.

"You said you believe God is all-powerful, correct?"

"Absolutely. There's no doubt God is omnipotent."

"So, is this all-powerful God capable of creating an object too heavy for Him to lift?"

"That's ridiculous."

"Why?"

"You might as well have asked me if God can clap with one hand. God's omnipotence extends only to things that are logically possible."

"But creating objects and lifting them are perfectly logical tasks."

"Yes, but what you are asking is whether God's infinite power to create is somehow more powerful than His infinite power to lift. The question is non-sensical."

"But can't God do anything?"

"Let me put it this way. Suppose God could do the logically impossible. And say He created an object too heavy for Him to lift. Since He's already performed one logically impossible task – creating the problem object – then what would stop Him from performing a second logically impossible task, namely, lifting the object that He couldn't lift in the first place? After all, is there any greater trick in performing two impossible tasks than one?"

"I see your point."

"Absurd questions like asking whether or not God can create a square circle only sound profound because they're incomprehensible. You will be a lot better off if you avoid the semantics and focus on the plain things."

Hunter nodded his head.

"I've got several books in my personal library that deal with all of these subjects and issues," Jamison said, then coughed behind his hand. "My favorite is a book by Thomas Heinze entitled *How Life Began.* You're welcome to it or any other book I've got for that matter."

"I just might take you up on that."

"Do you need my address?"

"No, it's in the file."

"The key is in the flower box under the window by the door."

"Thanks." Hunter stood to go. "I'll see you Saturday."

"By the way, how are you doing?"

"What do you mean?"

"I read the article in Sunday's paper. That kind of family tragedy is tough to carry around."

"You don't know the half of it."

"Do you want to talk about it?"

"No."

"Well, I understand a little better now."

"Understand what?"

"Why you're so angry with God."

17

Lakewood High School
9:45 A.M.

T
he bell rang, signaling the end of the period. Jason Saul fought his way through the flood of students in the first-floor hallway and made his way to his locker. He worked the combination then jerked the door open. An avalanche of books and papers spilled out onto the floor. Posters of Marilyn Manson and Ozzy Osbourne plastered the inside of the rat's nest of a locker. He grabbed his jean jacket, scooped up the materials from the floor, then slammed the door shut. He checked his Army Surplus watch then hustled down the hall toward the rear exit door.

The bell rang for 3rd period. A dilapidated, tan Chevy pickup skidded to a stop on the damp pavement just outside the door. A rusted flap of metal near the exhaust pipe fluttered in time with the engine's pulse. Jason Saul looked over his shoulder then made a dash for the get-away vehicle. He pulled open the door and dove in. The truck screeched off.

"Anybody see you?" Bruce Richards asked.

"I don't think so."

"Good. Stay down until we're off school property."

Jason examined the profile of his short, muscular friend. His shaved head, almost completely round, seemed to glow it was so white. Multiple loop earrings dangled from his right ear. Thin black eyebrows curved over his pale blue eyes; a pair of mirrored sunglasses perched midway down the bridge of his bulbous nose. Thick black stubble dotted his cheeks and chin. He wore a black leather biker's jacket over a T-shirt torn in ribbons down the front, a pair of faded jeans and a well-worn pair of Nikes. He retrieved a can of Copenhagen from his pocket and tucked a pinch of snuff inside his bottom lip.

"Coast is clear."

"Cool."

Jason popped up and turned up the music. Metallica blared from the speakers as the truck sped east on Madison Avenue.

"Did you score?" Jason asked.

"An eight ball."

"How many seals?"

"One."

"Cool."

The music blasted at ear-splitting level as they turned on West 117th Street. A few minutes later they merged onto the Shoreway, and Jason saw tiny dots of color bobbing out in the surf - sailboats of various sizes beyond the breakwall. They pulled into the main entrance to Edgewater Park. Richards stopped the truck a few yards from the shore. The engine sputtered then backfired.

The smell of fish and rotting driftwood greeted Jason as he climbed out of the truck. He trudged through knee-high grass and heard the rhythmic slapping of the waves against the retaining wall. About 100 yards down the beach a white-haired man in a yellow cardigan worked the strings of a massive, dragon-shaped kite; it swooped down a few feet above the water. Richards caught up to Jason and they walked to the end of the fishing pier, jutting out into the surf.

"Let me see," Jason said.

Richards reached into his front pocket and pulled out a folded rectangle of paper. He carefully unfolded it to reveal a white, almost translucent, powder.

"You got the kit?" Richards asked.

"Right here."

Jason dug his hand into his coat pocket and withdrew a

nylon pouch. He unzipped it and pulled out a square mirror and a short plastic straw. He held out the mirror, and Richards emptied the tiny packet onto it. Jason took out a switchblade, chopped the powder, then formed it into two lines.

"Go ahead, dude," Richards said.

Jason inserted the straw into his right nostril, lowered his head above the dope, and snorted the entire line. His nasal passage burned; his right eye felt like it would explode.

"Good ice."

Richards did the other line. They dropped down on their backs and stared up at the sky, saying nothing. Jason's heart pounded against his chest; he felt a cold sweat break out on his forehead. His stomach tightened; he couldn't wait for the euphoria, the escape, the heightened awareness. He knew it wouldn't be as good as when he first started using, and that frustrated him. He noticed some of the side effects he heard about - the tremors, hyperactivity and irritability - but he didn't care.

"How'd it go at the shrink?" Richards asked.

"I gave her the silent treatment."

"I bet that pissed her off."

"It didn't seem to." He closed his eyes and smiled. "I'll give her this much; she's got a killer rack."

They laughed.

"When are you supposed to see her again?"

"Today."

"No way."

"Why do you think I'm getting high?"

"You know, there's got to be a better way of getting off on this stuff. Tootin' it just ain't gettin' it no more."

"We could try smokin' it."

"Cool. Hey, what's the deal with your old man?"

"Stepdad."

"That blows he threatened to kick you out if you didn't see the shrink."

"Dude's the devil."

"Ever think about killing him?"

"Everyday."

"No, I mean seriously, like actually doin' it?" A thin brown syrup oozed out the corner of Richard's mouth.

"I don't want to talk about it."

"They say once you get the first one out of the way, the next one is easier."

"I said I didn't want to talk about it."

"Whatever you say, Jase."

It was one of those fall days when the sun shines hot and the wind blows cold. Jason leaned over the railing and watched a fisherman on the rocks cast a line into the rolling waves.

"What's that all over your boots?" Richards asked.

"What?" Jason looked down.

"Like red paint or something."

"Nothing."

18

The Key Tower Building
12:25 P.M.

Faith McGuire tapped her unpolished nails on the desk blotter, while scrutinizing the young woman with a long, mild, sheep-like face sitting across the desk from her. Ms. Douglas had been caught stealing money from her company and was in court-ordered counseling. She explained that the money was available, she wanted it, and she took it. The cash supplemented her income, and since she intended to give the money back, didn't see why all the fuss.

Ms. Douglas reminded Faith of her older sister Linda, the next youngest sibling 15 years her senior. With such a large disparity in age, Faith practically grew up an only child; her two older brothers and sister acted as auxiliary parents. Raised in a strict Jehovah's Witness household filled with oppressive dysfunction, Faith moved out when she turned 18, left the religion, and never went back. She believed in God but didn't identify with any particular religion or denomination.

While Ms. Douglas droned on and on, Faith's mind drifted to Hunter. His smiling face danced across her mind. She tried to suppress the image, but he wouldn't go away. Sparkling blue eyes. Disarming smile. He seemed harmless enough. And while establishing a professional relationship with him might not be romantic, at least it constituted a step toward—

"So, what do you think?" Ms. Douglas asked.

"Excuse me?"

"About my husband's obsessions."

"Well, I—"

The door flew open. A police officer barged in.

"You must evacuate the building at once."

The Rockefeller Building
4:37 P.M.

Hunter St. James pecked away at his computer, diligently working on the La Salle case. The tedious work didn't offer much intellectual stimulation, but it felt good to be making progress. He stopped typing for a moment to blow on his fingers. The room was unusually cold. He looked at the desk calendar. Tomorrow was his mother's birthday; she would have been 62. He closed his eyes and saw her frail form laying on the kitchen floor with a shattered bottle of whiskey in her hand. He longed for an explanation to the puzzling problem of suffering. He tried to imagine a world without pain. No headaches. No upset stomachs. No alcoholism. If God exists, then why did He create a world so filled with pain and suffering?

Hunter turned his attention back to the computer screen when someone knocked on the door.

"Enter."

Gordon Prescott walked in carrying a bundle of files under his right arm and a baseball in his left hand.

"Hunter, buddy, I'm about ready to head over to the airport, and I've got a little project for you."

"I'm already up to my eyeballs in these La Salle articles."

"I know, but I've got something a little more pressing. I just came from a meeting with Mr. Owens, and he's ranting over the need for a contingency plan in case the zoning board balks at the La Salle variances. He was spitting out scenarios more deranged than anything Timothy Leary saw after dropping four hits of acid."

"What do you want me to do?"

"Research the case law on Cleveland zoning and be ready to

present what you find at the La Salle meeting in the morning."

"Do I have a choice?"

"I already told Owens you would do it."

"That's what I thought."

"Here's the fax number at the hotel." Prescott handed him a yellow sticky note. "I need you, buddy."

"I'll take care of it."

"That's my boy." He dropped the files on his desk.

"What's with the baseball?"

"A little bribery in case you put up a fight. Here, catch."

Hunter caught the ball and examined it; a blue signature was scrawled over a black scuff mark. "Hey, this is autographed by Jim Thome."

"Damn straight, a home run ball his rookie year. It's already worth a mint."

"Thanks, Gordon." He leaned back in his chair, tossed the ball into the air, then caught it. "Before I forget, I bumped into your new girl."

"Which one?"

"Monica."

"Where'd you see that ditzy bimbo?"

"Over at Ms. McGuire's office."

"Where?"

"Monica's friend from the gym."

"Oh, her, the shrink. It's about time you had your head examined."

"She's a complete babe."

"She must be, because you're grinning like a hormone-enraged schoolboy."

"Can't a man just admire a woman's beauty without sexual overtones?"

"No."

"I know you can't, but I'm talking about the rest of us non-Neanderthals."

"So am I. Look, Hunter, you're the last romantic sap left on the planet."

"Everyone's a little romantic."

"Absolutely not."

Hunter spun his chair around and looked out the window. The orange-red sun hovered over Lake Erie just above the horizon, flanked by salmon-pink clouds; its dazzling rays shimmered off the unbroken surf.

"You're telling me when you see something like that, it doesn't inspire an inkling of sentimentality in your cold heart?"

"When I see a sunset, the only thing that comes to mind is, 'I bet my accountant is boning me every chance he gets.'"

"You're unbelievable."

"Look, I've got to go. Fax me the stuff tonight."

"Will do, as soon as I get back from Jamison's house."

"What?" Prescott's face soured. "Why would you possibly go there?"

"To borrow a book and snoop around."

"You're taking this case way too seriously."

"I'm doing my job."

"I would think with all the bad press, you'd try to get this fiasco over with as soon as possible." Prescott picked imaginary lint off his sleeve. "You should push for a plea bargain."

"He insists on a trial, and unless I can prove he's insane, a trial we will have."

"That's a mistake, buddy, a big mistake."

19

Marilyn Saul took the elevator up to the 3rd floor prosecutor's office. She dreaded facing Peter over yet another problem with Jason. She hated being stuck between her husband and son, always compelled to defend one against the other, but lately Jason's behavior was simply indefensible. And Peter's conduct had become increasingly erratic. He prided himself in his family and told everyone they meant the world to him, but somehow, he was never home for birthdays or family gatherings. She knew he abhorred weakness in himself and in those around him, so she bit her lip and absorbed the mood swings.

She saw Peter's silhouette through the opaque glass on the door to his office. Her stomach tightened as she knocked.

"What?!"

She pushed open the door. "It's me dear."

Peter Saul stood behind his desk, tall, with long thin legs, holding himself erect. His eyes were gray and large and presently fixed in a squint. A pair of half-moon reading glasses slid down his nose when he looked up; he grabbed them with his pale fingers and thrust them into his breast pocket.

"Marilyn, what are... what's he done this time?"

"Ms. McGuire called and said she wanted to talk to us about Jason's sessions. I thought it would be easier if I came down here."

"You should've called first; this isn't a good time."

"I know, but I wanted to make it easy for you."

"How long is this going to take?"

"Not long."

"Let's get it over with. Dial the number."

Marilyn rummaged through her purse and found the scrap of paper she had written the number on. Her fingers trembled as she made the call. After a few rings, a receptionist answered then patched the call through.

"Ms. McGuire, I've got you on speaker," Saul said. "My wife is here with me. What can we do for you?"

"I'd like to have a few words with you concerning Jason's session today. I'm afraid your son has some serious problems."

"I've known that for years," Saul said.

"Are you aware he's on drugs?"

"What?!" The Sauls erupted in unison.

"His behavior is pretty typical."

"What kind of drugs?" Saul asked.

"Judging from the sweating, hypertension, nervousness and paranoia, I would say some sort of amphetamine. Crystal meth is ravaging teenagers these days."

"Oh my God," Marilyn said, raising her hands to her mouth.

"Before I can diagnose his underlying psychosis, I need him clean."

"I'll have him arrested tonight," Saul said. "He can dry out in jail."

"I really wouldn't advise that," Faith said. "It will only further alienate him and could push him closer to the edge. I would recommend you confront him with love."

"I'll confront him all right," Saul said.

"What else is wrong with him?" Marilyn asked.

"Let's get him clean, and then we'll begin sorting out the underlying issues. He's on his way home. I told him I'd be talking to you tonight, but I didn't tell him about what. I'd recommend that you wait until tomorrow to speak to him about this."

"I'll handle it from here," Saul said. "Thank you."

"Allow me to—"

He turned off the phone, picked up a legal pad from his desk, and threw it across the room.

"Your son is ruining our lives!"

"It's not that bad."

"I'm the county prosecutor, Marilyn, it's my job to put guys like him in jail."

He glared at her; she looked away.

"I can't run for Attorney General with glitches like this. It's time Jason go live with his dad."

"No, Peter. Give him one more chance."

The phone rang.

He pushed a button on the console and shouted into the speaker. "I don't want to be disturbed!"

"I'm sorry, Mr. Saul," his secretary said, "but the caller said it was urgent and personal."

"Who is it?"

"A Mr. Templeton."

Lakewood, Ohio
5:45 P.M.

Hunter St. James drove his midnight-blue Jaguar down Lake Avenue. Don's Lighthouse emerged up ahead on the right, triggering a flood of memories. He dated a girl from Lakewood back in high school and spent many weekends along the shore. He smiled, thinking about Kelly Delphino. After roller skating they took late night strolls through the quaint town.

He turned onto West Clifton and compared the house numbers against the digits scribbled on the palm of his hand. He spotted the object of his quest - a white, wooden house with a large sloping roof. He parked his car at the curb then stepped out into the brisk night air. The sky was already darkening with the Cleveland skyline outlined in black against the milky strip of light diminishing over the horizon, the North Star visible opposite the moon. He walked up the uneven path then climbed the three concrete steps to the porch. He ran his hand inside the window box and found the key. *Odd. In a world filled with dead bolts and high-tech security systems, this is a man simply not concerned with protection.*

He rattled the key in the lock, and the door popped open. He groped the wall for the switch and flipped it. A lamp lit up on a small table between two frayed chairs to his right. The place smelled old, a combination of wet wool and warm dust. The avocado-green, threadbare carpet looked as if it had covered the floor for 50 years. A couch draped by a brown and orange afghan lined the wall to the left. An antique console stereo stood underneath a window to the right. No television. The place reminded him of his grandparents' house when he was a kid.

Hunter walked across the room, the floor creaking under each step, and into the dining room. To the left a staircase ascended to the second floor. He made a right, fumbling the wall for a switch. The kitchen looked like an advertisement from a 1950s *LIFE* magazine. The tile floor was yellowed and cracked. The fixtures on the metal sink pre-dated World War II. The rear door resembled the front; in fact, they were identical.

He walked through the kitchen and into a study where a small brass lamp blazed on the desk, casting its faint glow over the room. The desk drawers were open. Papers were strewn all over the floor. Floor-to-ceiling shelves lined the walls, filled with books of every size and description, each work cataloged and placed on a labeled shelf. Hunter fingered through a large commentary of the Bible, impressed by the heft.

He shuffled over to the next section loaded with books on the occult. Several paperbacks on the Ouija board stood next to publications on ESP, the Kabala, clairvoyance and voodoo. Odd reading for a pastor. At the end of the top shelf, all by itself, stood a worn Satanic Bible. He reached for it then withdrew his hand. Goose bumps raced over his body.

He quickly moved to the next shelf and stumbled onto the creation vs. evolution section. He rifled through the books with a sense of urgency and found *How Life Began* by Thomas Heinze. A suffocating sensation swept over him. He needed to get out of the house. He jogged toward the kitchen, but something on the desk caught his eye. A gold frame. He picked it up; the photo showed a youthful-looking Jamison dressed in a tuxedo with a head full of hair, embracing a beautiful blonde proudly displaying a new gold band. Funny, Jamison never mentioned having a wife. Hunter retraced his steps through the kitchen and for the first time noticed the silence. He turned the corner into the dining room.

Wham!

He buckled to the floor from a blow to the head.

A hail of fists and feet rained down upon him. He covered his face and cowered in the fetal position. Something heavy crashed against his skull. He heard the hollow thud then blacked out.

20

Marilyn Saul tormented a fingernail, while watching the steam waft off the chicken and dumplings. She hoped that by making a meal both Peter and Jason loved she could somehow defuse the inevitable blowout. But it appeared her effort was for naught. They were both late.

She looked over at the painting hanging on the wall beside the table, two candles touching at the wick, sharing a single flame. She painted it for Peter and gave it to him on their first anniversary. *How did life get so crazy? And what happened to that sweet little boy who used to climb onto Peter's lap to listen to Pip's adventures from Dickens'* Great Expectations. Those were happy times. For a couple years Marilyn thought she finally had the life she always wanted, then everything unraveled. *Why does God allow life to be so hard?*

She heard the distinct purr of Saul's BMW pull up on the drive. She braced herself. The door swung open and slammed against the wall. Saul stalked in with a malignant glint in his eye. She started to speak then stopped; anything she said would only make things worse.

"Where is he?" Saul demanded.

"He hasn't come home yet."

"His appointment ended two hours ago."

"Maybe he stopped over at a friend's house."

"He could've walked home from Cleveland in that time."

"Have some dinner, dear. He'll be along soon."

Saul stomped past the table without looking at her.

"Where are you going?" she asked.

"To search his room."

"Shouldn't we wait until he gets home?"

She chased and caught him at the base of the stairs in the living room.

"Dear, he deserves a little privacy."

"He deserves to be in jail."

Saul scaled the stairs two at a time. She raced up after him.

"Please don't do this."

She clutched his elbow. He jerked away.

"Not now, Marilyn."

He stormed down the hall and into Jason's room; Marilyn followed at a safe distance, stopping in the doorway. Dirty clothes littered the floor beside the unmade, twin sized bed. An inhospitable smell of cold sweat and hot smoke filled the room. A velvet poster of a red pentagram on a black background adorned the wall over his bed. A computer sat on a desk with a geometric screen saver weaving intricate designs across the monitor.

Marilyn watched as Saul jerked open the top drawer of the nightstand, dumped the contents on the floor, then rifled through the mound of junk.

Nothing.

He attacked the dresser, slung open the top drawer, and uncovered a stack of porno magazines. He smirked then tossed them at Marilyn's feet. He ransacked the next two drawers and found nothing. He yanked open the bottom drawer and discovered a nylon zippered pouch. He opened it, clenched his teeth, then handed it to Marilyn. She looked inside: a mirror with white residue, razor blade, roach clips, a straw and some other paraphernalia she had never seen before.

"That's what your boy does with the money we give him."

Saul stepped in the closet and bent over an army-style footlocker. Marilyn stumbled forward; someone pushed her.

She caught her balance and saw Jason grab Saul by the back of his pants.

Saul spun around and smashed Jason on the side of the head with a book. Jason staggered back, clenching and unclenching his fists.

"What the hell do you call this?" Saul thrust the burgundy-colored book in Jason's face.

Marilyn read the cover: *Hymns for God's Family, St. Andrew's Church.*

"A souvenir."

"Where'd you get it?"

Silence.

"Answer me boy."

"Ask me no questions, I'll tell you no lies."

Saul slapped him in the face with his left hand.

"Don't play with me, boy."

Silence.

Saul struck him again, knocking him to the ground.

Jason sprang up. He reached in the waistband of his pants and snapped open a switchblade.

Marilyn screamed.

He held the blade to Saul's face.

"Don't do anything stupid, boy."

Jason stepped forward.

Saul gave ground.

"The next time you put your hands on me," Jason said, his face twisted with rage, "will cost you your life."

"Put down the knife," Marilyn pleaded.

"Stay out of this."

"Listen to your mother."

"I'm tired of being pushed around." He thrust the knife an inch from Saul's right eye.

"Honey, please put down the knife."

Tears welled up in Jason's eyes and spilled over his lashes.

"It's just tough love," Saul said, holding up his hands.

"I hate you."

"Please look at me, Jason," Marilyn said, her voice a soothing whisper. "We love you. Please, put down the knife."

"Look at your mother."

Jason leered into Saul's eyes then darted his gaze toward his mother. She stretched out a tremulous hand.

Wham!

Saul hit him in the temple with a right hook. Jason fell hard on his right shoulder. Saul kicked the knife out of his hand then booted him in the ribs.

"Stop, Peter, stop!"

Marilyn rushed forward and grabbed Saul's arm.

Jason scrambled to his feet then bolted for the door.

"Don't come back!" Saul shouted after him.

21

Tuesday, October 24
Lakewood, Ohio
7:50 A.M.

Hunter St. James pried open his eyes to the sound of incessant chirping. *What is that noise?* He shifted his eyes to gain his bearing and found himself lying face down on the floor with lint in his mouth. It wasn't his floor. He pressed himself up on his elbows; his head felt like it would explode. Pressure surged behind his eyes and his temples throbbed. Searing pain shot up and down his neck. The chirping continued. *What is that noise?*

The phone.

He rolled onto his side, reached into his front pants pocket, and retrieved his cell phone.

"Hello."

"Hunter, where the hell are you?"

"Gordon?"

"Where the hell are you?"

"It's a long story."

"You didn't fax me the La Salle zoning cases."

"No, I know."

"The meeting starts in ten minutes."

Hunter checked his watch.

"Did you hear me?" Gordon asked.

"I heard you."

"Where are you?"

"Jamison's."

"You idiot."

"I can explain."

"Get to the meeting. You've got seven minutes."

The phone went dead.

Hunter struggled to his feet. Nausea swept over his body. Tiny white dots danced across his field of vision. He squinted and jammed his fists into his eye sockets. The spots disappeared. His mind focused. What was he doing here? The last thing he remembered he was searching the study for... the book. He looked around. It was gone. No time to worry about it now. He spurred his legs into a run toward the front door. The cold air on his face refreshed him. He dashed down the concrete steps then along the path towards his car. It looked different. The tires were flat.

"Wonderful."

He checked his wristwatch: 7:55 a.m. He goosenecked up and down the street, sprinted to the neighbor's house, then banged on the door.

No answer.

He pounded again. The door opened slowly, and a short Italian woman wrapped in a shawl peeped through the small opening.

"What you want?"

"Sorry to bother you, ma'am. But my car has a couple flat tires." He pointed to the crippled Jaguar over his right shoulder. "And I'm already late for work. Could I possibly borrow your car?"

"No." She started to slam the door.

He wedged his foot into the threshold. "I'll pay you."

"How much?"

"A hundred dollars, and I'll give you the keys to my car as collateral."

"No." She shoved the door against his foot.

"Two hundred, and here's my card. I'm a lawyer."

"A lawyer?"

"Yes ma'am."

"Three hundred."

"Deal."

"I get keys."

He reached for his wallet and for a split second feared he'd been robbed, but the cash was still there. *Odd.* She returned, and they exchanged keys and cash.

"Which car?" he asked.

"That one."

She pointed to a tan Dodge Aspen that looked like it was 25 years old. It would have to do. He slid onto the bench seat, and his knees hit the steering wheel. He reached between his legs but couldn't find the lever to adjust the seat. *Screw it; no time to waste.* He fired up the engine, slipped the gear in drive, and punched the accelerator. The engine stalled.

"No way."

He cranked the starter, pumped the pedal, and the engine sputtered to life. He eased on the gas, and the car lurched forward. He followed West Clifton to the intersection, made a left and merged into the morning traffic on Lake Avenue. He adjusted the rearview mirror and saw a plume of blue smoke billowing out the exhaust. Hunter checked his watch: 8:01 a.m. He phoned his secretary but got a busy signal.

The old Aspen sped along Lake Avenue, and by the time it reached Route 2, the speedometer needle flittered over 80. With no place for the Highway Patrol to hide for the next few miles, he pressed the pedal to the floor. The white center dashes looked like dots. The car shimmied; the steering wheel vibrated in his hands. He gunned the engine and passed a semi truck on the right. A red Ford Escort darted out. Horns blared. He swerved, sideswiped the guardrail, lost control, braked, regained command.

His heart thundered against his chest. He took short rapid breaths and pressed the redial button on his cell phone. Still busy. He checked his watch: 8:07 a.m. *What the hell am I doing? No use getting killed, since I'm already late.* He took his foot off the gas and looked in the side mirror to assess the damage. The rear quarter panel was crushed.

"Wonderful."

He ran his fingers through his hair and felt something crusty at the base of his skull. He checked his fingers. Dried blood. He examined his face in the rearview mirror. *No marks, thank God.*

Ten minutes later he dropped the car off with the parking attendant at the garage, trotted into the lobby of the Rockefeller Building, then waited for the elevator. He scrutinized his reflection in the polished brass doors. Black and white stubble spattered his face; his hair, parted in the middle, twirled up like horns. *What a mess.* His gray suit was rumpled, and the red tie looked like a hangman's noose dangling around his neck. *How apropos.* He suddenly felt his legs grow weak under him.

He stepped off the elevator to see his secretary frantically waving her arms.

"Hunter, Mr. Prescott's on the phone. Everyone's looking for you."

"I know."

"You look terrible. Are you all right?"

"I'm on my way."

He jogged down the hall, his black wingtips tapping on the marble floor. The jarring made him queasy. His head pounded. He took a deep breath then opened the main conference room door. A dozen men in dark suits turned to face him. A large-screen teleconference machine sat at the end of the mahogany table with the hazy image of Gordon Prescott squirming in a chair.

"Where've you been?" Owens asked, his lips parted like an angry dog.

"Sorry I'm late. I—"

"Two minutes is late. A half hour is irresponsible."

"I know, but—"

"You couldn't call?"

"I tried."

"You tried? I knew it was a mistake to give you this kind

of responsibility." Owens turned toward the teleconference machine and gave a look that singed Prescott's eyebrows thousands of miles away.

"I can explain," Hunter said.

"No need to do so." Owens held up his hand. "Security is already cleaning out your office. Turn in your keys, sir."

Hunter reached into his pocket.

"I don't have them on me."

"You must think me mad."

"Sir, please, this is all one big misunderstanding."

"The only misunderstanding is that you seem to think you still work here."

"But—"

"You're fired."

"I can explain."

"Get out!"

22

Peter Saul paced the floor in front of his desk, flipping through a stack of "tips" in the Jamison case. Since the story broke the previous week, a flood of calls from concerned citizens inundated his office. The information ranged from the partially helpful to the utterly absurd. But of all the calls, one in particular caught his attention: the one from a neighbor living near St. Andrew's Church who said Jamison often questioned people about a secret society he believed existed in the Cleveland area known as the *Templetons*.

Saul's secretary came in without knocking, carrying a cup of dark coffee and a stack of files. The 42-year-old looked ten years younger since the facelift back in March. Her hair, dyed golden blonde, hung in wisps around her face. She plucked her eyebrows into such high arches that her face wore the perpetual expression of surprise.

"Close the door behind you," he said.

"Yes sir."

She placed the files neatly on the desk and set down the mug. He took her face in his hands and kissed her passionately.

"And good morning to you too, sir."

She wrapped her arms around the small of his back and offered her mouth to him again. They kissed.

"How much longer do we have to wait?" she asked in a whiny voice.

"At least until after next year's election, and I'm safely behind the Attorney General's desk."

"I can't wait that long."

"Sure you can."

"I hate that you go home to her every night."

"It's temporary. Besides, I go to your bed every afternoon." He patted her on the butt. "Now, go send in Denholm and Myles."

She pouted her lower lip; he kissed it.

"Only because you asked nicely."

She walked away with a spring in her step. The affair had been going on for over ten years. She had been married to a county water department worker when it started. Saul managed to break up her marriage, but had no intention of divorcing Marilyn. He loved his wife, but his sexual appetite was a bit more ravenous and twisted than she could handle. So to keep the peace at home he cheated as often as possible, usually during lunch breaks or out-of-town conferences. In his mind the affair was more for Marilyn's benefit than his own. It prevented her from dealing with some of his perverted urges. From Saul's perspective, he cheated on his wife because he loved her. His twisted conscience justified adultery.

A couple of moments later Denholm and Myles came in wearing plain clothes, each carrying a box.

"What's this?" he asked.

"Evidence," Denholm said.

"Good, good." He walked around behind his desk and picked up the coffee mug. "Set them here."

"This is all of the background and statements from the neighbors and church members," Myles said, dropping the box with a thud.

"And this box is the case file on Jamison's wife," Denholm said.

"What wife?"

"The one who came up murdered five years ago in Charleston, West Virginia."

"Are you serious?"

"Totally."

"How'd she die?"

"Stabbed to death."

"You're kidding me."

"Nope. The case was never solved. They sent everything they had."

"Was Jamison a suspect?"

"The primary, but they couldn't nail him down."

"Is the autopsy in there?"

"Everything."

"Excellent."

"What do you think, Chief?" Denholm asked. "Do we have a serial killer on our hands?"

"Maybe. Do we know which cities he's lived in since his wife's murder?"

"No."

"Find out. Cross-check every town against unsolved murders, stabbings in particular."

"That's a tall order, Chief."

"Sun Tzu says, 'Do not demand accomplishments of those who have no talent.' I wouldn't ask if you couldn't deliver."

"We'll do our best," Denholm said.

"This is bigger than I thought." He leaned back and laced his fingers together behind his head. "We may have just stumbled onto another Jack the Ripper."

Cleveland, Ohio
11:20 A.M.

Hunter St. James returned the Dodge Aspen to the old woman and took a browbeating colored with such imaginative bilingual profanity, he was sure she could've been a Rap star. When she finally simmered down, they exchanged insurance information. He called Triple A to tow his car to the nearest garage. Twenty minutes later he climbed out of a cab at the corner of Lower Prospect and Huron Road intending to do what he always did when life grew unbearable – drink himself silly.

He walked along the green-trimmed windows of the Flatiron Building toward the neon sign of a lizard wearing a bow tie. The Winking Lizard had become a second home to Hunter over the past few years. He liked the small-town atmosphere inside the pub - wood paneling lined with sports memorabilia donated by the customers. He also liked the incredible selection of beer, with over 100 varieties available daily.

He sat at a table along the wall opposite the bar under a black and white photo of a Cleveland Indians batter smacking a ball toward the left field bleachers at the old Municipal Stadium. He ordered a plate of barbeque ribs and a beer and thought about the cesspool his life had become. An hour later he switched to vodka, and his depression turned to despondency.

At 40 Hunter found himself completely alone. Both parents dead. Girlfriend gone. His reputation ruined, and his career down the tubes. He tipped back his glass and motioned to the waitress for a refill. Suddenly, the splitting headache returned; it felt like someone had taken a dull knife and hacked a valley through his skull. He bowed his head and rubbed his temples.

Why would God allow so much misery? If God is good, wouldn't He want His people to be happy? And if He is almighty, couldn't He make them content? Hunter fished out an ice cube from the glass, chewed on it, and meditated on the quandary. He concluded that God wasn't good, or He wasn't powerful, or He didn't exist. In any case, life held no meaning, no purpose.

For as long as Hunter could remember, during despondent times like these, an invisible specter dropped by for a visit - his old nemesis Suicide. He thought back to the many lonely nights while driving down the highway, drunk, he heard an audible voice telling him to let go of the wheel. At times he struggled against an invisible hand jerking the wheel into oncoming traffic. *Maybe the time has come to stop fighting.* His father killed himself to avoid shame and humiliation, and Hunter hated him for it. But Hunter didn't have a little boy at home waiting to play catch.

Suicide didn't hurt; it ended pain. Unless, of course, there really is a Hell. No. He pushed that thought away and focused on his medicine cabinet at home. He had enough painkillers in there to drop an elephant. *Why not? Why continue on? Who would care?* But with pills there was no guarantee they would do the job. He needed something quick, painless, instant. His father's gun collection. It would be messy, but what did he care? He didn't have to clean it up. All he had to do was put the barrel of his dad's 16 gauge Savage shotgun in his mouth and pull the trigger. But first he needed another drink or two or three....

23

Faith McGuire sat in the teak-paneled sauna, wrapped in a fluffy white towel, watching beads of sweat form on the side of her calf then run down to the calloused heel of her foot then drip to the floor. She didn't particularly like to sweat, but something in the hot, dry air cleared her mind. Yesterday's meeting with Hunter started her imagination racing. He seemed like a decent enough guy, and more importantly, he sent butterflies fluttering in her stomach. That hadn't happened since junior high. Why shouldn't she take a chance? Things could work out. But the big question mark wrapped around Jeremy; would Hunter accept him? Or at least give him a chance? But then again, the man expressed absolutely no interest, so why even let her mind roam down that road?

The silhouette of a head filled the window. The door opened, and a whoosh of cool air blew across her body.

"I've looked everywhere for you," Monica said.

"You didn't look here."

"Why would I?"

"Close the door. You're letting all the hot air out."

Monica plopped down on the cedar bench in the corner. Her towel slid down a bit; she tugged it back up.

"What was the deal with the police evacuating your building yesterday?" Monica asked.

"Bomb threat."

"No way!"

"False alarm."

"I guess they can't be too careful since September 11th." Monica raked her fingers through her hair; sweat formed on her brow. "You want to go shopping tonight?"

"You need A.A."

"I don't have a drinking problem."

"Not Alcoholics Anonymous... Accessories Anonymous."

"I haven't been shopping in over a month."

"That's a lie."

"Name one time."

"You bought a Kate Spade purse last week."

"That doesn't count."

"Why not?"

"Because I went to the mall specifically to buy it."

"Yeah, that makes sense."

Faith looked down at Monica's perfectly pedicured feet; her red toenails even had decals on them. Once upon a time Faith pampered her own feet, exfoliating often and slathering them in peppermint foot lotion. But that was before Jeremy was born and before Tim left. Now she barely got around to shaving her legs. She suddenly felt self-conscious and covered one foot with the other.

"So, tell me all about your little meeting with Blue Eyes," Monica said with a lilt in her voice.

"He's cute."

"Cute? You practically melted in your chair. I was afraid I'd have to do CPR on you."

"Don't get excited, it's only business."

"When are you going to see him again?"

"I'm evaluating his client on Saturday."

"That's too far away. We need to come up with some reason for you to bump into him."

"You need to get a life."

"I've got a life, thank you." Monica put her arms up on the back support. Her towel slid down, revealing a mass of bruises in the green stage of recovery.

"What happened to you?"

"Nothing." She pulled up the towel.

"Are you all right? That looks bad. The Gargoyle did that to you?"

"It wasn't that bad."

"The man's a psychopath."

"He's kinky. And I'll have you know he called me from Paris last night and said he bought me a present."

"A little something from the Marquis de Sade collection?"

"No. And I shouldn't tell you because you're being mean."

"Tell me what?"

"Do you promise to be nice?"

"Tell me what?"

"Gordon said Blue Eyes just broke up with his girlfriend." Monica clapped her hands in front of Faith's face. "This is the perfect time for a budding new romance."

"Do I look that desperate?"

"Yes."

Faith rolled her eyes.

"At least think up some reason to give him a call."

Westlake, Ohio
12:45 P.M.

Jason Saul's mind jarred awake from the quaking of his bed. He pried open his eyes. The ceiling collapsed above him. He rolled to his right and bashed his head against the wall with a metallic thud. Someone pounded on the window. A muffled voice shouted at him. He looked up again. The ceiling hovered a few feet above him. This wasn't his bed. The wall split open and rolled back. A van. He slept in a van.

"Dude, you look like hell," Bruce Richards said, climbing in carrying a brown paper bag.

"I feel jacked up."

"Your old man did a number on you."

"He's not my old man, and that was only round one."

"You're not going back are you?"

"Hell no."

"Here, Dude, I brought you some breakfast." He offered the brown paper bag.

"Thanks, man. Cool, doughnuts."

"You gonna stay with your real dad?"

"I'd rather cut my throat."

"My mom's gonna want her van back soon."

"I'll think of something."

Jason devoured a jelly roll covered with white frosting and thought about the adventure of the previous night. After fleeing his home, he roamed the streets of Lakewood fuming, trying to simmer down. But the more he thought about it, the more he wanted to go home and stab Saul in the heart. In fact, for about an hour he debated going home and hiding in the bushes beside the garage, on the outside chance Saul had a late-night meeting. He could have been miles away before anyone discovered the body. But therein festered the problem; Jason figured his mom would be the one to find the body, and he couldn't put her through that kind of trauma. So, he got drunk instead.

He polished off a 12 pack before calling Bruce Richards to join the fun. The two drove around drinking and smoking blunts until Richards passed out. Jason drove the van down to the marina at Huntington Beach, parked in the weeds, then blacked out.

"You going to school this afternoon?" Richards asked.

"I ain't never going back. I can make a lot more money selling meth."

"You don't know how to make it."

"Bootsy does. I'll learn from him."

"If you're jumpin' into the dope game, I'm riding with you."

"That's cool. But I've got something else I need you to help me with."

"What's that?"

Jason looked at Richards then dug into his shirt pocket for a pack of Kools. He tapped the pack into the palm of his hand, extracted a cigarette, then lit up behind a cupped hand. He took a deep drag, held his breath, then expelled the smoke along with his words.

"Kill my stepdad."

24

University Circle
2:07 P.M.

Hunter St. James' hand trembled as he took the landline phone off the hook and placed it on the nightstand beside his bed. He felt oddly calm, almost relieved now that his mind was made up. *Why live in constant pain? Staying alive is simply not rational when faced with such hopelessness.*

He walked over to the dresser, slid the cardboard box of office personal effects out of the way, then fumbled with the lid on his antique jewelry box. He knew the key had to be in there somewhere. His fingers rummaged around the various compartments until they grasped his high school class ring with the aquamarine stone. He smiled. His mother paid over $200 for a ring he wore twice. Sophomore year, Colleen sported it on her index finger wrapped in argyle yarn until she caught him fooling around with Tracy. Senior year, Erin hung it from her necklace until she busted him with Diana. One broken heart after another seemed to be the story of his life.

He dropped the ring and picked up the Hamilton gold watch that once belonged to his grandfather and then his father. He remembered the night his mother gave it to him over Christmas break from freshman year at Ohio University. Some loudmouth at the campus bar started in about his father bilking people. They exchanged words then fists. Hunter ended up with a black eye, split lip, and a broken imitation-Gucci watch. His mom gave him the Hamilton to ease the pain.

He took off his Seiko and strapped on the Hamilton.

"Now where's that key?"

He lifted the tiny tray and searched the lower compartment. His eyes fell upon his Phi Kappa Tau fraternity pin. He thought back to the night it was affixed to his left lapel and the drinking extravaganza that ensued. When he woke up the next morning, after a night of violent retching, he found himself naked on the floor of his room, his body covered in signatures, drawings and homemade tattoos. Wild times indeed.

He dug around the bottom of the box and finally found the little brass key to his father's gun cabinet. Five years had passed since he last opened the case to clean the weapons. He clenched the key in his fist, walked out the door, then down the steps like a man on a mission.

The gun cabinet stood in the corner of the living room, a large oak structure with glass doors and brass fittings, displaying an assortment of rifles and shotguns. The key slid into the lock; the tumblers released with a bang. He stood for a few moments deliberating over a Marlin .22 semi-automatic rifle with scope. *No, a small caliber may not do the job. How about the Remington 20 gauge pump with recoil pad? The poly-choke muzzle may not fit into my mouth. What about the 16 gauge Savage single shot with the short barrel? Perfect.*

He grabbed the gun by the stock then pressed the lever, opening the barrel. He yanked open the drawer of the cabinet and tried several shells before the right one slid into the chamber. He snapped the gun closed, lifted the stock to his shoulder and looked down the barrel. He remembered the first time his great-uncle Ed took him out to the family farm to shoot it; he couldn't believe how hard it kicked. Before that day his uncle didn't spend much time with him, but after bonding in the woods the two were inseparable. Then Uncle Ed died. Somehow it seemed appropriate that the instrument that fused them in life would unite them in death. *But do people who commit suicide go to Heaven? I'll soon find out.*

He flipped the gun around and put the barrel into his mouth;

the gun oil tasted sour and puckered his lips around the cold steel. He braced the butt of the gun against the back of his leather recliner, so the recoil wouldn't affect the accuracy of the blast. He reached for the trigger; his heart thundered in his ears; his hand moved as if on autopilot.

Cleveland Justice Center
2:15 P.M.

Peter Saul preferred holding meetings in his office; it allowed him to remain in complete control. April Denholm fidgeted on the couch next to Kathy Myles. Special Agent Hartlieb from the FBI Behavioral Science Unit paced over to the wall next to the window and examined the enormous map of Cuyahoga County. Saul pressed the intercom button on the phone.

"Have you reached Mr. St. James yet?" Saul asked.

"Not yet, sir."

"Buzz me when he's on the line."

"Yes sir."

Saul turned off the intercom then looked over at Agent Hartlieb. "Where were we?"

"Discussing motives."

"That's right. Please continue."

"A serial killer's behavior and the physical evidence collected from the crime scene usually reflect sadistic and sexual overtones."

"Like mutilating the victim's breasts?"

"Precisely. But serial killers usually fall into distinctive sub-groups. Some are thrill seekers, some are goal-oriented, some are delusional, and some domineering."

"Where do you think our boy falls?" Denholm asked.

"If he killed both his wife and the Evans girl, he seems to fit the delusional profile."

"Why is that?" Saul asked.

"The crime scenes were in disarray. Both victims resisted and attempted to get away. He used some type of restraining device. Both were brutally assaulted with a knife, stabbed multiple times."

"That's our boy."

"But isn't it odd he's a minister?" Myles asked.

"Not really. Religious overtones are rather common among delusional killers. They usually hear a voice or see a vision. They say a demon, Satan, or God orders them to kill." Hartlieb walked over and sat on the corner of Saul's desk. "Take Harvey Carignan for example. He murdered women and claimed God told him to do it. On the other end of the spectrum, we caught a young boy who decapitated an elderly woman then stabbed her more than 200 times. Within the next several weeks, he killed four more old women by stabbing them repeatedly. When we finally captured him, he told us he was possessed by a red demon. In both cases the killers heard voices – one said God, the other said a demon. Theologians attribute all of the voices to Satan and demons."

The intercom buzzed.

"Your call is ringing on line one, Mr. Saul."

"Thanks."

Saul picked up the receiver and listened to the phone ring multiple times. He started to hang up when someone picked up on the other end.

"Hello Mr. St. James. This is Peter Saul, the Cuyahoga County Prosecutor. Sorry to call your cell phone, but my secretary tried your home number and kept getting a busy signal."

"This isn't a good time," Hunter said.

"We had a little incident down at the jail with one of your clients."

"I really could care less right now."

"It seems the pastor tried to kill himself last night."

"A lot of that going around."

"Excuse me?"

"Nothing."

"A couple of our deputies found him before he could finish the job. We have him in 4-way restraints, but he refuses to take any medication until he speaks to his lawyer."

"What do you want me to do?"

"Could you come down here, talk to him, and make sure he cooperates with the nurse?"

"This really isn't a good time."

"I wouldn't bother you if it weren't an emergency."

Silence.

"Mr. St. James?"

"All right."

"Very, very good." Saul cocked his head and lifted an amused eyebrow. "There's one more thing I need to discuss with you."

"What's that?"

"We're about to enter some documents into discovery that are pretty inflammatory. I wanted to give you a peek before we release them to the press."

"What is it?"

"I'd rather not say over the phone."

"I'll be there in 20 minutes."

"Thanks for the help."

Saul hung up the phone then looked over at April Denholm.

"I think he's drunk."

25

A middle-aged deputy wearing a crisply pressed, black uniform escorted Hunter St. James down a long corridor in the segregation unit. Inmates banged on the steel, windowless doors lining both sides of the hall; occasionally a faceless shout of profanity rose above the clatter. At the end of the hall on the right-hand side, a gray-haired deputy sat in a chair staring through a plexiglass wall at a naked man strapped spread-eagled to a steel table. A leather belt ran across the man's forehead, his eyes squinted shut, his lips moving slowly. Howard Jamison.

"What's this?" Hunter said.

"Suicide watch."

"Let him loose."

"No can do."

"You're torturing him."

"More like protecting him."

"I demand you remove those restraints."

"No offense, counselor, but you're in no position to be making demands." The deputy leaned over and whispered into Hunter's ear. "It smells like you've been hitting the sauce a little heavy today."

"So?"

"Think you could pass a breathalyzer?"

Silence.

"That's what I thought." The officer unlocked the steel door. "You've got 20 minutes."

Hunter walked in and was greeted by the sour stench of dried urine. The deputy slammed the door shut. Jamison opened his eyes.

"Excuse me if I don't get up."

"What the hell happened?"

"Come over here close."

Hunter looked around the room. A cloth-covered chair stood in the corner where the two plexiglass walls intersected. No sink. No toilet. Hunter wondered where that stink was coming from, then noticed the floor under the table sloped toward a large open drain. Hunter grabbed the chair and slid it over near Jamison's head and pointed it away from exposed flesh.

"Are you okay?"

"I'm a little cold."

"What happened?"

"I didn't try to kill myself." Jamison spoke in a confidential whisper.

"It's okay if you did. Believe me, I understand."

"I didn't and keep your voice down."

"These people are convinced you did."

"That's what they're telling you."

"Why are we whispering?"

"The room is probably bugged."

"Why would they bug your cell?"

"Because they tried to kill me."

"Who tried to kill you?"

"Keep your voice down. They did."

"Who's they?"

Jamison shifted his eyes toward the guards gawking in through the plexiglass. "They're afraid of what I know."

"The guards are afraid?"

"Whoever sent them."

"Do you hear yourself?"

"Listen to me. I was asleep in my cell last night until I heard somebody fooling around with the lock on my door. I opened my eyes in time to see someone jam a rag in my mouth and pull a plastic bag over my head. Then I felt a bunch of hands jerk me up, and the next thing I know they've got a sheet wrapped around my neck, my hands bound, and I'm hanging from the air vent. I couldn't cry out, so I kicked my feet against the wall as hard as I could. I felt their hands try to hold my legs, so I kicked even harder. I heard the muffled shouts of the guys in the cell next to me. That's the last thing I remember until I came to with a nurse doing CPR on me."

"Have you mentioned this to anyone?"

"No."

"Good, because you sound crazy."

"But you believe me, don't you?"

"That's not important. Mr. Saul says you're refusing your medication."

"I don't know what they are trying to give me. It could be arsenic for all I know. Besides, I don't need medication."

Hunter shook his head.

"If you don't believe me, I'm out of hope."

"If I'm your only hope, you would've been better off letting them kill you."

"You may not believe in yourself, but I believe in you."

"I don't know what to believe in." Hunter looked at the floor in a confused sort of way, as if he lost his train of thought. "I just came from Saul's office, and he handed me a file a foot thick on your murdered wife. It seems she was killed in much the same manner as the Evans girl."

"That's because the cases are related."

"That's what Saul said."

"I can explain everything."

"Don't you think a murdered wife would be something your lawyer should know about?"

"You said you didn't want to hear my side of the story."

"I meant with the Evans murder. I didn't know there were two."

"There's possibly more."

"You killed more than two?"

"Haven't you listened to anything I've said?"

"I'm more concerned with tomorrow's headlines."

"I can explain."

"This better be good, because the evidence against you is stacking up faster than dirty dishes at Rosie O'Donnell's place."

"Just let me start at the beginning."

"Go ahead."

"It all goes back to my childhood."

"We've only got 20 minutes."

"I'll try to be brief." He licked his cracked lips. "From the time I was young I was into mystical things and the occult. I tried all kinds of psychic trips, everything from tarot cards to astrology. In high school my friend Jack introduced me to the Ouija board. A lot of people could never get it to work and said it was only a game. But every time I touched the guide, it took off and ran around the board spelling out all kinds of words. Half the time I didn't even have to ask it anything. It just started talking to me."

"Whoa there. Are you telling me the Ouija board told you to kill these women?"

"I told you I didn't kill anyone, but I've got to start at the beginning."

"Continue."

"Through the Ouija I contacted a spirit guide. He told me he was a 7-year-old boy who drowned in one of those kiddie pools in his backyard. He spoke so readily that I sat there some nights for hours talking to him through the board. He encouraged me to use drugs to further open my mind to the spiritual realm. It wasn't until years later that I learned that Bible scholars translate the Greek word *pharmakeia* to English as sorcery."

"You expect me to believe you really communicated with a dead boy through a Ouija board?"

"No, not a real little boy. A demon acting like a little boy. Please hear me out."

"Go ahead." Hunter loosened his tie.

"As I became more deeply involved with the Ouija, it opened me up to receive other demonic spirits. At first they talked to me through the board, then their voices started speaking inside my head - two of them. They even argued among themselves sometimes, but usually they gave me advice on making decisions."

"And you did what these voices said?"

"Yep. And between the demons and the acid, I became a raging paranoid. No one wanted to be around me. Then over summer vacation after my junior year in high school the voices pushed me over the edge - and convinced me a big hurricane was coming to destroy and flood Savannah where I was visiting my brother. They kept repeating, 'The hurricane is coming tonight.' I panicked. I knew I had to get to the mountains, somewhere high where the waters wouldn't get me. The voices said, 'You have to steal your brother's car. Time is running out.' But I knew if I stole his car, he'd call the police and they would put me in jail, and I'd drown with everyone else. Then the voices told me, 'You have to kill your brother.'

"So, I went into the kitchen and picked up a butcher knife. My brother was taking a shower when I broke in the bathroom and hacked him six times. He collapsed. Blood everywhere. I thought he was dead, so I walked out to pick up his car keys when I saw his son playing in his crib. I decided to take him with me. As soon as I had him in my arms, I heard a pounding at the door and someone shouting 'Police!' I grabbed my nephew, hid in the closet, and put my hand over his mouth to keep him from crying. I heard the police break down the door and start searching the place. Then I heard the siren of the ambulance as it came to take my brother to the hospital.

"The police continued searching for about ten minutes. At one point an officer opened the door and looked in, but he didn't see me. A couple minutes later he returned and found me cowering in the corner, clutching my brother's little boy. By this time, I was dazed and unresponsive and squeezing my nephew so tight they had to pry my arms apart to get him loose. I didn't know it at the time, but I had choked him unconscious."

"Did he die?"

"No, thank God."

"Go on."

"They put me in jail, and I ended up in a padded cell completely out of touch with reality. They later told me I didn't respond to anyone or anything for over a week. But one night I had a dream. I was at the mall trying on a tuxedo, but instead of a bow tie, the clerk put a large gold cross around my neck. I walked out of the store and everywhere I looked were these magnificent cathedrals. Then all of a sudden, a three-headed dog appeared out of nowhere and started chasing me. And I ran and ran down a long street lined with real tall wrought-iron fences. No place to hide. I turned the corner and found a polygonal-shaped building, and I ducked inside just as the beast bashed against the door. I could hear his claws tearing at the wood. I knew I didn't have much time. I looked around the big room to find some sort of weapon to defend myself with, but the room was empty except for a simple wooden table with a loaf of bread, a bunch of grapes, and a gold chalice on it. Then all of a sudden, the beast stopped scratching. The door disappeared, and Jesus stood in the doorway with His arms outstretched. I walked over to Him, and He picked me up from under the arms like I was a little child and held me in the air. I looked down into His radiant face and in the background, I heard a beautiful choir. When He set my feet back on the floor, I woke up in my right mind.

"My brother found me a lawyer and a team of psychiatrists. I told them everything I could remember and answered all their questions. When we went to court all the experts came to the same conclusion: I was totally sane as I stood there that day, but at the time I attacked my brother I was insane. They testified they believed I would never use drugs again or ever go back to that crazy, demonic lifestyle. The judge found me guilty on two counts of attempted murder but not guilty by reason of insanity. I walked out a free man.

"I knew God had intervened in my life and would direct

me. Right after this I ran into Anne, an old friend. She was a Christian, and she talked to me about Jesus. I went to church with her that night, heard a powerful sermon on sin, judgement and Hell, and I got down on my knees in repentance to a merciful God. I then publicly confessed my sins, and received Jesus Christ into my heart as Lord and Savior. Two years later I entered seminary and became a pastor. And Anne became a wonderful wife."

"And none of this came out after your wife was killed?"

"No. I was 17 at the time. The records were sealed and later expunged."

"Unbelievable."

"It's the truth."

"I believe it is, but I don't see how this helps you. It only proves you have a history of violence and mental illness."

"But it also proves I have a history with Satanism and explains why, after I became a minister, I specialized in reaching out to those trapped in the occult - including Lucy Evans."

"If you tell that story on the stand, I can promise they will execute you."

"But you haven't heard the rest of the story. During my first pastorate in Charleston, West Virginia, I stumbled onto something." His voice became halting. "My wife was murdered because of it."

"What did you find?"

The door popped open. Hunter startled. The deputy shouted in.

"Time's up!"

"Give us five more minutes," Hunter said.

"You'll leave now, or I'll arrest you for drunk and disorderly conduct."

26

J ason Saul felt oddly calm sitting in the passenger side of Bruce Richards' pickup as the old jalopy sped east on I-90. After all, you would think a man would be a little nervous on his way to kill his stepfather. But in Jason's mind, some people just needed a good killin', and Peter Saul was one of them. Besides, how else could he free his mother from her secret nightmare and get his life back in the process? Saul would die tonight.

The truck drove past an old industrial park off to the right; the stench of sulfur filtered in through rusted-out holes in the floorboard. A misting rain sprayed across the windshield. The wipers only managed to smear streaks across the glass. Jason looked into the October sky; the Harvest Moon hid behind angry clouds. A perfect night for a murder.

"Let's go over the plan one more time," Richards said.

"Are you a moron? How many times do I have to repeat myself?"

"Take it easy. I just don't want to screw this up, that's all."

"My stepdad is at the commissioners' meeting. He goes every week just to make an appearance. The meeting breaks up around ten. His private parking spot is in the lot beside the county building at the end of a long alley. When he strolls down, we cut his throat, take his wallet, and make it look like a mugging."

"Who cuts his throat?"

"I get the honor."

"Got it."

"You straight now?"

"I said I got it."

"You got the gun?"

"Right here." Richards patted his side pocket.

"No shooting unless things go bad."

"I got it."

A few minutes later the truck pulled off the exit ramp at Carnegie Avenue then turned onto Ontario Street in front of Jacobs Field, home of the Cleveland Indians. The stadium floodlights looked like giant toothbrushes against the sky. On one corner a couple of young thugs stood with their pants sagging down in the back, Starter hats twisted to the side. They wouldn't sell much crack on a night like tonight.

Richards parked the truck on the street in front of the Cleveland Convention Center, and they climbed out. Both men wore dark blue jumpsuits Richards "borrowed" from his father's gas station. To anyone who happened to drive past, they looked like a couple of mechanics taking a break. They jogged across the street. Jason felt the switchblade bouncing in the pocket against his right leg. When they safely crossed the street, Jason held his hand out to see if it trembled. *Steady as a rock.* This was going to be easier than he thought.

"What time you got?" Jason asked.

"Five till."

"We're right on schedule."

They looped around the block and emerged in the alley next to the parking lot. Jason could see Saul's black BMW parked in its designated spot. Everything proceeded according to plan. They slipped down into the narrow corridor behind the county building, their backs pressed up against the rough limestone blocks. Both men goosenecked up and down the alley. The coast was clear. They melted into the recess in front of an emergency door about 30 yards from the rear exit. Rain dripped from the rusted fire escape dangling overhead.

"This is the spot," Jason whispered.

He reached into his back pocket for a black ski mask, shucked it over his head, and adjusted the fit so the material didn't obstruct his vision. He looked over at Richards who had done the same. He suppressed a laugh. They were really going to do it. And in a few minutes, it would all be over. Jason reached into his left front pocket to retrieve a pair of leather work gloves, pulled them on, and worked his fingers to ensure full range of motion.

"It's ten o'clock," Richards whispered in his ear.

"He'll be the first one out. He always is."

Jason's heart pounded against his chest. He took deep breaths through his mouth. *What a rush!* He could hear the exit door open then shut. He peeked his head around the corner. There he was, Peter Saul, in all his pompous glory. Jason watched him turn his collar up against the cold evening mist then descend the stairs.

"Here we go."

Richards pressed up against Jason's back and stretched his neck around the corner. Saul headed right for them then stopped. Another man approached Saul from the end of the walkway, a stocky man with a powerful build and dark glasses.

"Who's that?" Richards whispered.

"I don't know."

"What do we do?"

"Maybe he'll go away."

Saul and the man spoke in a confidential tone, but Jason could tell from his stepfather's mannerisms the meeting was unexpected and upsetting. Jason hooked Richards with his left arm and pulled him back into the recess.

"This is what we do. If the dude walks away, we go ahead as planned. If they both walk this way, you jump out first and tackle the dude, then I spring out and do the deed. Got it?"

"Whatever you say."

Jason peeped his head around the corner.

"Here they come."

"Both of them?"

"Yep."

"All right."

Richards shuffled in front of Jason and positioned his body for the attack. The sound of leather-soled shoes tapping on the pavement grew louder with each approaching step. Jason slid his gloved hand into his jumpsuit pocket and grabbed the switchblade. Adrenaline surged through his body. He pressed the release button on the handle; the blade snapped into place. The footfalls thundered in his ears. He pumped his fisted hand around the hilt of the knife. Any second now.

Richards pounced.

"What the—"

A tangle of arms and legs rolled on the ground. Saul froze then turned his back. Jason surged forward, the blade extended.

"Look out!" somebody yelled.

Saul pivoted. The blade missed his neck and struck him in the shoulder. He yelled. Jason withdrew the knife. The two men faced each other; Saul grabbed the wound.

"If it's money you want, here, take it all."

Jason grunted.

Saul reached for his wallet. Jason thrust the blade at Saul's throat. Saul twisted. The blade nicked his ear. Saul grabbed the outstretched arm and twisted. Searing pain shot through Jason's wrist, elbow and shoulder. He felt the knife slipping from his fingers. He drove a knee into Saul's gut. The powerful grip persisted. A second knee to the groin broke the hold. Saul staggered back, doubled over.

Jason heard the two men behind him locked in combat; he ignored them and pressed the attack. A well-placed front kick sent Saul to his back. Jason pinned the older man to the ground, straddling his chest with his knees. He raised the knife above his head with both hands, poised to plunge. A sharp pain exploded in the small of his back - a surge of electricity. His hand sprang open. The knife rattled to the pavement. Jason's body writhed to the ground. He fought to stay conscious.

Boom!

Jason darted his eyes toward the sound. Richards pointed a pistol at the stranger who cautiously backed away with his hands in the air. Richards shifted his aim at Peter Saul. Jason tried to shout, *Shoot him!* But his lips wouldn't move.

27

Hunter St. James lay on the couch in his living room, wrapped in a brown and orange Cleveland Browns afghan, surveying the utter shipwreck of his life. His temples throbbed; cold sweat covered his body. Getting drunk at 9 o'clock in the morning meant the hangover arrived early in the evening. Six cups of black coffee and a half-dozen Tylenol did little to clear the cobwebs. He focused his eyes on the unopened home-pregnancy tests standing on the glass coffee table; he could hear the twin boxes taunting him with questions that could forever go unanswered: *Was she really pregnant? Did Pamela kill your baby?*

He glanced over at the shotgun leaning against the La-Z-Boy recliner. The metallic taste returned to his mouth. He gagged. *How do you screw up your own suicide?* Why didn't he pull the trigger? It would have been so easy. Why did his cell phone ring when it did? Was it just dumb luck? Or was some cosmic eye watching over him?

Whenever Hunter's mind pondered such eternal mysteries, he always started at the same point – his own consciousness. He could rightfully doubt everything else, but he knew he existed. Even when he doubted his own reality, he inevitably came to the same conclusion as the renowned philosopher René Descartes, "I think, therefore I am."

So, if Hunter was real, then the world outside of him was

probably real too, and by extension the universe must also be real. But where did the universe come from? As far as he could tell there were only two options: either the universe was eternal, or it was created by someone eternal. But an eternal universe didn't mesh with his newfound knowledge of thermodynamics, which stated that all available energy in the universe is constantly winding down. And as far as that goes, where did all the energy come from in the first place? Did the universe explode into being by some act of self-creation? But in order for the universe to create itself, it would first have to exist in order to do the work of creation, and that's a logical impossibility. Something cannot come from nothing.

The law of cause and effect further disqualifies an eternal universe; after all, every effect must have a sufficient cause. The universe is the *effect,* so there had to be a *cause* prior to and outside of the universe. *Could God be that first cause? But where did God come from?* Wrestling with that enigma made Hunter's head hurt. *Could God really transcend the universe?*

Transcendence, as Hunter understood the concept, had nothing to do with geography. If he rode a space shuttle to the top of the universe and looked up, God would not be sitting there on His throne. So that means God's transcendence pertains to His being, not to His location. God is transcendent because He is a higher order of Being who would alone have the power of self-existence. Transcendence means that God is outside of time. He doesn't experience reality moment by moment as we do. If God exists, He must do so outside of time so that everything is eternally present for Him.

These were hard concepts for Hunter to ponder in his present state of mind. He felt as if he was trying to squeeze the entire ocean of reality into the tiny thimble of his mind. Maybe he could only grasp an infinitesimal snippet of God, just as only a miniscule amount of the ocean would fit into a thimble. How do you understand a whale or shark when only salt water and algae fit inside your thimble? Maybe his finite human mind was incapable of comprehending the infinitude of God. After all, the world of academia held many subjects his puny mind couldn't perceive, even though other human minds could. His inability with astrophysics did not invalidate that branch of science. The epitome of arrogance would be to deny something simply because he could not fathom it. He simply needed to swallow his pride and admit that he need not comprehend the incomprehensible. *What a revolutionizing concept!*

An overwhelming sense of relief swept through Hunter's mind. The world finally made sense. Some things were not for him to know, and he felt at peace with that. But the concepts he did know, he knew for sure: something cannot come from nothing; mindless forces do not give rise to minds; and God is the cause that brought the universe into being. Hunter may not fully comprehend God, but from this day forward he would seek to apprehend everything God revealed about Himself.

28

J ason Saul lay on his back, his body screaming with pain. The acrid smell of gunpowder surrounded him. The misting rain turned into a steady downpour. The large, splashing drops blurred his vision. The ski mask grew heavy with saturation. He tried to lift his arms to wipe his eyes but only managed to flop his hand across his forehead. Bruce Richards stalked forward, his legs spread wide, both hands on the pistol grip, darting the barrel back and forth. Peter Saul and the stranger backed down the alley with their hands in the air. Richards lowered the gun. The two men dropped their hands, turned, and ran.

"You shot me," Jason said, his words sounding slurred in his own ears.

"I didn't."

"My back."

"Dude got you with a stun gun."

"It hurts like hell."

"We've got to split, can you move?"

"Help me up."

Jason heard a commotion at the end of the alley. The silhouette of a gathering crowd appeared, pointing and mumbling.

"I said, get me up."

Richards stashed the gun in his back pocket, bent down, and

scooped Jason up under the armpits. Jason tested his legs, but they wouldn't respond.

"Hey you two!" a booming voice yelled from the crowd. "Stop right there!"

"Get me out of here!" Jason shouted.

The would-be assassins struggled down the alley, arms laced over each other's shoulders like a couple of drunks in a three-legged race. Jason looked back; the crowd pursued. The feeling gradually returned to his legs along with the sensation of a thousand bees stinging his feet with each step. He grimaced behind the mask and began carrying his own weight. Another ten strides, and he ran under his own power.

"Stop! Police!"

They sprinted toward the streetlight at the end of the alley then dashed into the parking lot. They stopped to look around. A tall, chain-link fence encompassed them. Richards bolted for the fence and started climbing. Jason laced his fingers through the links but couldn't sustain his grip.

"Can you make it over?!" Richards shouted.

"I'll manage."

Richards jumped down and gave Jason a boost.

"Hurry, Jase, they're comin'."

Jason reached the jagged top, pulled himself up and over, and then belly-flopped onto the cement with a ghastly thud. Richards shinnied up the fence, jumped down, then helped Jason up. The makeshift posse raced across the parking lot, but by the time they reached the fence, the perps were gone. Jason and Richards peeled off the masks and quickstepped toward the waiting truck parked about 50 yards up ahead on the right.

"We... made... it," Richards said between heaving breaths.

"Not yet we ain't."

"You okay?"

"I think so."

They climbed into the truck. Richards fired up the engine. The wipers slapped out their cadence, providing absolutely no visibility. The windshield fogged with their rapid breathing.

Richards wiped the glass with his hand but only made it worse.

"Go!" Jason yelled.

"I can't see."

A police siren wailed from the end of the block. Richards stomped the accelerator; the back wheels spun out on the wet pavement.

"I can't see, I can't see."

Jason rolled down his window then stuck his head out. The rain stung his face.

"Go straight!"

"I can't see anything."

"Drive."

The truck weaved down the street, nearly side-swiping a row of parked cars.

"I said go straight!"

"I'm trying."

Jason looked behind. The police car tailed right behind; the flashing red light glowed on his face. He turned around in time to see a telephone pole whirl past. He ducked back inside. Something ripped off the side-view mirror.

"You trying to kill me?!"

"I told you, I can't see."

Jason climbed back out the window, bracing himself on the windshield. The wiper slapped his knuckles.

"Turn those damn things off!"

"Sorry."

"Make a right!"

The truck lurched around the corner and swerved into oncoming traffic. Horns blared. Cars darted past on both sides.

"Come right, come right!"

Jason heard the police cruiser squeal around the turn. Up ahead three cars waited at the intersection.

"Pass 'em on the left!"

Richards jerked the wheel. The truck clipped the bumper of the last car as it passed, spinning the car across the left lane. The tailing police car veered to the left, went up on the curb, then screeched through the intersection in hot pursuit. The truck vibrated and clattered up the I-77 ramp. The police car quickly closed the gap.

"We'll never outrun him!" Jason yelled, looking back, the wind whipping through his hair. "Hit the brakes!"

"What?!"

"I said hit the brakes!"

Richards slammed the pedal with both feet. The police car smashed into the tailgate. The truck surged forward from the collision. The police car spun off the road.

"Did we lose him?!" Richards asked.

"Yep!"

"Awesome!"

"Get off the highway at the next exit. They're not done with us yet."

29

Peter Saul looked out his 3rd floor window. He leaned forward to get a better look, and pain shot through his shoulder. His left arm hung in a sling, and the slightest movement brought instant agony. He spent most of the night in the Emergency Room at Metro Hospital. Luckily the stab wound in the shoulder only caused soft tissue damage. The slash across the ear required a dozen stitches and throbbed with every beat of his heart.

Saul spun his chair back around and pressed the intercom button on his desk.

"Send in Lt. Denholm."

The petite blonde strolled in with a manila file tucked under her arm. Saul had never noticed her lithe figure before; police uniforms did nothing for her. She sat down in the green vinyl chair across from his desk.

"What happened to you, Chief?"

"I had a little altercation last night. It wasn't serious."

"Looks serious."

"I'm fine."

"Did they catch the perp?"

"No, but we will. Sun Tzu says, 'Invincibility depends on one's self; the enemy's vulnerability depends on him.'" Saul gingerly reached for his coffee mug. "What do you have for me?"

"The FBI identified the bootprints we found at St. Andrew's."
Saul's face darkened; a crease appeared down his brows.
"Is there something wrong?" she asked.
"Why would there be?"
"You don't seem too pleased."
"I'm a little preoccupied, that's all. Continue."
"It turns out the boots are replicas of Nazi jackboots worn by the SS in World War II. Very rare. Only two companies in this part of the country import them, and one is right here in Cleveland. I've got calls in to both of them."
"Good work."
"I can't imagine vintage jackboots are in much demand."
A knock at the door. Jimmy Graham stuck his head in.
"Boss, St. James has arrived at the Justice Center."
"Did you take care of that thing?"
"Sure did."
"Excellent."
"I'm headed over there right now."
"Keep me posted."
"Will do."
Graham closed the door behind him. Denholm opened the file and laid the contents out on the desk.
"Here's a copy of the FBI's findings. And here are a couple of black and white photos of the bootprints. Notice the wear pattern on the left heel is remarkably similar to the tennis shoe impressions found at the church window."
"That's odd." Saul set down the mug and picked up one of the photos. "What size are the boots?"
"Eleven."
"And what size are the sneakers?"
"Eleven."
"You've done—"
Another knock at the door.
"What?!" Saul yelled.
A uniformed officer walked in and stopped directly in front of the desk, looking nervous.

"Can't you see I'm in the middle of a meeting? What do you want?"

"I just came to tell you we found a good set of footprints in the mud next to the sidewalk where you were attacked."

"Any distinguishing characteristics?"

"They have an unusual tread."

"What did they look like?"

The officer thought a moment, peered down at the desk, then pointed at the photos. "They look exactly like those."

30

H unter St. James waited in the attorney's visiting room feeling refreshed. He slept remarkably well the night before, and he didn't even mind the morning headlines: "Alleged Serial Killer Attempts Suicide." The lurid story detailed the Lucy Evans murder in grisly detail, drawing parallels to Jamison's wife's death a few years earlier. Of course, the reporter recounted Hunter's father's misdeeds once again.

A few minutes later the door opened, and Howard Jamison entered wearing a pair of blaze orange pants and a bright-white straightjacket. Scant strands of hair, usually combed over the top of his bald head, stood up on end giving him the appearance of a baby bird. The three gouges running down his forehead and cheek had healed nicely, leaving only three pink lines.

"You've got 20 minutes max, counselor," the black-uniformed deputy said before slamming the door shut.

"I see you made it through the night," Hunter said.

"I didn't sleep well."

"I don't imagine you did. Do you need help sitting down?"

"I'll manage." Jamison scooted the chair back with his butt then plopped down heavily.

"We made the front page this morning."

"What did it say?"

"You're a serial killer."

"Mom will be proud."

"You might as well get used to it. You're going to be national news by the end of the day."

"That can't be a good thing."

"Listen, Howard, the first time we met, you said I needed to believe in God to understand what happened on the night of the murder. Well, I do, and I'm ready to listen."

"Are you serious?" Jamison's face brightened.

"I'm not saying I'm a Christian or anything, but I do admit God does exist. He must."

"Why the change of heart?"

"To make a long story short, I finally acknowledged with my mind what I always knew in my heart. But I still don't understand why God allows so much pain in the world."

"Pain is actually beneficial. If you didn't feel pain when your hand touches a flame, you wouldn't know to pull back your hand before third-degree burns set in. Pain allows you to know something is wrong. But pain also has a spiritual use. The author C.S. Lewis said, 'God whispers to us in our pleasures, speaks in our conscience, but shouts in our pains; it is His megaphone to rouse a deaf world.'"

"I'm not talking about physical pain as much as suffering in general."

"You mean like poor people starving to death in Africa, or terrorism, genocide or COVID-19, that sort of thing?"

"Precisely."

"The answer to that question dates back to the Garden of Eden and disobedience, ever since man started abusing his free will. His sin brings about terrible consequences to himself and everyone around him. After all, it was man, not God, who invented war and slavery and prison."

"But God allows it?"

"He does, but He is still in control. Let me give you an illustration from the Bible. Judas, by his own free will, chose to betray Jesus. But in so doing he fulfilled God's plan that Jesus would die for the sins of the world. From a worldly perspective, Jesus suffered terribly for the consequences of Judas' actions, but from a heavenly perspective, Jesus' suffering opened the doors to Heaven. Judas, by doing evil, inconceivably produced a tremendous good. God is able to allow sin sinlessly."

"So, man causes suffering, but God allows it for His own purposes."

"It seems contrary to human nature, but suffering is what God uses to draw us to Him."

"Interesting."

"God can also use it to prevent greater suffering or evil."

"I've never looked at it that way before." Hunter grabbed a legal pad from his briefcase. "But right now, I need to hear your side of the story."

"Where do you want me to start?"

"Lucy Evans. How did you meet her?"

"She came into my office one day for counseling."

"How often did you see her?"

"About a dozen times."

"Did you often meet her alone at night?"

"Never. I have a strict policy against meeting alone with any woman, anytime. I make sure my secretary or someone else is present at all times."

"Was someone else at the church the night in question?"

"No."

"But you just said—"

"Ms. Evans didn't have an appointment. She just showed up."

"Is that common?"

"No."

"So why did she drop in out of the blue?"

"She said it was an emergency, that she was in really serious trouble."

"What kind of trouble?"

"Spiritual."

"Explain."

"Let me back up. The first time Lucy came to see me, she told me she had been involved with the occult – satanic stuff – and she feared a demon possessed her."

"Like Linda Blair in *The Exorcist*?"

"No, it's not like the movies. She was hearing voices in her head, male voices, and they kept telling her to kill herself."

"Sounds like she was schizophrenic."

"She said the voices started about a year after she got involved with the Ouija board."

"That happened to you."

"Yes, just like me. It made me take her very seriously and then..." Jamison fidgeted in the plastic chair.

"What?"

"She knew everything about me."

"How?"

"The voices told her. They even told her the name of my former demon."

"No way."

"I documented everything."

"Go on."

"She showed up at St. Andrew's that night, Friday the 13th. It's the second highest day of the year in the Satanic calendar."

"What did she want?"

"She was agitated, said the demons told her tonight was the night she must die."

"Suicide?"

"That's what I thought, but it didn't turn out that way."

"What did she want you to do?"

"Cast the demons out."

"You can't be serious."

"Jesus did it all the time."

"You're not Jesus."

"No, but I believe in Him."

"So, what happened?"

"I tried to cast them out, but without time for fasting and prayer."

"How?"

"First I made sure she wasn't wearing any pentagrams or satanic charms. Then I read the Scripture passage from Mark where Jesus casts out the legions of demons from the guy living in the tombs. All of a sudden, she started hissing and spitting and coughing. Then she let out a scream like a wolf being roasted alive. It made my skin crawl. Then she dropped to the floor."

"No way."

"She didn't move. I thought she was dead. I called her name. She didn't answer. I bent over and touched her cheek..."

"And?"

"And she attacked me. Only it wasn't her."

"Who was it?"

"I weigh about 230, and she can't go more than 125, but she threw me around the office like a rag doll. She had the strength of a powerful man. I tried grabbing her arms, but she broke my grip and slashed my face."

Hair stood up all over Hunter's body. "Then what happened?"

"She bolted out of the office and into the sanctuary."

"What did you do?"

"I followed after her, but when I turned the corner, I blacked out."

"Blacked out?"

"I don't know what happened. One minute I'm right on her heels, and the next thing I know I'm on the floor and regaining consciousness. I looked up and saw poor Lucy draped over the altar covered in blood, her clothes torn off..."

"What did you do?"

"I ran over and checked for a pulse." Jamison's voice broke. "She was dead. That's how her blood got on my hands, shirt, pants and shoes."

"And there wasn't anyone else in the church before the murder?"

"Not that I know of."

"And she was alive before you blacked out?"

"Yes."

"This is our defense? Demons and a blackout?" Hunter leaned back and shook his head. "We're screwed."

146

"It's the truth."

"What makes you so sure you didn't kill her during the blackout?"

"I didn't."

"How do you know?"

"I know because my wife was killed the same way, and I wasn't anywhere near my house when it happened. That's why I told you both killings were related."

"This is not much of a defense."

"The same people who killed my wife killed Lucy Evans."

"And your evidence for this is?"

"I know who did it."

"Who?"

"I started to tell you yesterday." Jamison leaned forward and whispered. "When I started pastoring in Charleston, I stumbled onto a secret organization, a powerful organization... a satanic organization."

"There are deviant punks in every city in America drawing pentagrams and killing goats."

"But this was a group of the leading families in Charleston with money and position and power. I was on the verge of exposing them when they stabbed my wife to death on Friday the 13th."

The door swung open. An angry-looking deputy stormed in and grabbed Jamison by the back of the straightjacket.

"We've got 10 minutes left," Hunter said, looking at his watch.

"Not anymore. Emergency count."

31

F aith McGuire sat in the lower arcade area outside the Sans Souci restaurant feeling like a junior on prom night. A breakfast meeting never before caused a sleepless night, but then again, this was the first with Hunter St. James. His phone call caught her off guard, and she worried she sounded too eager in accepting. She kept telling herself this was strictly business, but her emotions didn't believe her.

She kept an eager eye on the entrance. An elderly man opened the door for his wife, then the two shuffled toward the hostess hand in hand. *Soul mates. How wonderful for two people to go through life sharing triumphs and tragedies together.* Faith longed for her "other half." Her mind drifted back to her ex-husband Tim. *He certainly wasn't the one; he didn't even look like the one.* But she was 19 and stupid and settled for him. A terrible mistake. A disaster. But didn't she deserve to be happy now? Wasn't there someone out there for her?

Hunter St. James walked through the door, and her pulse took off at a gallop. His dreamy blue eyes scanned the room then fell on her. His mouth spread into a disarming smile. Her stomach tightened. He walked toward her; his herringbone, double-breasted suit outlined his athletic frame.

She stood, and they shook hands.

"Good morning, Ms. McGuire."

His hand felt thick and powerful.

"Good morning."

"Thanks for seeing me on such short notice."

"No problem at all."

They walked over to the hostess and were promptly seated at a corner table. The bright morning sun blazed in through the windows and illuminated Hunter's face like a floodlight. He looked a little pale, and dark signs of sleeplessness hung beneath his eyes. He must have shaved in a hurry, because a little crescent of dried cream dotted his right cheek.

"You've got a little something right here," she said.

He rubbed the wrong cheek. She shook her head. He swiped at the other side but missed the smudge. She reached over, caressed the side of his face, then rubbed the spot with her thumb. His skin felt warm and smooth. She allowed her hand to linger too long and felt embarrassed. She pulled back her hand and looked away.

"Thank you," he said in a tone that seemed to show he guessed what she was thinking.

"So, what did you want to discuss before the evaluation?"

"A couple of things."

"Background."

"No. I just didn't want any surprises to give you the wrong impression of Mr. Jamison. He's got enough strikes against him already."

"Like what?"

"Well, I've been to see him twice in the last four days. The first time he was stripped naked and tied down in 4-way restraints, and the last time he was in a straightjacket. They wouldn't let me in yesterday, because the jail was locked down."

"What did he do?"

"They claim he attempted suicide, but he says the guards tried to kill him."

"Do you believe him?"

"I want to."

"He might be delusional."

"He might be, but something happened this week that lends a little credibility to his story."

The waitress came over and filled their cups with steaming black coffee. She took their orders then hustled back toward the kitchen.

"What happened?"

"I was over at his house picking up a book, and on my way out I was attacked."

"Were you hurt?"

"Knocked cold until the next morning." He rubbed the back of his head. "When I came to the book was gone."

"What kind of book?"

"Creation vs. evolution."

"Why would somebody mug you for that?"

"I have no idea."

"That is strange."

"Nevertheless, I wanted to prepare you for when they bring him out. And secondly—"

The waitress returned and placed a pink grapefruit in front of Faith, and a plate of two fried eggs and toast in front of Hunter.

"Secondly?" she said.

"Have you ever been to the Justice Center before?"

"No."

"I thought you might want to ride over with me, since it's a little tricky to find your way around inside."

"That would be nice." *There I go again, sounding too eager.*

They ate quietly for a few minutes, exchanging glances and smiles then looking away. Her grapefruit tasted tart and puckered her mouth. She sprinkled a spoonful of sugar over the fruit, then once again caught herself staring into his eyes. She had never seen such a marvelous shade of blue, like the reflection of cloudless sky against a mountain lake.

"So, what do you think of your friend dating Monica?" she asked.

"You mean Gordon?"

"That's not what I call him."

"What do you call him?"

"I shouldn't say."

"Go ahead. I won't tell him."

"The Gargoyle."

Hunter laughed through his nose. "That's appropriate."

"What do you think?"

"Off the record?"

"Off the record."

"I think it's a recipe for disaster."

"Why do you say that?"

"I know Gordon." He tossed the last fragment of toast into his mouth. "What do you think?"

"Monica is naïve and superficial."

"Sounds like they're perfect for each other."

"They'll probably be married for 50 years."

"He's due back from France tonight."

"I know. Monica is picking him up at the airport."

"Just tell her to be careful."

"I already have."

"What about you?" He looked at her with the keenest interest on his face. "Are you seeing anyone?"

"Just my son." *That was stupid.*

"You're married?"

"Divorced."

"Sorry."

"I'm not."

Hunter's cell phone chirped and broke the awkward silence. He dug into his suit coat and retrieved the phone.

"Hello... this is he... what... can't be." Hunter dropped his head and rubbed his eyes with his thumb and forefinger. "Are you sure? I'll be right there." He didn't look up for several moments. He lifted his head with a jerk and looked at her with glazed eyes.

"What is it?"

"Our appointment with Mr. Jamison has been cancelled."

"Why?"

"He's dead."

32

J ason Saul awoke to the sound of a fist pounding on the side
of the van.

"It's time to get up," said the muffled voice.

Jason sat up and rubbed his eyes, trying to clear the cobwebs
from his mind. The past three days were a blur. After the
debacle downtown, he and Richards spent the night driving
back streets and alleys from Parma to Westlake, careful to avoid
the swarm of police they knew must be after them. Once they
parked inside the garage behind Richards' house, they covered
the truck with a tarp. Then the adrenaline wore off and Jason
collapsed. Later that night Richards removed the stun gun's
arrow-like projectile from Jason's back with a pair of greasy
pliers. The next morning a fever set in, and Jason had been
resting and sleeping in the van in a pool of his own sweat.

More pounding.

Jason reached for the lock, and a wave of nausea swept over
him. He looked out through the windshield at the side of a
dilapidated garage. The white paint, long ago faded a dirty gray,
lay in blisters along the rotten wood siding. The side door of the
van slid open. Bruce Richards climbed in. His shaved head was
riddled with knots and bruises. His left eye looked puffy and
blackened.

"How're you feeling, Jase?"

"Like death warmed over."

"You look it."

"Dude probably had the tip of that thing dipped in poison."

"Is it getting any better?"

"Worse."

"Let me see."

He lifted up his shirt. A yellowish-brown liquid saturated the makeshift gauze bandage. The flesh around the wound was red and swollen. He mopped the cold sweat from his forehead with his sleeve.

"Dude, that looks bad."

"Could you have used a rustier pair of pliers?"

"I ain't no surgeon."

"No duh." Jason gingerly lowered his shirt. "And how are you feeling?"

"I've been better, but I'll tell you what. I got some pretty good shots in on that dude myself."

"I hope you broke his neck."

Jason winced and laid back down.

"I should take you to the hospital."

"Not."

"It could be infected."

"I'm sure my stepdad's got cops waiting for someone to show up in the emergency room with burns from a stun gun."

"We've got to do something."

"I'll be all right." But tiny sparkles danced in Jason's field of vision. He took a couple of deep breaths. "It was really stupid to try and kill him in public like that. I don't know what I was thinking."

"It's probably best it worked out this way."

"The hell it is!"

"I just mean—"

"The man has to die."

"I don't know, Jase."

"Don't punk out on me now."

"I'm not."

"I've been giving this a lot of thought. We can do this. Every year my stepdad has a big Halloween party for a bunch of his big-wig friends."

"A costume party?" Richards pulled a can of snuff from his coat pocket and put a pinch inside his bottom lip.

"Exactly. They wear these stupid robes, and before midnight all the men go out in the woods near our house and the lake."

"And do what?"

"I don't know. I tried to follow them once, but my mom busted me. Anyway, when they go out to the woods, we'll take him down then."

"How will you know which one is your old man if they're all wearing costumes?"

"He wears the same thing every year. They all do."

"Kill him on Halloween, huh?"

"Has a nice ring to it, don't it?"

"I like it."

"We've got three days to scope out the woods and set everything up."

"This could be cool."

"I know those woods like the back of my hand."

33

P eter Saul eased into the 3rd floor conference room, his shoulder throbbing with every heartbeat. Last night he went to bed thinking it was humanly impossible for the pain to get worse, only to wake up this morning discovering he was wrong. He took his seat at the head of the table where a styrofoam cup of coffee waited for him. He gingerly settled into the chair and surveyed the room. To his left sat Kathy Myles and April Denholm in crisp blue uniforms, their eyes glued on Saul. At the far end of the table Jimmy Graham scribbled something in a small notebook. Sheriff Joseph Baker sat ramrod straight on the edge of his seat; his eyes darting around the room yet not making contact with anyone. Coroner Russell Mansfield reviewed a stack of papers.

The room seemed extremely bright. The morning sun blazed in through the eastern window and reflected off the polished tabletop. A stale scent permeated the air; the ventilation system wasn't working.

"All right, people. Let's get down to business. What the hell happened at the jail last night?"

"We had a little incident," Sheriff Baker said.

"A fight is an incident. The death of a serial killer is a major event."

"Everyone knows that Jamison was unstable." Lines of strain appeared around Baker's eyes. "I'm on record with the Psych people stating he needed to be on constant watch."

"Nobody is blaming you, Joe. Just tell us what happened."

"The 3rd-shift log shows that everything was quiet at the 4 o'clock count, but when the doors broke at six for breakfast, Jamison didn't come out. A few minutes later a couple of inmates found him on the floor of his cell with a broken pen shoved into his arm and the walls spray-painted with blood."

"Technically, it was only the pen casing," the coroner said. "He apparently disassembled the pen and stabbed the hollow tube into his right subclavian artery. An efficient way to bleed the body."

"Have you completed the autopsy already?" Saul asked.

"No, but I did do a visual before I came up here."

"We'll get back to that later. Now, Joe, which deputy was the first on the scene?"

"Farris."

"Why does that name sound familiar?"

"His father is a big Party contributor," Graham said.

"That's right. Continue, Joe."

"Well, here's where the problem comes in."

"I would have thought the dead inmate was the problem," Denholm said.

Sheriff Baker shot her a look that could have etched glass. "As I was saying, Deputy Farris is rather inexperienced. After the body was removed, he sort of panicked and had the trustees clean out the cell."

"What?!" the coroner roared, half standing. "Before it was examined?"

"I'm afraid so."

"This is clearly an obvious case of suicide," Saul said with a dismissive wave of his hand. "Sun Tzu says, 'To distinguish between sun and moon is no test of vision.'"

"But the scene is essential in corroborating the autopsy."

"There will be no autopsy."

"But it's the law."

"I'm the law here, and I say it's not necessary." Saul slammed his fist on top of the table. The cup bounced, slopping coffee on a stack of papers. "We will not waste the taxpayers' money on an obvious case of suicide."

"Whatever you say, Chief."

"I want that stinking carcass incinerated by noon."

"I'll get right on it," Baker said.

"Does this mean the case is closed?" Denholm asked.

"Officially, yes. I will be holding a press conference making it clear that the book is closed. But as far as I'm concerned, the investigation will not stop until I have the man who left his shoeprints outside the church window standing in my office."

"So, you want us to keep looking for him?"

"No. I'm assigning the cold file to Graham. It will keep the press off the trail." Saul tugged at the bandage on his ear. "I've got another job for you two."

"What's that?"

"Go arrest my stepson."

"Are you serious?"

"Do I look like I'm joking?"

"On what charges?" Myles asked.

"Leave that to me. He moved out a few nights ago, and I haven't seen him since. I've assembled a list of his friends and usual hangouts. Just be discreet. I don't want a big production."

"Will do, Chief."

A knock at the door.

"What!" Saul shouted.

His secretary pushed open the door and positioned herself where only Saul could see her. She bent over straight-legged, allowing her V-neck blouse to drape open. "Don't forget your lunch appointment."

"I'll be there. Is there anything else?"

"Oh, yes. There's a Mr. St. James waiting to see you in your office."

34

Hunter St. James waited alone in Peter Saul's office, sitting in the green vinyl chair that made an annoying sound every time he moved. He felt angry, confused and relieved all at the same time – angry over Jamison's death, confused whether Jamison actually killed himself, and relieved he no longer had to deal with this nightmare that already cost him so much. In the back of his mind he wanted it to be cut and dried. If Jamison killed himself, then maybe he really was schizophrenic, maybe he did kill his wife and the girl Lucy Evans, and maybe Hunter could finally return to his normal life.

But his heart said something different. After all, Hunter looked into the man's eyes the day he was strapped down in the 4-way restraints and saw genuine fear and a desire to live. But if Jamison didn't kill himself, then someone killed him - and that was more than Hunter could handle at the moment.

On the cosmic side of things, why would God allow this to happen? Jamison claimed to love and serve the Lord, and now he's dead. What kind of gratitude is that? Hunter remembered him saying that God allows suffering in order to prevent a greater evil or to bring about a higher good. But what grand purpose could this tragedy serve? Such concepts were hard to grasp. Evil existed. What rational person could deny it? But how do you reconcile evil in a world created by an omnipotent and benevolent God? Jamison mentioned the sinfulness of mankind.

Hunter's mind searched for something pleasant to

contemplate for a few moments, and Faith McGuire's beautiful face appeared. Breakfast with her was magical. He could still feel her hand against his cheek, so soft and gentle. *What a remarkable woman. Smart. Beautiful. Yet so down to earth.* But now with Jamison's death, he no longer had a professional reason to see her. So he felt cheated. Who knows where the relationship may have gone with a little more time?

The door to the office swung open. Peter Saul strolled in, tall and stately, scrupulously dressed with a wad of gauze taped to the side of his head. Saul offered his hand. Hunter stood to meet him.

"What happened to you?" Hunter asked.

"Cut myself shaving."

"Rough shave."

"What can I do for you, Mr. St. James?"

"A couple of things actually."

"Name them."

"I'd like the final discovery file on Jamison."

"I'll call and have it released to you as soon as we're finished."

"Thanks. And maybe you could explain why my client came up dead."

"Suicide."

"Aren't you supposed to make sure things like that don't happen?"

"We had him in 4-way restraints until you made a stink about it."

"Are you saying this is my fault?"

"I'm not accusing you of anything."

"It sure sounded like it to me."

"I'm a busy man, Mr. St. James. Is there anything else I can do for you?"

"I want... no... I demand an independent autopsy."

"You what?"

"He died in your custody, and I want an impartial set of eyes to make sure the official ruling is legit."

"Are you challenging my integrity?"

"I want the truth."

"Out of the question."

"What is? The truth or the autopsy?"

"Watch yourself." Saul turned red from the neck up.

"Then I want to be present when your people do the autopsy."

"What part of *no* don't you understand?"

"What are you trying to hide?"

"I don't like your tone."

"My client has rights."

"Those rights ended along with his pulse."

"Convenient for you."

"I've heard enough out of you."

"You haven't begun to hear enough from me."

"Your father challenged me once and look what happened to him."

"What did you say?"

"That's right. I'm the one who took him down. You want to be next?"

Saul's words struck him like a blow. The day of his father's sentencing came surging forward from the recesses of his mind. Hunter, just 9 years old, stood holding his mother's hand; tears dribbled off her once proud face. The judge slammed his gavel, and just at that moment the brash young prosecutor turned and looked directly at his mother with a stupid, smug smile that fit his face so well, and winked at her. Saul.

"What's wrong, St. James, cat got your tongue?"

Hunter struggled to focus. A voice from somewhere inside shouted, *Hit him!* Hunter's hands clenched and unclenched. The impulse to attack welled up inside and retched against every ounce of his restraint. *Knock his block off!*

"That's what I thought." Saul pressed past him and snatched a file off his desk. "I've got my copy of the Jamison discovery right here. You can have it."

Saul slammed the file against Hunter's chest.

"Here sport. Now get the hell out of my office."

Hunter stepped forward and stood nose to nose with Saul,

glaring deep into his soul.

Silence.

Saul stepped back; his face flushed.

"I said get out!"

35

Cleveland, Ohio
11:15 A.M.

Hunter St. James sat in his Jaguar, parked in the Justice Center parking lot, flipping through the Jamison discovery file. He couldn't believe what he found. Most of this stuff didn't appear in the "official" record of evidence he'd been given. According to this, the police found two other sets of suspect footprints in the blood at the crime scene through Luminol testing. The FBI identified the prints as coming from boat shoes and a pair of replica Nazi jackboots. He turned a few pages and discovered a color photo of an emerald found near the altar. *Why would Saul violate the law by withholding exculpatory evidence?*

His cell phone chirped.

"Hello."

"Mr. St. James?"

"Speaking."

"This is Peter Saul. I gave you the wrong file. I need you to return it to me at once."

"I don't know what you're talking about."

"Cut the crap. I gave you my personal file on the Jamison case, and I want it back."

"You're not supposed to have a personal file on the Jamison case. Ever hear of public record?"

"You're really pissing me off here. Don't make me send the sheriff to retrieve it."

"The battery on my cell phone must be going dead. I can't hear a word you're saying. I'll have to call you back later."

Hunter put down the phone, started the engine, and backed out of the parking space. The file represented political dynamite, and in a matter of moments Hunter knew that every cop in Cuyahoga County would be looking for him. He put the car in drive and headed for the tollbooth. A police cruiser pulled in front of him, blocking the exit. The uniformed officer motioned for him to open his window.

Man, they work fast.

Hunter first thought to stomp on the accelerator and push the cruiser out of his way, but common sense prevailed. Instead, he opened the window and tried to sound calm.

"What can I do for you, officer?"

"Sit tight, and I'll be with you in a moment."

The officer turned his attention to something on the console; probably running the license plates. Hunter stuffed the file under his seat then popped back up. The cop got out of his car and approached Hunter with his hand on his pistol.

"I need your driver's license and registration."

"Certainly."

Hunter handed him his wallet, then reached across to the glove compartment and retrieved the registration.

"What seems to be the trouble, officer?"

The cop didn't answer. He scrutinized the license info and compared the photo against Hunter's face. His brow wrinkled then relaxed.

"I guess that's you."

"Have I done something wrong?"

"Your headlight is broken. I'll have to give you a citation."

"Is that all?" Hunter exhaled audibly. "How much is this going to cost me?"

"Nothing. Just show up at the police station tomorrow before 5 o'clock with the light replaced, and I'll rip up the citation."

"Sure thing."

"Have a nice day."

The officer returned to his car.

That was close.

The patrol car moved out of the way, and Hunter pulled out into traffic. He drove to the corner, stopped at the red light, and pulled the file out from beneath the seat. He examined a couple of black and white photos of shoe impressions. Someone had scribbled in black marker on the top picture: *Found outside the church window.* A BCI report stapled to the picture indicated the impressions were made by a pair of NIKE Air Jordans, size 11. So at least two people had to be involved in the murder while another stood outside and watched. Such evidence didn't point to a lunatic acting alone. In fact, this file indicated conspiracy. Hunter knew if he returned the file to Saul the contents would be destroyed. He couldn't take the file to his home. The police were probably there waiting for him. What to do?

The light turned green. He drove through the intersection and made a left on Euclid Avenue at the Soldiers and Sailors Monument. He noticed the Dollar Bank Building. The tinted glass façade and new balconies gave the place a modern feel. He remembered *Cleveland Magazine* announcing the condos, and he thought it might be nice to live downtown, right in the heart of all the action. But before he considered buying a quarter-million-dollar condo, he needed a job.

His cell phone chirped.

"Hello."

"Hunter."

"Pamela?"

"It's me."

"To what do I owe this pleasure?"

"I can assure you it's nothing personal."

"I didn't think it would be."

"I left my Rolex on your nightstand."

"So?"

"I want it back."

"Come and get it."

"I thought you'd bring it over."

T

TO KILL A SAINT

"You must be out of your mind."

"Then give it to Gordon."

"Can't. He's in France."

"Since when?"

"Monday."

"No he's not."

"He's there on business."

"He was at my father's office on Tuesday."

"Impossible."

"He came over to use the teleconference machine."

"What?"

"I helped him set it up. He even left his book here."

"What book?"

"Some book on creation or evolution. I know I've got it here somewhere." Hunter heard shuffling sounds. "Here it is. *How Life Began* by Thomas Heinze."

Silence.

"Hunter. Are you there?"

"I'll be right over. I've got to make a stop first."

36

F aith McGuire placed a $5 bill in the vending machine, pressed the button for a pizza sub, then watched her impromptu lunch land with a thud. She hated eating in the lobby and would rather be at the gym, but emergencies do happen. Besides, Hunter wouldn't be there so her incentive disappeared. The rugged outline of his handsome face seemed emblazoned on her retinas; she saw his face everywhere. Her pulse quickened just thinking about him. She headed for the elevator considering this morning's news. She felt no sympathy for Jamison – she didn't know the man – but it did ruin her day with Hunter. So much for professional detachment.

Faith stepped off the elevator chewing a mouthful of her sandwich. She stopped in front of her receptionist's desk and swallowed.

"Are they here yet?"

"They're waiting for you in your office."

"Thanks."

She took another bite then threw the remainder of the sandwich into the trashcan next to the desk. She pressed open the door and saw her clients sitting on the couch.

"I can't thank you enough for seeing us on such short notice," Marilyn Saul said. "Jason called and I insisted we meet together."

"Your voice sounded frantic on the phone. Allow me to get situated, and we'll begin."

Faith walked over to her desk, grabbed her notebook, then sat in the high-back leather chair beside the couch. She examined Jason Saul's face. His black hair stood up in spiky rows as usual, but not with the precision of past visits. His face looked more pallid than she remembered, his skin resembling gray paste. The silver rings piercing his eyebrows were dull and unclean, and a little redness radiated from where the loops entered the skin. He slouched with his gaze on the ground, occasionally glancing up with a half-resentful and half-puzzled expression. His mother, Marilyn, fidgeted next to him on the couch, her red hair pulled back accentuating her milky-white skin. A latent sadness filled her Irish-blue eyes.

"What brings you to my office today?"

"Things came to a head at home a few days ago. Right after Peter and I talked to you on the phone."

"I was afraid that might happen."

"Peter came home from work like a wild man. He went straight to Jason's room and tore it up. Every time he found something, he got more crazy."

"What did he find?"

"Nothin'," Jason said.

"He found some pornography and drug paraphernalia, but the thing that really set him off was a hymn book."

"Why would that make him mad?"

"I don't know."

"Do you know, Jason?"

"Beats me." He shrugged his shoulders, winced, then tucked his arm against his side.

"There must be some reason."

"Then Peter hit him."

"Hit him how?"

"Slapped him, punched him, knocked him down, kicked him."

"Are you all right, Jason?"

"Dude's a punk."

"You could press charges."

"Yeah right. He's the frickin' county prosecutor."

"What should we do?" Marilyn's eyes turned watery; she rubbed one then the other. "Peter kicked him out of the house and has forbidden me to even speak to him. If he knew I was here there'd be big trouble."

"Would Peter be willing to see me?"

"He's too proud."

"The way I see it, these problems involve everyone in the family, and the only way to solve them is with everyone's involvement."

"That sounds real good and all," Jason said, his face twisted with rage. "But I'm going to take care of this problem my own way."

"What do you mean by that?"

"I don't want to talk about it."

Jason stood up; his mother grabbed his arm; he shook her off.

"I'm outta here."

"Jason, wait."

"The time for talking is over." He headed for the door with Marilyn and Faith right behind.

"Jason, wait."

He jerked open the door and bumped into a man standing with his back turned, knocking a file out of his hand. The man bent over and gathered up the loose contents. Jason stood on a paper; the man tugged; Jason moved his foot.

"Nice boots kid," the man said before standing up. "Nazi SS jackboots, right?"

"Hunter?" Faith said.

"Am I interrupting?"

"We're outta here."

"I'm really sorry about this," Marilyn said.

Jason stormed off toward the elevator with Marilyn following.

"Did I come at a bad time?"

"No, no, come right in."

"I can't stay long, but I needed to see you."

"Come right in."

She directed him toward her office with a sweep of her arm. She followed close behind. A great pack of muscle shifted when his shoulders moved under his coat. She liked the way his black hair grew down and slightly covered a small, puckered scar, a white seam against his dark skin. She wondered why he needed to see her. Her heart thundered against her chest. She pulled the door closed; her sweaty palms felt cold against the brass knob. She casually dried her hands on her skirt.

"Are you all right, Mr. St. James? I mean after this morning and all?"

"I'm fine, and please call me Hunter."

"All right, Hunter. And please call me Faith. What happened to Mr. Jamison?"

"They called it a suicide."

"You don't sound convinced."

"I'm having serious doubts."

"What are you going to do?"

"I'm not sure. I need more information before I can make any official inquiries."

"Is there anything I can do?"

"As a matter of fact, there is. I came here hoping you could do me a favor."

"What is it?"

"Could you hold onto this file for me?"

He offered the file. She took it.

"Does this have something to do with Jamison?"

"Oh yeah."

"Why do you want me to hold it?"

"Because the man who gave it to me wants it back, and I don't want anything to happen to it until I get some answers."

"For how long?"

"Awhile. I'll make it up to you. How about dinner tonight? Anywhere you want to go."

Yes, yes, yes! "I couldn't let you do that."

"It's the least I can do."

"But I can't leave my son alone."

"I'll pay for a sitter."

She paused, her nostrils dilated, her shoulders straightened. "All right, sounds like fun."

"Great. All I need is directions to your home, and I'll be out of your way."

She scribbled the instructions on a piece of paper, hoping he didn't see her hand trembling. *A date! A real live date with Blue Eyes!* She tore the paper from the pad and handed it to him.

"What time should I expect you?"

"Seven."

"Perfect."

"On another topic, didn't you say your friend was picking Gordon up at the airport tonight?"

"Nine o'clock."

"Interesting."

"Why is that interesting?"

"It's nothing. I was just thinking out loud." He started for the door and then stopped. "One last thing. Who was that kid who bumped into me out in the lobby?"

"Jason Saul."

"Any relation to Peter Saul?"

"His stepson."

37

Cleveland, Ohio
1:20 P.M.

Hunter St. James hesitated before pulling open the door to the suite of offices leased by Edward J. Marsh atop the Terminal Tower Building. Odd for Pamela to want to meet him here. She could have stopped by his house if she wanted her Rolex back. But then again, this was neutral ground. He took a deep breath then jerked open the door to the lavishly appointed offices.

A young blonde sat at an ornamental desk in front of a mahogany paneled wall emblazoned with brass letters that spelled out "Edward J. Marsh Enterprises." She looked up from her computer screen.

"Good afternoon, sir, may I help you?"

"I'm here to see Pamela Marsh."

"And you are?"

"Hunter St. James."

"Oh. Go right in, she's expecting you."

Hunter pulled open the interior door and was greeted by a lean, greyhound-looking woman with an arrogant beauty about her face; she wore no makeup except a dash of carelessly applied lipstick.

"How nice to see you again, Hunter." Her voice sounded as plastic as her smile.

"Hello, Mrs. Marsh."

"You simply must come to Key West for Thanksgiving. The

weather here is so gloomy."

"I'm not sure Pamela would appreciate your invitation."

"She's waiting for you in her father's office."

Hunter walked down the corridor lined with aerial photos of various industrial properties. Pamela Marsh waited at the end of the hall; her golden hair reached down to her shoulders in gentle ringlets. A smug expression contorted her usually pretty face.

"Congratulations on your performance at Owens, Ryder and Scott."

"Very kind of you to mention it."

"Did you bring the watch?"

"Here." He dug into his suit pocket and quickly withdrew the platinum watch. "Now where's the book?"

"I left it out front with the receptionist. You can pick it up on your way out."

"When did you say Gordon was here?"

"Tuesday."

"But he left for France on Monday."

"Are you calling me a liar?"

"Somebody is lying."

"Yes, that's right, I made the whole thing up to get you to come over here so I can spit in your face. You caught me."

"But why would he come here?"

"How the hell should I know? He used the teleconference machine, and he left the book behind. What that means, I don't know, and I don't care. I've got my watch back, and you can go to Hell for all I care."

"Your compassion moves me."

"You know what, Hunter? I actually worried I made a mistake when I aborted your baby. Now I'm glad I didn't bring another loser into the world."

Her words stabbed his soul. His chest heaved as if a wild animal was trapped inside, kicking itself free. He tried to speak, but his tongue lay paralyzed. She killed his child.

"Go ahead, Hunter. Say something smart now."

"What's there to say? You're the devil."

He spun around, strode down the corridor past Mrs. Marsh, and out into the anteroom. He snatched the book off the receptionist's desk and took the elevator to the lobby. Hunter stepped out, walked across the marble floor, then out the revolving door. The crisp autumn air relieved some of the nausea. He climbed into his car and drove through the streets of Cleveland in a daze. *How could she do it? She killed my child. Probably a little boy. What kind of cold-hearted snake gloats over something like that?* Her capacity to inflict emotional pain amounted to sheer genius.

He arrived in front of his brick Victorian home just as the mailman turned the corner. Hunter opened the window. The mailman handed him a stack of letters, mostly bills, except one embossed envelope with a return address, handwritten, that he didn't recognize. He ripped open the envelope and pulled out a letter written front and back on yellow legal paper:

Dear Hunter,

Hello and how are you? I hope this letter reaches you in good spirits. In fact, I hope this letter reaches you at all. As you can see, I had one of the men here fill out the envelope in his own hand, using his own name. I knew the jail would never allow one of my letters to leave the facility.

I am writing now because I have the unmistakable premonition that I will be martyred tonight. Now, don't think I'm crazy. God didn't speak audibly, but I know His still, small voice. Read your Bible. Anyway, as my lawyer, I want you to consider this letter as my Last Will and Testament. But before I get into bequeathing my meager possessions, you and I have a little unfinished business to attend to concerning my case and the things about to happen.

On a number of occasions, I have sought to tell you about the secret organization I've investigated for many years – the group responsible for murdering my wife and Lucy Evans. The group is known by various names throughout the country; in and around Ohio they are known as the *Templetons*. Their members include the most powerful and influential men in the state. I will not go into detail about how I obtained this information, but suffice it to say my quest is well documented. They have no permanent meeting place; subsequently, they gather at a different member's home each week. They keep an extensive archive, and each new member is required to study the history. Their motto is, "Those who know the secret do not speak it; those who speak it do not know it." So those records are the key to exposing the entire organization.

At their core the *Templetons* are satanic, and their major activities are tied to the occult calendar. Friday the 13th is a sacred day used for ritual killing, hence the fate of my wife and Lucy Evans. But the most significant day of their year is Halloween. Here in the Cleveland area, at least one murder or report of a missing young woman occurs on Halloween every year. Ohio has the second highest rate of ritual murders in the nation; only California has more. I could go on and on, but I'd only be repeating what you will soon read for yourself. I have compiled a file of my research, which should aid you in your work. It's hidden in the fruit cellar in the basement of my house. I believe you still have the key. Be very careful, everything is not as it seems.

As for the disposition of my belongings, I would like my house and furniture sold with the proceeds going to the Institute for Creation Research. My library I give to you, Hunter St. James. You have an inquisitive mind that God will use for His glory if you will allow Him. I know God brought us together for a significant reason. It is up to you to discover that purpose and then fulfill it.

We have talked about the existence of pain and suffering in the world. No doubt you have already pondered my demise. Let it be an object lesson to you. Death is only frightening because we look at it from man's perspective

– not God's. Death is the doorway to Heaven for those redeemed by His grace. Isaiah wrote, "The righteous perish and no one ponders it in his heart; devout men are taken away to be spared from evil. Those who walk uprightly enter into peace; they find rest as they lie in death." But before death arrives, God uses suffering to produce morally and spiritually virtuous beings with whom He wants to have fellowship. So, you see, we must have challenges that teach us the worth of the virtues that God possesses perfectly. I know, very philosophical, but indulge a man about to depart and be with the Lord.

You are a good man, and I know the Lord will lead you to Him in time. I have accepted the Lord's will for my life with a heart filled with peace. And the peace He has given me, He will give to you. All we have to do is repent and believe He exists and that He is a rewarder of those who seek Him. May God bless and keep you.

Sincerely,

Howard Jamison

38

J ason Saul climbed down the steps of the bus in front of Bruce Richards' house, a two-story rectangle with faded yellow siding. The jostling trip from the Rapid Station sapped his energy. He paused beneath a large oak tree beside the driveway, its massive roots buckling the cement. A cold sweat covered his body; he knew his wound was infected. He walked along the side of the house to the back yard. A rusted chain-link fence surrounded a patch of knee-high grass bent over in heaps, nearly engulfing a dilapidated lawn mower that certainly hadn't seen action in a decade. The old garage at the end of the drive listed to the right and looked like it would tumble with the slightest breeze. In the yard beside the garage stood his home away from home – the van.

He climbed in the van, closed the door, then eased himself down on the mattress. He pulled up his shirt to check the wound. A reddish-brown discharge seeped through the gauze bandage stuck to his back by strips of gray duct tape; he cursed his stepfather. The man never ran out of ways of inflicting pain in his life.

Jason thought back to the earlier years when Saul first started dating his mother. He seemed so nice and playful and fatherly. Even after the wedding things went well. Then one night Jason sneaked downstairs for some cookies about two in the morning, and he stumbled upon Saul watching television in the living room. Jason stood in the doorway unnoticed for several minutes. He had never seen such images; naked people wrestling with each other. He felt sick to his stomach. Then Saul discovered him and made him come sit on his lap... and the touching began.

A coldness swept over Jason's back at the horrendous memories of Saul creeping into his bedroom in the middle of the night, leaving Jason bloody and in tears. He could still smell the putrid breath and hear Saul's words whispered demonically in his ear at the end of each session: "If you tell anyone, I'll kill your mother." For ten years he carried his secret burden, but it all would end soon – along with Saul's pulse.

The van door slid open. Richards climbed in carrying a McDonald's bag.

"I brought you some grub."

"Thanks, dude, my stomach is growling like a German Sheperd."

"How'd it go with the shrink?"

"It didn't."

"What happened?"

"Nothing. She had no answers, none that I wanted to hear anyway."

"Did she look hot?"

"Oh yeah. She wore this tight turtleneck. Man, her body was slammin'."

"So, it wasn't a complete waste."

"I only went to humor my mom." Jason bit into the Big Mac. "Funny thing was, that lawyer from the paper showed up."

"Which lawyer?"

"The pastor's lawyer."

"No way. What was he doing there?"

"I don't know."

"You got the guns?"

"Under the mattress." Jason pointed downward then took another bite.

"Cool. Halloween is just around the corner and your stepdad's party."

"Change of plans. I'm killing him tonight."

"What?!"

"He goes down tonight."

"But you said—"

"Shssshh. Listen."

A car pulled up in front of the house. They both strained their necks to peer out the rear windows. The house and oak tree at the end of the drive obscured the view to the street.

"Is your mom due back?" Jason asked.

"Not till 5:30."

"Go see who it is."

Richards quietly slid open the door then tiptoed along the side of the house. Jason watched him crouch down at the corner of the porch, peep around the corner, then come sprinting back.

"It's the cops."

"How many?"

"Two women."

"What do they want?"

"How the hell should I know? I didn't stop and kick it with them."

"My stepdad must have sent them."

"What do we do?"

"Grab the guns and go."

"Go where?"

"We'll hide in the garage."

Jason reached under the mattress and nabbed the two rifles; he handed one to Richards. They dashed across the short distance to the garage. Richards fuddled with the door.

"Hurry up," Jason whispered.

"The damn thing is stuck."

"Put some muscle on it."

Richards lowered his shoulder and pressed. The door popped open and banged against the old pickup covered by a tarp. They ducked inside. Jason gently closed the door. The place reeked of moldy cardboard and rotten wood. Stacks of newspapers, boxes and junk crammed every inch of space. Daylight glinted through rotten slat walls.

"Now what do we do?" Richards asked.

"Take up positions. If they come this way, we bust some caps."

"I ain't shooting no cops."

"It's us or them, man. Us or them."

"You do what you want, Jase, I'm gonna find us a way out of here."

Jason peered out through a hole in the wall. The two female cops stalked along the side of the house with their weapons drawn. They scanned the back yard, climbed the rickety steps to the porch, then banged on the door. He heard their muffled voices.

"Is there anybody home?!"

"We've got a warrant for the arrest of Jason Saul."

More banging on the door.

"Is there anybody home?!"

The cops climbed down the steps and headed for the van.

"Here they come, dude."

No reply.

Jason raised the rifle to his shoulder. Twisting his torso shot pain through his body. Tiny spots danced in front of his eyes. He squinted. His vision cleared. The petite, blonde cop walked directly into his line of fire. He touched the pad of his index finger against the trigger. He held his breath. Squeezed. Click.

What the...

He checked the action.

No bullets.

He heard their footsteps only a few feet away. Something moving caught the corner of his eye. Richards frantically waved his arms from the front of the garage, motioning for Jason to come to him. He heard the van door pop open.

"There's nobody here, April."

Jason froze, listened, then maneuvered through the maze of garbage strewn across the floor.

"Let's check the garage and head on back," Denholm said.

Jason made it past the front of the covered truck as the garage door opened. Daylight filled the dank building. Richards squatted down in a pile of rotten timber beside a newly constructed hole in the corner of the wall.

39

H unter St. James drove along Warrensville Center Road juggling Faith and Jamison in his mind. This was not a good time to follow his heart. He spotted Geraci's Restaurant, a great place to take a date, with old Italian men hand-tossing pizza. But was this really a date? She probably just felt sorry for him. What would he do if she were interested? He didn't have clue.

He also didn't know what to do about the Jamison situation. He considered filing a complaint against Saul with the Ohio Supreme Court for withholding evidence during discovery, but he figured Saul would use his connections to quash it. He then thought about leaking the information to the press through a friend at *The Plain Dealer.* That was still an option. And Jamison's letter would certainly look good in print. Hunter wanted to walk away, but he knew that unless he did something nobody would. He dreaded the idea of going back to Jamison's house to retrieve the file. If he decided to go – and that was a big *if* – he would go in broad daylight. He had no desire to repeat the last escapade.

Then there was Pamela. *The snake.* She knew he wanted children, and she murdered his first child. If she were a man, he would've pummeled her. He thought of the final resting place for his son, probably some dumpster in a back alley somewhere. Or maybe his tiny body lay frozen in some laboratory cooler, waiting to have his stem cells harvested. *What a nightmare.*

He stopped at the intersection of South Green Road, and his mind drifted to the task at hand. According to the directions, Faith lived up ahead on the right. The light changed, and he eased on the gas until the house number matched his directions. He found it: a red-brick ranch with an unusually wide sidewalk in the middle of the lawn. A pine tree swayed in the breeze and brushed up against the corner of the house. He stepped out of the car; his breath floated like smoke in the brisk autumn air. His hands felt clammy; his heart seemed to wrench itself free from his chest. Why such nervousness?

Get a hold of yourself, Old Boy, she's just a woman.

He walked up the smooth cement walk, holding behind his back a white rose he purchased earlier from a street vendor. He knocked on the door then took a step back. The door opened. On seeing her beautiful face, a swarm of butterflies in his stomach took to flight. Her shoulder-length hair spilled around her neck like a silky, fawn-colored waterfall. Her almond-shaped eyes sparkled. The corners of her exquisite mouth curled up in a smile that made him hold his breath. She wore a turtleneck, revealing a curvy yet athletic body. Her expression deflated. She dropped her gaze to the floor.

"What is it?" he asked.

"I'm not going to be able to make it tonight."

"Oh..." The news struck him like a blow. "Why not?"

"I couldn't find a babysitter."

"I see." *Think fast, Old Boy.* "Well, couldn't we take your son along with us? I'm good with kids."

"I don't think that's such a good idea."

"I understand." *She's blowing me off.*

"I don't think you do."

"No, it's all right." He turned to go, then remembered the rose. "Here, this is for you."

"How sweet, thank you."

"I'll see you."

"Hunter, wait." She wrinkled her forehead. "Would you like

to meet my son?"

"I'd be glad to."

"Come on in."

Confusion set in. Such contradicting signals so close together confirmed his suspicion that women are from another planet. He stepped into the foyer. Loud music blared in from the adjoining room.

"Jeremy, turn it down!" Faith yelled. "We've got company!"

The music tapered off. She led Hunter into a delicately decorated living room with pastel-gray carpeting and dusty rose walls. The music wafted in from a doorway at the far end of the room.

"Jeremy, come and meet Mr. St. James."

Hunter didn't see a child at first; he only heard an odd whining sound of an electric motor. A power wheelchair rolled into the room carrying a contorted little boy. His talon-like hand gripped the joystick on the armrest. He held his head at a severe angle over his fragile shoulder, mouth open and drooling. Hunter's heart melted. The wheelchair stopped in front of him. The boy released the joystick and with great effort swung his hand across his lap and tapped it against some sort of electronic device. A digitized voice spoke.

"Hello – how – are – you?"

"I'm fine, and, how are you?"

"Cool."

Hunter smiled then looked at Faith who seemed choked with emotion.

"It's an electronic talker," she said. "It's also a universal remote, which is how he manages to rattle the windows with his stereo." She put her hands on her hips and raised her eyebrows at the boy, who smiled and rocked his head from side to side.

"You can go back to your room now," she said.

Jeremy pecked at the machine. "It – was – nice – to – meet – you."

"My pleasure."

The chair spun around, motored across the living room, then

disappeared in the bedroom.

"He's a good boy, with a great heart." Her bottom lip quivered. "But now you see why we can't take him with us."

"No, I don't."

"Please don't play with me."

"He'd probably love the Great Lakes Science Center. I went nuts for that kind of stuff when I was a boy."

"Are you serious?"

"Absolutely."

She drew her breath sharply; tears spilled over her eyelashes and trickled down her alabaster cheeks.

"Okay." She stretched out a tremulous hand, touched his cheek, then withdrew it. "You're an angel."

40

J ason Saul climbed out of Bruce Richards' van, parked behind a clump of trees on the outskirts of Clifton Park. His stepfather had bought a brick colonial on a wooded lot bordered on the north by a 20-foot cliff above Lake Erie. The best way to approach the house unnoticed was through the woods.

"I'll be back in 20 minutes," Jason said.

"I've got your back, dude."

"Whatever happens, don't panic and drive away."

"I told you, I've got your back."

Jason eased the door closed then checked his pockets to make sure he had everything – most importantly the knife. Richards had argued that a gun would be more efficient. But the only guns they had, now that Richards ditched his pistol, were hunting rifles. Aside from being awkward to handle at close range, if something went wrong it would be impossible to explain why he was creeping around in the dark with a thirty-ought-six. The knife easily fit concealed in his pocket; besides, it was his weapon of choice.

He started walking through the woods. Off to his left he saw a lighthouse on the breakwall where he spent many happy summers fishing with his friends – friends he never dared bring home for fear Saul would molest them too.

He wiped his forehead with the back of his sleeve. In spite of the chilly air, a layer of perspiration blanketed his face. The infection grew worse by the hour. No use worrying about it now. After tonight he'd have plenty of time to rest. He emerged from the edge of the woods and trotted across the exposed green in a half-crouch. The moon overhead shone intermittently through the clouds and cast his shadow on the ground. He darted into another patch of trees, stopped, and looked around. No movement. No sound except the chirping of nocturnal insects, until his first step crunched through the underbrush.

The tree line stopped about ten yards behind his house. He crawled across the expanse deftly silent, his fingers clawing at the wet grass. He peeped his head over his mother's flower box, and to his relief darkness shrouded the rear of the house. If Saul were true to form, he would have drunk a highball about an hour ago and should be soundly asleep by now. Jason crept up to the sliding glass door to the recreation room. He tried his key; it slid into the tumblers. Thankfully Saul didn't change the locks.

Jason tiptoed across the floor in total darkness, relying on memory to avoid furniture. He stopped where he believed the bottom of the stairs to be, and snapped open the switchblade. He fished around for the bottom step then began the ascent that would end his nightmare. About halfway up, his boot heel caught the lip of a step. He stumbled, fell face first, and his ribs crashed into the steps with a thud. An explosion of pain erupted from his wounded back. The knife clattered down the wooden steps.

He froze, panicked. A voice in his head told him to run. He gathered his thoughts and listened. Nothing. No stirring up above. No one coming to investigate. Saul must have slept through the disturbance. He resolved to complete his mission. He would not give Saul another chance to defile his mother. It ended tonight.

He probed around in the dark for his knife. From the sound it made, it couldn't have gone far. Two steps down to his right, he felt something cold. The blade of his knife. He grasped it. Pain. The blade bit into his flesh. The knife tumbled back to the steps. His hand felt wet. He reached into his pocket with his left hand, grabbed his lighter, and lit it. The gash ran across all four fingers just below the knuckles. He moved his fingers and everything worked. Just a superficial wound.

He reached into his back pocket and pulled out a bandanna. He wrapped it around the wound and cinched it tight. He flicked on the lighter again and found the knife. Anger welled up in his heart. This was Saul's fault, and he would pay for this and a lifetime of other offenses.

Jason advanced with wicked resolve. He pressed open the door at the top of the steps and walked into the kitchen. A shaft of light peered in through the window above the sink. Absolute silence. He practiced a few thrusts of the knife in his left hand. It felt awkward. He couldn't get much leverage. He took the knife in his injured right hand and squeezed it in his fist. His own blood trickled down the blade. Anger turned to rage. He moved across the living room and up the curved stairway as if walking on thin ice. He stopped outside his parents' bedroom. His neck quivered with nervous weakness. His throat felt full of burs. His mind was in a frenzy.

Show time!

He kicked open the door.

His mother screamed.

Jason surged toward the bed, leapt in the air, then plunged the blade into... the empty pillow beside his mother.

"What the hell?!"

She crawled away from him, her scream vibrating with horror and frenzy. Jason bounded out of bed and went for the light switch near the door.

"Look, Mom," he said, flipping the switch. "It's me."

"Jason."

"It's me, Mom."

"What are you doing?!"

"I can't—"

"Peter! No!" she yelled.

Jason turned to see the blade of a golf club just miss his head and slam into his right shoulder. The blow dropped him to his knees. The knife flung to the floor. Saul took another swing. Jason ducked. The club head buried into the door. Saul struggled to get it loose. Jason saw the knife a few feet in front of him. He lunged for it. Saul mashed the outstretched, bloodstained hand with the heel of his shoe.

Jason howled.

Saul jerked the club free and repeatedly slammed it against the small of Jason's back, each blow landing with a ghastly thud.

"Stop! Peter! Stop!" Marilyn yelled, running at the two combatants.

Jason looked up to see his mother reach out to stop the next blow. The club struck her forearm. The bone snapped. Her hand dangled at an impossible angle. Jason jerked his hand from under Saul's shoe. He surged forward and tackled Saul, driving him into the wall in the hallway. Jason grabbed the shaft of the club, blood pulsating out of his hand. He heard his mother's whimpering cry. He wrestled the club down over Saul's throat and pressed it against his windpipe with both hands.

"Die! Die!"

Saul gasped. His eyes popped open.

"Die!"

Saul drove a knee into Jason's groin then punched him on the side of the head. Jason crumpled to the floor. Saul pressed past him into the bedroom.

"Run, Jason, run!" Marilyn screamed. "He's got a gun!"

Jason took off down the hall.

Boom! Boom!

Plaster exploded near Jason's head. He darted down the stairs.

Boom!

A chunk of the banister blew apart, showering him with splinters. He dove headfirst down the remaining steps.

Boom! Boom!

Bullets slammed into the floor at the bottom of the landing. Jason sprinted for the door.

"Run, boy, run!" Saul shouted in a maniacal voice. "When I catch you, I'll kill you!"

41

Sunday, October 29
University Heights, Ohio
8:40 A.M.

F aith McGuire sat at her kitchen table, mindlessly stirring a spoon in a cup of coffee. On the other end of the table, a stack of magazines, papers and mail leaned precariously close to the edge. She reflected on the previous day. *What a roller coaster.* Breakfast with Hunter started with boundless potential only to be dashed to pieces by the Jamison news. Who knew the evening would turn out so special? Hunter made her feel like a woman again. When he looked into her eyes, she felt he was staring into her soul. She hadn't thought much about God since her divorce, but after the amazing night with Hunter, she closed her eyes and said a prayer of thanksgiving.

Growing up in an oppressive Jehovah's Witness household, Faith entered adulthood with a bad taste in her mouth for all things religious, especially once it came to light that her father had sexually molested her older sister for several years. The hypocrisy. The man held himself out as a pillar of the community; meanwhile behind closed doors he did the unspeakable. Once the scandal became public, the elders at the Kingdom Hall refused to discipline him, no doubt because of his influence upon the governing board and the substantial financial contributions he made to the Watchtower headquarters.

While this episode of her life turned her sour against

organized religion, she always believed in God. She repudiated the Jehovah's Witnesses doctrines and longed for spiritual fulfillment. She knew God existed, and she wanted to please Him; she just didn't know how. But through it all, she never stopped praying...

Dear God, thank you for all the blessings you've given me over these years. Thanks for Jeremy just the way he is. And thank you for bringing Hunter into my life. If nothing comes out of it, I had a wonderful time last night, and you know I needed it—

The doorbell rang. A moment later Monica walked in, wearing pink sweats and carrying a bag from Jack's Deli. Faith waved her into the kitchen.

"Hello, Miss Faith, and how are we this morning?"

"Morning? It's almost noon. You're late."

"Gordon got back from France last night, and we had a little catching up to do."

"What did he do this time, electrocute you with a cattle prod?"

"No, but he did—"

"Stop right there, I don't want to know."

Monica opened the bag and reached inside.

"I've got latkes and blintzes, which do you want?"

"Blintzes."

"You look different today," Monica said, handing Faith a container. "Did you get a facial?"

"No."

"You must have done something different; you've got a glow about you. Wait a minute." Monica's mouth parted into a half-moon of glimmering teeth. "I know that look."

"No, I didn't."

"Then what is it?"

"I had a date."

"With who?"

"Hunter."

"No way! With Blue Eyes?"

"He's so sweet. He took me and Jeremy to the Great Lakes

Science Center."

"Hold on a minute, sister. You took your son on a date with you?"

"I couldn't find a sitter."

"That's why you didn't—"

"Monica, get your mind out of the gutter. Not everyone thinks with their glands."

"Really?" she said with a lilt in her voice.

"Hunter was so gentle and attentive with Jeremy. He even helped him in the restroom when the attendant wouldn't let me take him into the ladies' room."

"When did he ask you out?"

"It wasn't really a date. He wanted to thank me for doing him a favor."

"What favor?"

"None of your business."

"But what about the date? Give me the juicy stuff. Did he kiss you good night?"

"Nope." Faith drew up her feet onto the wooden chair and hugged her knees. "But I wanted him to. All night long I kept thinking about what it would be like to kiss him."

"You should've planted one on him."

"I'm not that kind of girl."

"I am."

"No kidding."

"Are you going to see him again?"

"I invited him over for dinner tonight."

"Wear something seductive."

Faith rolled her eyes. "What did the Gargoyle bring you from Paris?"

"A pair of earrings."

"What do they look like?"

"I don't know. He got mugged on the way to the airport."

"Yeah, right."

"No, he really did. He's got an eye that is nearly swollen shut and his neck is all scratched up."

"Poetic justice if you ask me." Faith gave her a scornful look. "Are you seeing him tonight?"

"He's got some sort of a meeting, but he's coming over afterward. Maybe we'll drop in on you and Blue Eyes."

"I don't think that's a good idea."

"Oh, come on. It'll be fun."

"I'd rather you not."

"Don't be a stick in the mud, we'll help you break the ice with Blue Eyes, then we'll leave."

"You promise?"

"Promise."

A bell rang in Jeremy's bedroom.

"What's that?" Monica asked.

"That's our signal if he doesn't feel well." Faith stood, drank the last of her coffee, then headed into the living room. "This may take awhile."

"I'm in no hurry."

Monica watched Faith disappear into Jeremy's room, took a bite of cookie, and noticed a *People* magazine sitting on a stack of stuff. She reached for it and knocked the whole pile onto the floor.

"Ooops."

She bent over and picked up a couple of magazines then discovered a thick manila file.

"What's this?" she whispered, looking over at Jeremy's room.

She flipped through the contents: photos of a naked woman stabbed to death, police reports, and an autopsy. She closed the file and looked at the front cover. In the upper right-hand corner in bold black letters it read, "Property of the Cuyahoga County Prosecutor's Office." In red pen someone had written *State of Ohio v. Howard Jamison.*

"What's Faith doing with this?"

42

Hunter St. James drove west on Route 2 feeling apprehensive about his return trip to Jamison's house. Getting knocked out again didn't sound like much fun. Don's Lighthouse came into view, and Hunter's mind drifted to Gordon Prescott. Somewhere along the line there would have to be a confrontation. After all, Gordon ended up with the creation vs. evolution book, and Jamison's letter certainly tied the *Templetons* into this sordid affair. But before he could decide what to do next, he needed to find Jamison's file.

He drove down West Clifton and thought about his date with Faith. His heart went out to her for carrying the burden of raising a handicapped child alone. It took a special woman to nurture a special son. The night went by too quickly, and he had fun with little Jeremy, but ruminations of his own aborted child kept cropping into his mind all evening. Even so, he wouldn't have changed a thing, except maybe he should have kissed her. He wanted to, and her lips looked so inviting. But having her son with them removed the romantic dynamic typical of a first date. It wasn't a bad thing as it allowed him to focus on getting to know her in a casual setting. But he still wanted to kiss her.

The invitation to dinner surprised him but made him feel really warm inside. He couldn't help comparing her to Pamela, and the contrast was jarring. Pamela epitomized selfishness, whereas Faith seemed selfless. Pamela was materialistic... no, he wouldn't go any further down that road. It wasn't fair to hoist

Faith atop some towering pedestal, only to topple her as soon as her flaws worked their way to the surface. Besides, he already felt a tinge of guilt over leaving Saul's discovery file with her. He didn't like getting her involved, but then again, whom would she possibly tell?

He pulled over at the curb in front of Jamison's house. It didn't look so ominous in the daylight. A robin pecked at the bird feeder hanging from the side of the porch. Hunter walked up the sidewalk and noticed the old Italian woman – whose car he wrecked – peeking at him from behind a curtain. He nodded to her; she disappeared. He climbed the cement steps and tried the door. It was unlocked.

"That's odd."

Then he thought back to his hasty exit a few days earlier. He never stopped to lock the door. He walked inside, through the musty living room, and into the dining room. He stopped to examine the thread-worn, avocado-green carpeting at the spot of his attack. Nothing out of the ordinary. No clues. He continued into the kitchen; the floor creaked under his weight.

Bright sunshine filtered in through a dirty window and fell on a small breakfast table. To the left of the refrigerator, a door caught his attention. He pulled it open; stairs descended into darkness. He flipped the light switch on the wall, and nothing happened.

"Wonderful."

He searched the shelf inside the door to the right and found a yellow flashlight. He pressed the button, and a dim bulb lit up. It would have to do. He ventured down the stairs, a luminous circle of light bobbing with each step. Cobwebs brushed his face. He swatted the silky strands away and continued. A dank, moldy scent encompassed him as he reached the bottom of the stairs. He scanned the faint light around the room. A rusted-out washer and dryer stood in the corner. A plywood door was unlatched to his right. He pulled it open and looked inside. A chain hung from a light fixture in the middle of the low ceiling. He tugged it, and to his relief it lit up.

He thought he heard a creaking noise.

Must have been his imagination. He rummaged through shelf after shelf of canned goods and found nothing. He checked behind a row of glass jars; a small leather satchel lay underneath a stack of paper bags. *Pay dirt!* He pulled it out and looked inside.

The handwriting on the loose-leaf pages matched Jamison's letter. Most of the contents seemed to be dedicated to Jamison's wife's murder, including a list of men who belonged to the Charleston, West Virginia, chapter of the *Templetons*. He ran his finger down the list. None of the names looked familiar. *Wait. Brandon Marsh. That's Pamela's uncle, the real estate developer.* He double-checked the list. No other name rang a bell. He flipped through the file looking for a roster from the Cleveland area.

"Ah ha."

He found a list of 13 names under the heading "Templetons Alpha Delta Chapter" based in the greater Cleveland area. He scanned his finger down the list: Albert Owens, his former boss; Edward Marsh, Pamela's father; Peter Saul, his nemesis; and at the bottom of the list Gordon Prescott, his lifelong friend. A heavy foreboding engulfed him as he closed the file. The most influential men in his life belonged to a secret society that Jamison claimed was satanic and involved in ritual murder.

He ran the list of names through his mind again. These men had the power and position to kill people and get away with it. Over the past few months Hunter managed to run afoul of all of them. Is that why the Jamison case fell into his lap? Why he lost his job? If he fought back, what would stop them from burying him alongside Jamison?

The injustice enraged him. What gave these arrogant jackals the right to victimize these innocent women? His anger rose. He would expose the *Templetons*. He would set their privileged rat's nest on fire. But how? This file amounted to information, not evidence. He needed something tangible that would stand up in court. He needed the *Templetons* archive. And Gordon Prescott was going to give it to him.

He heard something on the steps.

"Damn."

He jammed the paperwork back in the satchel then reached for the light chain. A wide-shouldered man stooped through the doorway and stood with his legs wide apart. He pointed a rifle at Hunter's forehead.

43

J ason Saul staggered out of the van in the Kroger's parking lot, dead drunk. His body ached. The wound in his back continued to ooze a yellow fluid. He felt sure he cracked a couple of ribs during his swan dive down the steps at his parents' house. The alcohol took the edge off, but not completely. He grasped Bruce Richards' forearm, and the two stumbled toward the main entrance. They needed food, beer and money.

Jason caught his reflection in the window of a Ford Bronco. His normally spiked hair lay limp and matted to his scalp with grease and sweat. Two of the rings looping through his right eyebrow were tangled together. For an instant he remembered the bright-eyed face that used to smile at him from the mirror. *What happened? How did life get so bad?*

Following the second failed assassination attempt, the duo drank nonstop, driving from town to town trying not to leave a trail for Peter Saul's bloodhounds to follow. Jason took his stepfather's parting words to heart: "When I catch you, I'll kill you."

All Jason wanted in life was a happy family. Peter Saul dashed that dream. Jason loathed the idea that at any moment Saul could defile his mother just as he had been violated so many times over the years. He hated Saul for stealing his innocence, for infecting him with self-disgust. No little boy should have to endure such nightmares.

Richards leaned over and whispered in Jason's ear.

"I'll get the booze; you get the grub."

"What the hell are we doing here?"

"Making a pit stop, dude. It was your idea."

"Not this." He swung his arm around his head. "I mean this."

"You lost it, dude."

"We can't live like this."

"We sure as hell can't go back."

"We're screwed."

They went inside and split up. The floor seemed to list to the right. Jason countered by stumbling to the left; his unlaced jackboots clopped with each step. He found himself in the baby food aisle. Suddenly the Gerber's creamed corn looked appetizing. He reached for a jar then noticed all the women staring at him.

"What are you looking at? Ain't you ever saw a freak show before?"

The women stood open-mouthed as he fumbled into the row of dry goods. Cereal didn't appeal to him. He wanted something substantial. He weaved through the maze of shelves and found the frozen food section. He looked around, didn't see any clerks, then stuffed two packages of bologna down the front of his pants. He strolled beside the cooler, running his hand along the frosted edge, nabbing a block of cheese here, a package of lunchmeat there. In a few moments, with pockets bulging, he set off to find Richards.

Flashing neon signs pointed the way to the cold-beverage section on the far wall. No one seemed to watch as he covered the distance, trying to walk a bit more erect. He turned the corner. No Richards.

"Where the hell is he?"

He first thought to head back to the van and start eating. Richards would eventually turn up. Then again, Richards was the kind of guy to do something stupid and get them both busted in the process. Jason headed off through the cavernous store playing his own brand of Marco Polo.

The canned fruits aisle.

"Richards."

No answer.

The feminine products section.

"Richards."

No reply.

Off in the corner he heard a distinct laughter, a high-pitched whining like the sound of a siren winding down.

"What did the idiot do now?"

Jason walked in the direction of the disturbance with long strides and arrived at the same time as the white-smocked manager. Richards sat with his back propped against the base of the Reddi-wip display case. Half a dozen cans were strewn along the floor, caps off, foam spilling out. Richards held the nozzle of a fresh can in his mouth, pressed the trigger, and inhaled the propellant until foam blasted into his mouth.

"What the hell are you doing?" Jason asked.

"Wip-its," he said with a giggle. "I can hear spaceships."

"Someone has to pay for this," the manager said.

"We will." Jason bent over and grabbed Richards by the armpits. A package of bacon fell out of his coat.

"What's going on here?"

"I was going to pay for that."

"You two stay right where you are." The manager jogged over to a wall-mounted phone, pressed a few digits, then spoke over the loudspeaker. "Security to Aisle 5, security to Aisle 5."

Jason nodded at Richards. They broke for the door.

"Stop!"

Jason tripped over his own feet and fell headfirst into a dog food display. Richards returned to help him up. A brown-uniformed security guard sprinted up the aisle behind them.

"Go, go!" Jason shouted in Richards' face.

They stormed through the store, dodging old ladies carrying baskets and shopping carts loaded with groceries. Up ahead people at the checkout registers clogged the lines. No way out. Where to go? Jason headed toward the row of grocery carts, dove on top of them, then crashed to the floor. Richards followed right behind.

"Stop!" someone yelled.

They frantically scrambled to their feet then headed toward the exit. A security guard posted himself at the door, gun drawn, and terror on his face. The boys headed straight for him.

"Grab my arm!" Jason shouted.

They joined arms.

The guard flinched.

They clotheslined him on their way out the door.

44

Lakewood, Ohio
3:10 P.M.

Hunter St. James threw his hands in the air. The cold steel of the barrel dug into his forehead.

"Take it easy there, fella'. Don't shoot."

"What do you think yer doin' here?" The man's face was all pushed over to the left; he had the biggest eyebrows Hunter had ever seen. "What's in that there case yer holdin' over yer head?"

"Some papers."

"They's yer papers?"

Hunter stammered.

"Well, are they's?"

"I can explain."

"I don't think you can, that's what I think." He cocked the trigger. "In fact, I think I blow yer brains out, and the cops'll give me a medal."

Hunter took a small step back. The light chain brushed his hand. He yanked it. Darkness.

BOOM!

The muzzle flash singed Hunter's right ear. He grabbed the scalding hot barrel and jerked it with all his strength. He stumbled back into the shelf, holding the gun. Darkness. He got tackled. They struggled on the cement floor. A blow struck Hunter in the jaw. He swung the butt of the gun blindly and struck something hard. The assailant collapsed on top of him. He shrugged the man off, got to his feet, and turned on the light. The stranger lay in a puddle of blood; his jaw unhinged; his front teeth knocked out. Hunter grabbed the satchel, bolted up the steps, then calmly walked out the front door, checking both ways to see if anybody was watching.

He climbed in his car and noticed his pants felt wet. Blood saturated both legs.

"He shot me."

He ran his hands up and down his thighs. *No pain. It must be the stranger's blood.* He fired the engine and headed home with his heart racing. *What the hell just happened, Old Boy?*

Twenty minutes later he parked his car in the driveway and went inside his Victorian home on Overlook Road. He dropped the satchel on the kitchen table then went to the sink and ran cold water over his head. *Who was that guy?* No matter. He'd gotten in too deep; now there was no turning back. He changed his pants, went to the gun cabinet, and grabbed his father's .357 revolver. He wouldn't be caught unprepared again.

He drove east on Route 322, heading for Gordon Prescott's house in Gates Mills, wondering how he should go about getting the information his life depended on. Maybe he should appeal to their years of friendship? Or maybe he should just jam the gun into his face and demand the archive. He knew he could never shoot his old friend – or anyone else for that matter – but striking the fear of God into Prescott was another matter.

Hunter drove along the two-lane road mustering up the courage to pull off his grand coup when he spotted an oncoming car that looked a lot like Prescott's black Mercedes. A couple moments later the two cars passed, and sure enough, Prescott gave a nod and wave. So much for Hunter's plan. Now what should he do? He could turn around and come back later. No. If he didn't go now, common sense would get the best of him.

His cell phone rang.

"Hello?"

"Hey buddy, where are you going?" Gordon Prescott asked.

"Orchard Hills."

"To do what?"

Think fast. "Hit a bucket of balls at the driving range."

"I thought you might be coming up to visit me."

"Why would I do that?"

"To see your buddy after his trip to France."

"I thought I was *persona non grata* since Owens fired me."

"Not to me."

"Do you want to turn around and meet me at your house?" Hunter asked, trying to sound casual.

"Can't. Got a meeting."

"On Sunday?"

"Unofficial business."

"*Templetons*?"

"I can't say."

"Maybe we'll get together later."

"Sure."

They hung up.

That was a close one. Hunter hoped that Prescott didn't sense any hesitation in his voice. But with Prescott on his way to a *Templetons* meeting, that meant he'd be gone for at least a couple of hours. That would give Hunter plenty of time to get into Prescott's house, find whatever he could, and get out. This might work out yet.

A few minutes later Hunter pulled onto the red-brick driveway in front of Prescott's palatial home, a three-story monstrosity of lobster-colored brick and stone the hue of unripe tomatoes. Prescott boasted of its Gothic architecture; Hunter thought it looked pretentious. He parked in front of the six-pillar portico jutting out from the center of the house. He tucked the .357 in the back of his pants.

What to do? He stood staring at the front of the house, trying to figure out how to get inside. He knew Prescott had installed a security system. He jogged around the side of the building, his white Nikes sinking into the soggy turf with each stride. He was careful to stay 20 yards from the house to avoid setting off potential motion detectors. Manicured shrubs and trees grew along the base of the house. He scanned the gutters and awnings for a siren or bullhorn or motion detector. He didn't want to trip the alarm and alert the neighbors before he had the chance to disarm the system.

He made his way around the back of the house. A green tarp covered the in-ground pool. He scrutinized the back of the house. Nothing. He worked his way around the other side of the house, searching every crevice, but found zilch. He jogged to his car, popped the trunk, then rummaged through his toolbox and grabbed a pair of wire cutters and a long-necked screwdriver about a foot long. He followed the telephone line to a box on the right side of the house. Dampness saturated his jeans as he squeezed in between a gap in the foliage. He popped open the box, snipped the telephone line, then sprinted back into the trees and hid. He figured if he tripped the alarm, the police would show up within ten minutes. If not, he was safe to go inside. With the phone line out, the internal alarm was harmless since it could not send a signal to the police. He checked his watch. Ten minutes. Fifteen minutes. No sign of the police. He trotted around the back of the house and climbed up on the extravagant brick decking. He scaled the railing and jammed the screwdriver into the lower right-hand corner of the window beside an exterior vent. He rocked the screwdriver up and down, prying it deeper into the frame. He pressed down with all his strength. The wood cracked. The lock snapped. Hunter stumbled back then caught his balance. He tried the window. It slid open. He crawled inside and found himself in the laundry room.

He took a few deep breaths then stepped into the hall. A whooping siren went off at ear-splitting decibels. He covered his ears and fought the urge to panic. The noise emanated from the kitchen. He ran down the hall, found the siren, and pummeled it with the butt of the .357. The noise stopped, thank God.

A surge of adrenaline coursed through his veins. He stood still for a couple of moments listening to the silence. No time to waste. He went straight for Prescott's office on the far side of the house. The room was testimony to a rich boy's ego, walnut-paneled walls lined with photos of Prescott standing next to other rich and powerful people.

Hunter dug into the filing cabinet behind the desk. Zippo. He searched the desk. Nothing. He grabbed the handle of the closet door behind the desk; a chirping noise startled him. Another alarm? No. His cell phone.

"Hello."

"Hunter, this is Faith. How are you?"

"Fine."

"I can barely hear you. Are you whispering?"

"I must be on the edge of my phone's range."

"I won't keep you long. I was just wondering if you'd like to watch a DVD after dinner?"

"Sounds great."

"Are you all right? You sound out of breath."

"I'm fine. Fine."

"Is there anything you'd like to see?"

"Pick whatever you like."

"All right then, I'll see you tonight."

"I can't wait."

"Ba-bye."

Hunter raised his hand to his chest. His heart thundered with each beat. He turned off the phone. He didn't need any more shocks like that. He turned his attention back to the closet behind the desk and jerked open the door. A set of golf clubs leaned against the wall in one corner. A few coats hung from brass hooks on the rear wall. To the right, a pile of newspapers sat on a blanket covering some sort of box.

He picked up the papers, careful not to get them out of order. He lifted the blanket to discover an ancient wooden chest that looked like it had been around since the Civil War. He hoisted the lid. A small velvet case sat on top of stacks of leather-bound ledgers and files. He opened the case to reveal a dagger with rubies, sapphires and emeralds encrusted into the golden handle. He'd never seen such a thing. It looked like it belonged in a museum in a glass case. He pried the knife out of its form-fitted cradle. Something jagged pinched his middle finger. He rolled the handle over in his palm. A large jewel was missing from its setting. *Why is that significant?* His mind locked onto the discovery file. *An emerald found at Lucy Evans' murder scene. This is the knife.*

"Gordon, what have you done?"

Hunter wiped the dagger on his shirt, carefully put it back in its case, then returned to the chest. The dates on the ledgers went back to 1863. He found the most recent book. Inside he found what appeared to be a family tree. Each entry listed a member's name, a date, and a name in parentheses. Below each entry a vertical line connected it to the member below. The dates on the first page began in the 1970s. He flipped through a few pages and found Gordon Prescott, the date October 13, 2017, and the name in parentheses – Lucy Evans.

"Wow!"

The date must correspond to the initiation, and the name the person he had to kill to become a member. Unbelievable! He turned back a few pages in search of the entry for Peter Saul. He found it. The date June 13, 1986, and he killed... David St. James – Hunter's father!!!

Hunter staggered back with tightness clutching his chest. The walls seemed to recede and waver. The ledger distorted like a shape in water. He started hyperventilating. He cupped his hands over his nose and mouth. This couldn't be. All these years hating his father for abandoning and disgracing the family was a baseless lie? White spots danced in front of his eyes. If his father didn't kill himself, then maybe he didn't embezzle from his clients either. Hunter rubbed his eyes with his thumb and forefinger. Why did the *Templetons* kill his father? There must be a reason. He pictured Peter Saul creeping into his father's cell with a garrote in his hands. The scene was too terrible to contemplate. He forced himself to focus and get back to the records. Time ticked away.

He looked through the membership entries above and below Peter Saul. None of the names meant anything to him. Although, one of the names in parentheses stuck out. Melissa

Phillips. What was it about that name?

A noise. A car engine outside.

Hunter scrambled to the window. A blue car he didn't recognize pulled in behind his Jaguar. A woman he didn't know climbed out of the driver-side door.

"Oh no."

He ran back to the closet, stuffed the ledgers and dagger back into the chest then tossed the blanket over it. He set the newspapers back in place, grabbed a pair of stained boat shoes, and took off for the laundry room. He dashed across the kitchen floor, his footfalls reverberating off the walls.

"Who's there?!" a female voice shouted.

45

Peter Saul parked his black BMW in the reserved space on Euclid Avenue in front of the Cleveland Athletic Club. The *Templetons* had been holding their annual meeting behind these hallowed walls since the building was first constructed in 1911. Saul felt proud to be a part of that power-wielding legacy. He climbed out of the car and looked up at the Harvest Moon shining in the cloudless, copper-green sky, the smell of autumn in the air.

Once inside Saul took the elevator to the 7th floor. The meeting was held in the Sterling Room. Members milled around in the anteroom, getting ready. Saul slipped into his black robe and took his place with the rest of the *Templetons*. Apprehension seized him. Gordon Prescott's initiation turned into an absolute debacle, and the more he tried to cover it up, the more it unraveled. No doubt the Worship Master would demand an explanation. He noticed a smudge on his black wingtips. He bent over, and a spasm seized his back. Last night's brawl with Jason left him hurting all over. In hindsight, he was glad he didn't shoot the boy. Aside from the mess, Marilyn would never go along with the cover-up. He didn't want to kill her, but he would if he had to. Nevertheless, the punk had to die. Soon.

Saul heard the muffled bang of a gavel. The arched doors in front of him opened, and the men marched into the grand hall in two lines on either side of the yellow and cream pilasters.

The overhead brass chandeliers burned dimly. His leather shoes sank into the ornate, lavender carpet. A semi-circle of 13 empty chairs arched in front of an elevated podium, where Edward Marsh stood waiting in the scarlet robe of the Worship Master. His fierce, bulldog face was framed in a tangle of silver hair; two dark eyes gleamed from behind thick-tufted, overhung eyebrows. Saul looked over at the 11 men marching in with him, all dressed in black robes except one – Gordon Prescott – clothed in the brown robe of a neophyte. Saul's neophyte.

Marsh rapped the gavel. The man to Saul's right stepped forward.

"As the sun rises in the east to open and adorn the day, so presides the Worship Master in the east to open and adorn his lodge."

"The high meeting of the Alpha Delta Templetons is now in session," Marsh said, "you may be seated. Sergeant at arms, call the roll."

A tall, broad-faced, square-shouldered man stood and methodically called out the 13 names. Each responded with, "Present."

"All present and accounted for."

"Brothers, before we get into tonight's ceremony," Marsh said, "we have a mound of old business to attend to. It seems this Jamison saga will just not go away. Brother Saul, give us the status report."

"The situation is under control, sir."

"You had the man killed in a public facility, and you call that under control?"

"The location was unavoidable."

"Rain is unavoidable. The scene of a murder is arbitrary."

"But the problem is solved."

"St. James is still out there snooping around." Marsh glared at Prescott. "He's your responsibility."

"We shouldn't expect any more trouble out of him," Prescott said.

"Correct me if I'm wrong, but aren't you the same man who

said St. James could be manipulated like a puppet?"

"Yes, but—"

"Such mistakes could prove fatal. We really don't know what Jamison told him."

"Yes we do," Saul said. "I have the attorney rooms bugged."

"If he's not a concern, then why are we tailing him?"

"He has a discovery file from my office."

"How did he get that?"

"I gave it to him by accident."

"You what?!" Marsh's enraged face flushed red. "I don't know how you morons muster the mental capacity to keep your hearts pumping. Does it implicate us?"

"No."

"St. James is a loose end that needs to be cut."

"If you give me just a little more time," Prescott said, "I'm sure I can convince him to relocate to another part of the country."

"Just like you managed to get him to sell out Jamison?"

Prescott opened his mouth as if to speak then closed it.

"I allowed my daughter to get involved in this elaborate scheme of yours, because I thought I saw potential in you," Marsh said with a snarl of contempt. "The matter is no longer open to negotiations. St. James must die."

"Yes, Worship Master." Prescott bowed his head then lifted it with a look of determination in his eyes. "You can count on me."

"I don't care how it's done, but I want him dead this week."

"Yes, Worship Master."

"High Priest Coleman, have you selected the offering for All-Hallows Eve?"

"I've got a 16-year-old virgin lined up."

"Is she a Christian?"

"Yes."

"Excellent."

"Excuse me, Worship Master," Saul said. "I strongly suggest that we consider using this opportunity to purge ourselves of another loose end."

"Who would that be?"

"There's a woman St. James has been seeing, a psychologist. A few days ago, I had her building evacuated in order to bug her office."

"Good work. What has he told her so far?"

"Only superficial facts relating to Pastor Jamison. But he has recently started seeing her outside the office. I don't think we should take the chance of pillow talk. Sun Tzu says, 'When the thunderclap comes, there is no time to cover the ears.'"

"Priest Coleman, do you have any objection to using this woman... what's her name?"

"Faith McGuire."

"Do you have any objection to using this Faith McGuire woman instead of the girl you already found?"

"No, Worship Master."

"Very good. So, it is decreed, Faith McGuire will be sacrificed on Halloween."

46

Hunter St. James froze in Prescott's kitchen. The laundry room door beckoned from a dozen feet away. He strained to hear the unexpected visitor's footsteps. *Which way is she moving?* He couldn't tell. He tiptoed across the ceramic tile floor toward the laundry room, looking over his shoulder in the direction he last heard her voice. He knew she would walk into the kitchen at any moment. What could he possibly say?

"Who's there?" the female voice called in a strained pitch. She sounded closer.

The center island stood a few feet away. Hunter ducked down behind it. He peered out from between its legs.

"This isn't funny, Gordon. Is that you?"

Should he knock her down and bolt for the front door? His eyes scanned the room. A set of knives on top of the island caught his attention. He pulled one out of its slot – a serrated blade about a foot long. *That should scare her. What am I doing with a knife when I've got a gun right here?*

He slid the knife back into the slot, then pivoted his weight on the balls of his feet so he faced the laundry room.

"All right, whoever you are. I'm calling the police."

She was in the kitchen, only a few feet away. He heard her pick up the receiver from the wall-mounted phone. He heard her press three digits. Certainly 9-1-1.

"I don't know what you did to the phones, but it won't work

on my mobile."

What to do? His eyes darted around for a projectile. He saw a glass saltshaker on the counter a couple feet away. He snatched it, squatted down, then threw it at the window over the sink.

The glass shattered.

She screamed.

Her footsteps raced down the hall. *Now.* He broke for the laundry room. He closed the door, dove on the dryer, then shinnied out the window. He sprinted around the corner of the house. His feet slipped on the wet grass. Down he went, landing on his hip and sliding several feet. He bounced up and dashed for his car. His hands trembled; he fumbled with the keys. The engine fired. Tires pealed out on the red bricks. The car fishtailed to the end of the drive, slid to a near stop, then accelerated down the two-lane road.

"Thank God I made it."

Something dug into Hunter's back. The loaded gun. He tossed it on the seat next to him. He glanced into the rearview mirror. No one followed. He took a deep breath and tried to collect his thoughts. *What the hell is going on?* His mind vacillated from his father to Prescott to the *Templetons. How could this be?* His father murdered. His best friend a killer. What should he do? Go to the police? No. The *Templetons* probably controlled them. He needed someone outside the local jurisdiction. Maybe the FBI. He needed more proof. The story sounded ridiculous even in his own mind. He needed the archive chest. He needed the dagger to match against Lucy Evans' wounds. He needed to go back. But right now was out of the question.

Something caught his attention in the rearview mirror. A car pulled out behind him from a side road. A police car.

"Wonderful." He pounded the steering wheel. "Don't panic, Old Boy. He can't possibly—"

The flashing lights lit up.

"Damn. She must have given them a description of my car."

What to do? Make a break for it? No. He would just pull

over and deny everything. Surely there must be more than one midnight-blue Jaguar on the streets of Geauga County. He was just a lawyer on his way to Orchard Hills for a round of golf. *What's so hard to believe about that?* Hunter slowed down and veered over to the side of the road, the tires crunching over the gravel. The squad car pulled over behind him. The trooper climbed out of his car and adjusted his mirrored sunglasses. A thought struck Hunter like a punch in the gut. *What if she gave the police my license plate number?*

No amount of rhetorical gyration on his part could extricate him from this trap. Too late to worry about it now. He would have to take his chances. The trooper approached the driver-side door and motioned for Hunter to open the window.

"What can I do for you, officer?"

"License and registration, please."

"Yes sir."

Hunter reached back for his wallet then noticed the gun sitting on the passenger seat. He froze. His stomach knotted. Did the cop see it? He turned his head toward the window. The trooper pointed his drawn pistol at the tip of Hunter's nose.

"Put your hands on the wheel."

Hunter complied.

"Is that firearm loaded?"

"Yes sir."

"Why do you have a loaded firearm?"

"Officer, I'm an attorney, and I am notifying you that I intend to exercise my right to remain silent."

"All right, lawyer boy, step out of the car. Slowly."

Hunter grasped the handle and surged against the door with all his strength, knocking the trooper to the ground. He fired the engine and put the car in gear. The tires squealed on the pavement.

Boom! Boom!

The rear window shattered.

Hunter ducked.

Boom!

The bullet thumped into the trunk. Hunter turned around to see the trooper scrambling back into his car.

"What have I done?"

He pressed the accelerator to the floor. A siren blared from behind. The squad car closed the gap. Hunter slammed on the brakes, slid sideways through the four-way intersection at State Route 306, and nearly clipped a car pulling out of the Shell station. He swerved through the oncoming traffic and made it back to the right-hand lane. The squad car screeched through the intersection in a controlled skid and got right behind him.

"This guy is good."

Hunter weaved around the slow-moving traffic, heading south. Up ahead a line of cars waited at another intersection. He steered over onto the berm, laying on the horn. He made a hard right and fishtailed onto a two-lane road heading out into the countryside. A few moments later the squad car turned the corner about a hundred yards behind. Hunter looked ahead. The road stretched out fairly straight for as far as he could see. He stomped on the gas pedal. The speedometer darted up over 100. The squad car kept gaining. Hunter turned his attention back to the road. He blew through a stop sign. A yellow sign with a black arrow pointing right appeared over the crest of the hill. A dead end into a side road.

Hunter stomped on the brakes and jerked the wheel to the right. The car didn't respond; it blasted through the sign then went airborne. Silence. A house. The garage door open. Hunter turned his head and shielded his face with his arms. The airbag inflated. The car burst through the back of the garage and roared into a field. Corn stalks struck the bumper and flew over the hood, blinding him. The speeding car broke into a clearing. Sapling trees dead ahead. He braced his arms against the wheel. The impact launched him into the windshield, striking the side of his head and shoulder.

He sat for a few moments, dazed, but relieved to be alive. He chuckled.

"At least the cop couldn't have followed that path."

He forced open the door, struggled out of the car, and staggered off in the general direction of Old Mill Road. He reached into his pants pocket, pulled out his cell phone, and dialed 9-1-1.

"Hello, this is Hunter St. James. I'd like to report my car was stolen about 20 minutes ago from the Tavern of Chester."

47

University Heights, Ohio
5:17 P.M.

F aith McGuire stirred the marinara sauce on the stove in her kitchen. She decided a pasta dish for dinner made more sense than trying to impress Hunter with something elaborate, plus there was less chance of something going wrong. She wanted everything perfect for him. She spent the day scouring the house, changing the drapes, and primping herself. Earlier she ironed a pair of low-rider jeans that showed just a touch of midriff, then pulled a peach sweater out of the closet that accentuated her figure. The ensemble lay on her bed waiting for the precise moment. Right now, she wore an old pair of sweats.

She sipped the sauce from a wooden spoon. Perfect. She headed for the living room for her final preparations. Music thundered in from Jeremy's room.

"Turn it down in there, kiddo! You trying to go deaf?!"

The volume diminished.

"Thank you."

She sat on the sofa and inserted pink foam spacers between her toes, then shook a bottle of Raspberry Freeze nail polish. She looked at her feet and thought she should have had a pedicure. Hunter would arrive in about an hour and a half, and she hadn't started on her hair and makeup. She hoped he'd be a little late.

She started with the big toe on her left foot and worked her way down to the sliver of nail on her pinkie toe. That little appendage always gave her trouble. She tried to keep the brush on the tiny nail, but the polish dribbled onto her skin.

"Darn it."

She used her thumbnail to scoop up the spillage then fanned her toes with her hand. They needed a good half hour to dry. She examined her handiwork. Not bad at all.

The doorbell rang.

"Who could that be?" she said just above a whisper. "This is not a good time."

Faith hobbled over to the door, walking on the heel of her left foot. A smudge at this point would set her back precious minutes she couldn't afford to spare. She tried to suppress the feeling of irritation at the untimely interruption before opening the door.

"Hunter! You're early."

He forced a smile, but he didn't look good. Scratches lined the side of his face, and a large bump protruded from the right side of his forehead.

"I had a little accident."

"Come in, come in. Are you all right?"

"I think so."

She opened the door and stepped back. He walked with a slight limp. Both knees were grass-stained, and his button-down shirt was stuck to his chest by dried blood. His eyelids sagged.

"What happened?"

"I wrecked my car."

"Maybe I should take you to a hospital."

"No. I'm okay. I just need to rest for a minute."

"Here. Sit on the couch."

She saw the bottle of polish on the coffee table, then suddenly became aware of how she looked. Her damp hair was pulled back in a ponytail. No makeup.

"What happened?"

"It's a long story." His voice sounded weak. "I have so much to tell you. Just let me catch my breath."

"That looks bad." She brushed the hair off his forehead. "Let me get you some ice."

She hurried off to the kitchen. *What a disaster.* She looked a mess. She hadn't started the noodles yet. He wrecked his car. *How come things never go according to plan?* She found a Ziploc bag in the cupboard and filled it with ice from the refrigerator door dispenser, spilling some on the floor. She bent to pick up the ice and noticed lint from the carpet stuck in the fresh toenail polish. *What a mess.*

She hustled back to the living room. Hunter had taken off his leather jacket and slumped back into the overstuffed couch.

"Here you go, sweetie." She winced. *Did I say sweetie out loud?*

He opened his eyes.

"Thank you."

She gently cradled the ice over his wound.

"I really should take you to the hospital."

"I'd rather spend the evening with you."

"That's sweet."

"I don't know how to say this so…"

Starting with the day he met Jamison, Hunter told her everything. She listened intently trying to digest the avalanche of information. At first the stuff about the *Templetons* sounded too outlandish to be true. But as he discussed the items he discovered at Prescott's house, the story rang true. She never liked the Gargoyle; something about him gave her the heebie-jeebies. Her intuition told her Hunter was right about the *Templetons* being responsible for the Lucy Evans murder and Jamison's alleged suicide.

Hunter explained the contents in Saul's discovery file. The emerald found at the crime scene no doubt came from Gordon's jewel-encrusted dagger. That was solid evidence. And his bloodstained boat shoes would match the boat shoe prints in the church. BCI determined that the smooth-sole shoeprints were Pastor Jamison's. Hunter still wondered about the third set of footprints, thinking that Jason Saul's Nazi jackboots might match. As for the tennis shoe prints outside the church window, it could have been anyone. The presence of three people at the church crime scene indicated a degree of conspiracy.

Faith's heart melted when, with tear-rimmed eyes, he told of the demise of his father. So much pain filtered through his tremulous voice as he talked about the years of misplaced anger he felt toward his dad. Hunter paused for a moment, looked into her eyes, and said, "That's it."

"Only one question remains."

"What's that?"

"What do we do about it?" she asked.

"We?"

"We, as in you and me."

48

Hunter St. James awoke to the sound of an electric motor whining a few feet from his head. He didn't recognize the sound or the room. He sat up. His head throbbed; his ribs hurt when he breathed.

"Where am I?"

His eyes followed the sound of the motor. A wheelchair. Jeremy McGuire's wheelchair. He remembered telling Faith the whole story and she seemed to take it pretty well, and he vaguely recalled her going to the kitchen to stir the sauce, but that was it. He stretched his neck toward the kitchen. No sign of her. A couple moments later the wheelchair returned.

"Hey, Sport, where's your mother?"

"In - the - bedroom," the digitized voice said as Jeremy pecked at the computerized talker. "Getting - dressed."

"I must've fallen asleep."

"I - thought - you - were - dead."

Hunter checked his pulse. "Oh no, Sport, I think you're right."

Jeremy's face lit into a smile; his twisted frame convulsed in a full-body laugh.

"What's going on here?" Faith asked, standing in the doorway of the hall adjoining the living room. Two braided strands clenched her chestnut hair at the back of her head, allowing the rest to cascade down her back. Her form-fitting sweater didn't quite reach the top of her jeans, revealing a taut abdomen and an adorable belly button.

"Wow, you look amazing."

"Oh this? Just something I threw together."

"You throw rather well."

"How are you feeling?"

"Much better," he lied.

"Did you sleep well?"

"Sorry about that. I didn't come here to crash."

"You had a rough day." She walked across the living room, her bare feet sinking into the pastel-gray carpet. "I dressed that wound."

"I didn't know it was bleeding."

"You got pretty banged up."

"Thanks." He pulled up his shirt and examined the bandage.

"Are you ready to eat?"

"Absolutely."

"Just give me a couple minutes to get Jeremy to bed, and I'll be right in for dinner."

"Good night, Jeremy," Hunter said.

"Good - night."

Jeremy drove the wheelchair into his bedroom; Faith walked close behind. Hunter stood up and couldn't believe the pain. Stiffness seized his shoulders and back. He twisted at the waist a few times trying to limber up. It didn't help. He walked into the kitchen and was greeted by the inviting aroma of simmering marinara sauce mingled with a hint of garlic. His mouth watered. He looked at his watch and realized he hadn't eaten in over 12 hours. To his right in the breakfast nook, a pink cloth draped the round table. Tiny tongues of flame danced atop two long-stemmed lavender candles. Beads of sweat ran down the side of a brass ice bucket. He grabbed the bottle by the neck and pulled it out far enough to read the label.

"Stone Cellars Chardonnay."

A hand touched his shoulder. He startled.

"I didn't mean to frighten you," she said.

"Today's got me a little edgy."

"I can only imagine."

"You didn't have to go to all this trouble."

"Nonsense. I love to cook. Have a seat."

He eased himself into the chair then watched Faith working over the stove. *What a remarkable, special woman. A successful professional. A dedicated mother. Intelligent. Beautiful. Simply amazing.* She turned around holding a platter of noodles. He smiled. She smiled back.

"I hope you like pasta," she said.

"My mom was 100 percent Italian. I grew up on pasta."

"Then I hope mine doesn't pale by comparison." She walked over and set the platter on the table. "Why don't you pour the wine while I get the sauce."

"Certainly."

He picked up the corkscrew from beside the ice bucket, inserted it into the cork, and pulled. Pain shot through his right shoulder. The bottle slipped from his hand. He caught it inches from the floor. He glanced over at Faith. Thank God she didn't see him. He switched hands and pulled with his left. The cork released with a pop. He poured the wine into the crystal stemware. She returned with a glass bowl of sauce and a basket of rolls still steaming from the oven.

"This looks wonderful."

She filled both plates with pasta then ladled the sauce over it.

"Would you like to say grace?" she asked.

"Ah... ah... sure." He bowed his head and folded his hands across his lap. He tried to remember what his mother used to say before meals. "Dear God, I ask you to... um... bless this food and um... bless the hands that prepared it... amen."

"Amen."

"Sorry about the abbreviated prayer. I'm not a real religious person."

"You did fine."

"In fact, I was pretty much an atheist until a couple weeks ago."

"What changed your mind?"

"Pastor Jamison. He made me see things differently. And he

did it through rational, logical arguments, stuff I could relate to." He rolled a mound of angel-hair pasta around his fork and stuffed it into his mouth. "This is exquisite."

"Thank you."

"What about you? Are you religious?"

"I never cared for the word *religious*. It makes me think of organized self-righteousness. I came out of the Jehovah's Witnesses background, so I recoil from such things. But I do consider myself spiritually open."

"Sounds like we're in the same boat."

"Was there anything in particular Mr. Jamison said that hit home with you?"

"He said, 'Something cannot come from nothing.'"

"That's it?"

"Sounds simple, doesn't it? But that little truth changed my whole way of thinking. I mean, obviously I exist, and I'm something. The universe exists, and it's a something. All this something had to have a beginning, and that beginning could not have been nothing."

"I never had trouble believing God exists. My problem is discovering the right way to reach Him, the right way to get to Heaven."

"Pastor Jamison talked about a prayer of repentance and faith in Christ. I know he believed the Bible holds all the answers."

They ate quietly for a few minutes.

Hunter gazed into her lovely brown eyes; he could see the candle's reflection flicker in her pupil. He longed to tell her she was the most beautiful woman he had ever seen, that she could make his life complete, that he could love her more deeply and passionately than anyone in the world, that together they could reach levels of intimacy and happiness neither of them dared imagine. He knew they just met, but he saw in her the rare combination of qualities he so desperately wanted in a wife. He tried to unlock the floodgate of his heart, but his tongue refused to move. He froze like some love-struck schoolboy.

She crossed her legs, and her bare foot brushed against his

knee.

"Don't your feet get cold?"

"Not really. I hate wearing shoes. Always have. When I was a little girl, I used to cry when my mom made me put on my shoes for school. To this day the first thing I do when I get in my car is kick off my shoes and drive barefoot. Silly, huh?"

"I think it's adorable."

She blushed.

They stared into each other's eyes. Several times they both strove to speak, but stopped short and again gazed speechless, their eyes fastened on one another. He wanted to kiss her. Her lips beckoned him. But he didn't want to frighten her or seem pushy. He wished he could read her mind.

"More wine?" he asked.

"Please."

He picked up her glass and filled it nearly to the brim. He handed it to her, their hands touched, she didn't pull away. *Kiss her, Old Boy, before the moment's gone.* He leaned over. She closed her eyes. The silken touch of her hair against his cheek sent electricity through his body. Her breath cascaded over his skin. His lips parted.

The doorbell rang.

Their eyes popped open.

"Are you expecting anyone?" he asked.

"No."

Hunter stood and looked out the window. A black Mercedes was parked on the street.

"That looks like Gordon's car. What would he be doing here?"

"That's right." She slapped herself on the forehead. "Monica said they might drop by."

"Here? Why would they do that?"

"She thought it would be like a fun double date." Her brow wrinkled. "What should we do?"

"Let them in."

"Are you crazy?"

"If they saw us from the street, and we don't let them in,

Gordon will get suspicious."

"But he's a killer."

"He doesn't know we know."

The doorbell rang again.

49

9:15 P.M.

Hunter St. James stood behind Faith in the foyer of her home, struggling to control his emotions. Gordon Prescott, his best friend since childhood – murderer – stood on the other side of the door. Hunter didn't know what to say, terrified he would betray his enhanced knowledge of the *Templetons* and put Faith in danger.

"Are you ready?" she asked.

"I guess so."

"Here goes."

She swung open the door.

"Surprise," Monica said, shimmying her shoulders, and revealing ample cleavage through her V-neck sweater. Her blonde hair was teased up on top of her head in a short twist.

Hunter forced a plastic smile and scrutinized Prescott's face. Dark eyes glistened back at him, bright and hard under hairy eyebrows. Impossible to tell what Prescott was thinking.

"Come in," Faith said. "You're just in time for dinner."

"We won't stay long," Monica said.

Faith took their coats, hung them on brass hooks on the wall behind the door, then led the group to the dining nook.

"How romantic," Monica said. "Look, Gordon, candles."

"I'm familiar with wax-based luminary devices."

Faith retrieved two plates from the cupboard. Hunter poured wine into two additional glasses. Once Faith served the food, Hunter pulled out her chair for her then took the seat across the

227

round table from her. Monica sat to his left and Prescott to his right. The group ate quietly for a few moments.

"Where's Jeremy?" Monica asked.

"In bed. He's not feeling well."

"I hope it's not serious."

"Just a sinus infection. He'll be fine."

"So, Faith," Prescott said, pausing to sip the wine. "Monica tells me you are holding some sort of file for Hunter."

Hunter coughed; fragments of food ejected from his mouth and flew about the table.

"Easy there, Old Boy." Prescott slapped him on the back. "Can't have you choking to death."

"I don't see how the file is any concern of yours," Hunter said, reaching for his own glass of wine.

"Lighten up. I'm just trying to make conversation."

Faith glared at Monica.

Hunter thought he saw a malignant gleam in Prescott's eye. *Was that a threat? Or was he just testing the waters?* Hunter forced the muscles in his neck to relax, putting on his best poker face. He felt a slight headache coming on.

"So Hunter, have you decided what you are going to do about a career now that old man Owens gave you the boot?"

"I might go into practice for myself."

"I could put a word in for you at the firm once things cool down. They may take you back."

"No thanks. I'd rather be the head of a fly than the tail of a lion."

"Suit yourself."

"How was France?"

"Marvelous. You really should go sometime."

Hunter could scarcely focus on the repartee for the throbbing in his temples. It felt like an iron ring slowly tightening around his forehead. He forced himself to think. He raised a hand to the lump on his head; it felt hot.

"Are you all right, Old Boy?"

"I'm fine. Just a little accident."

"I thought your car was stolen."

"I didn't say the accident was in my car."

"My mistake."

"How did you know my car was stolen?"

All eyes turned to Prescott. He coolly sipped his wine then answered.

"You see, Old Boy, someone broke into my house today. My cleaning lady told the police she saw a midnight-blue Jaguar in the driveway when she arrived. By the time the police notified me, they already received a report that your car was stolen." He paused then said in a different voice. "Quite a coincidence really. The same guy who stole your car broke into my house. And an even more amazing coincidence is that your stolen car gets crashed, and you're sitting here all banged up. Astounding really."

"What are you trying to say?"

"I don't believe in coincidences."

Prescott's stare lasted so long it made Hunter blink.

He knows.

"Strange things like that happen to me all the time," Faith said, sounding unconvincing.

Silence.

Hunter tried to concentrate and say the right thing to diffuse the situation. But the throbbing headache robbed him of his wit.

"Shame about your client Jamison. Suicide wasn't it?"

"So they say."

"Most unfortunate." Prescott's lips curled into something between a sneer and a smile. "I guess that means the case is closed."

"Not if I have anything to say about it."

"You're making a serious mistake Hunter. Let it go."

"I will not sit by and be a silent accomplice to murder."

"What murder? An old religious nut killed a girl then killed himself. Why is that so unacceptable?"

"It's not the truth."

"There's no such thing as truth." Prescott leaned forward, his hands on his knees. "Truth is whatever we say it is."

"I disagree."

"That was your father's problem."

"What about my dad?"

"He believed in absolutes. Not a good career move."

Hunter's mind locked onto the name from the *Templeton* ledger. Melissa Phillips. His father defended a young black man accused of killing Melissa Phillips. The media had the man convicted from the moment the story broke, just like the Jamison case. His father put up a tenacious defense, and after two hung juries, the man was acquitted. That was it. The *Templetons'* scapegoat wasn't supposed to be found not guilty. He refused to cave to the *Templetons'* false accusation, so they ruined him. And when that didn't silence him, they killed him.

Rage boiled to the surface. Hunter leapt to his feet, nearly knocking the table over.

Prescott rose to meet him.

They locked eyes.

Tunnel vision set in. Fight or flight. Adrenaline coursed through Hunter's veins. He knew he was the stronger man. He waited for Prescott to flinch.

50

Hunter St. James seethed with anger. Betrayal stabbed his heart. Thirty-one years of frustration bubbled up inside. He wanted to wipe that smug look off Prescott's face. A cell phone chirped from Prescott's pocket. He took a step back and raised the phone to his ear, never taking his eyes off Hunter.

"Prescott here... uh huh... right... very good... bye." He lowered the phone. A slow, cunning grin spread over his face. "Come on, Monica, we're leaving."

"This isn't over," Hunter said.

"You don't know how right you are."

"Where are we going?" Monica chugged her glass of wine then hustled over to Prescott's side.

"No need to see us to the door."

Prescott backed across the living room, groped the wall for their coats, then slammed the door behind them. Faith sprang to Hunter's side.

"He knows I know. He flaunted it in my face."

"I thought you two were going to kill each other," she said, grabbing his arm, her voice choked with emotion.

"Things are going to get ugly."

"What are we going to do?"

"I don't know yet, but one thing for sure, I've got to get that file you're holding as far away from you as possible."

"When?"

"Now."

She stared at his face, her eyes flitted back and forth, her forehead furrowed.

"Right now," he said.

She ran off to her bedroom.

He needed to hide the file somewhere safe. A bank vault. He would drive somewhere unexpected, maybe Pittsburgh, and put the file in a safety deposit box. First, he needed to get the information Jamison compiled on the *Templetons.* The pieces of the puzzle started falling into place. His stomach sank. Did he leave Jamison's satchel in his car? *Think, Old Boy, think.* No. He left it on the kitchen table at his house.

Faith ran back into the kitchen and handed him Saul's discovery file.

"I've got to go," he said.

"Where?"

"It's best you don't know."

"Call me."

"As soon as I get a few things settled."

"Please be careful."

He looked into her tear-filled eyes. His heart fluttered. Such a beautiful woman. He opened his arms; she hugged him. Her body felt good pressed close to his, her heart thumping against his chest. Such a perfect fit. A desire to protect her swept over him. He squeezed her tight. She tilted her head back. The exquisite line of her lips summoned him. He lowered his face to hers. Their eyes closed; their lips met.

Glorious!

The moment lingered. He felt the room spinning around him. He heard the music of angels, felt the warmth of her tender lips. Paradise. A surge of emotion overwhelmed him; he fought back tears. His eyes opened. Urgency gripped his mind. He broke the embrace.

"I've got to go."

"Stay a little longer."

"I can't."

"Please."

"I'm endangering you just being here."

"Please be careful."

"I will."

"Call me."

"I promise."

He headed for the door then remembered he took the bus.

"Could I borrow your car?"

"Sure. It's in the garage."

She led him by the hand through the house and into the attached garage. He climbed into her wheelchair accessible van then put down the window.

"I've got two questions," he said.

"Ask."

"First, where's the garage door opener?"

"In the glove compartment." She pointed to it. "What's your second question?"

"How did you get so beautiful?"

She blushed.

They kissed again.

He started the engine then backed down the driveway. Something in the crisp autumn air slowed his racing mind. He left the window open as he drove down the street in front of her house. The van weaved through the back streets of University Heights. Even though no one would associate him with the van, he wasn't taking any chances. Lives were at stake.

Fifteen minutes later he parked on the street in front of his home, and slid Saul's discovery file under the driver's seat. It seemed like forever since he had been here. He climbed the three brick steps to his front door and noticed a tight, pinching pain in his right knee. God only knew the damage he inflicted on his body over the past few days. He slid the key into the lock, pressed open the door, then flipped on the lights. Everything looked the same as when he left; yet something seemed out of place. He couldn't put his finger on it.

Jamison's satchel lay on the kitchen table 30 feet away; he

could see it through the doorway on the far side of the living room. He tried to move, but a strange premonition halted him near the door. Was someone in the house? He reached for the gun in the back of his pants. It wasn't there. No good.

He crept over to his father's gun cabinet in the corner, darting his eyes around the room. He grabbed a chrome-plated Colt .45 and quietly loaded it. His pulse accelerated as he approached the closet at the bottom of the stairway. He took a couple deep breaths, slung open the door, and pointed the gun at a rack of coats.

"Thank God," he whispered to himself.

He eased up the stairs, running the list of potential hiding places through his mind. Thankfully old Victorian homes were sparse on closets. He tiptoed up to the door across from his bed, jerked it open, and brandished the gun. Nothing. He checked the bathroom. Nothing. What a relief. He walked back to the bedroom and felt suddenly exhausted. The exertions of the day caught up to him. His king sized bed summoned from the midst of the alcove of windows. Maybe a short nap would take the edge off before hitting the road again. He sat on the edge of the bed.

KABOOM!

An explosion ripped through the house!

51

Lakewood, Ohio
10:25 P.M.

Peter Saul sat in his den, feet propped up on the desk, waiting for a phone call. He drained a decanter of rum into a glass tumbler and chugged the burning tan liquid. Things had to go well tonight. He couldn't afford another screw-up. His career – his very life – hung in the balance. If tonight's mission went according to plan, nothing stood between him and the Attorney General's office. The *Templetons* guaranteed the financing and political connections. The brass ring dangled at his fingertips, and all he had to do was grab it.

The phone rang.

"Tell me."

"It's done," the voice said.

"Was the bird in the cage?"

"Watched him go in myself."

"Excellent."

He hung up the phone feeling euphoric. With St. James dead, the Jamison nightmare ended. The Halloween sacrifice would eliminate any potential loose ends, and then he could set his sights on the campaign trail. All those years of paying dues finally paid off. Life didn't get any better than this. He wanted to celebrate. Who better to share the moment with than his lovely wife Marilyn?

He heard her go up the stairs a few minutes before. She couldn't possibly be asleep already. He headed for the steps singing, "I Did it My Way". He thought about the last time he made love to his wife; must've been weeks ago. His secretary eagerly indulged his perverse affection on an almost daily basis, so by the time he got home at night there wasn't much left for his wife. But tonight was Marilyn's turn.

He pressed open the bedroom door and said in a boyish voice, "Is my lover girl ready for a little romance?"

Marilyn lay perfectly still on the bed with the comforter pulled over her head; she didn't move. He kicked off his shoes and unbuttoned his shirt as he approached the bed.

"Is my little lover getting her beauty sleep?"

No response.

He shucked off his pants then climbed into bed. He pulled back the comforter to discover his wife wide-awake, silently sobbing, tears streaming down her face. A plaster cast covered her left arm. He genuinely felt bad that the golf club meant for Jason's skull broke her arm. But she shouldn't have interfered.

"What's wrong lover girl?"

"Nothing."

"Does your arm hurt?"

"No."

"Then what's the matter?"

"Nothing."

"Don't give me that. Something obviously must be wrong."

"I don't want to talk about it."

"Suit yourself." He reached under her nightgown.

She pushed his hand away. "What are you doing?" she asked.

"Making love to my wife."

"Not tonight. Please, Peter, I'm not in the mood."

He leaned over to kiss her; she turned her head.

"I can't."

"What the hell's going on here?"

"I'm still shaken up from last night." She sat up and tugged a few tissues out of the box on the nightstand. "I'm worried about Jason."

"Not that little punk again."

"He could be freezing to death out there."

"He's lucky I didn't shoot him when I had the chance."

"You don't mean that."

"He tried to kill me. You saw the whole thing."

"He's a little confused."

"You're as crazy as he is."

Saul sat up on the edge of the bed and laced his fingers through his hair. He pulled a flask out of the top drawer of the nightstand, took a belt, then threw it across the room.

She gasped.

"Your little demon seed is ruining me." His voice sounded maniacal.

"You're scaring me."

I'm going to do more than that.

52

Monday, October 30
University Heights, Ohio
8:15 A.M.

F aith McGuire paced the kitchen floor, sipping coffee and fretting over Hunter St. James. She sat up until 3 a.m. waiting for his call; it never came. She alternated between worrying something went wrong, to thinking she offended him during their evening together. After hours of tossing and turning she closed her eyes to fitful sleep, only to be awakened by Jeremy experimenting with the recording feature on his remote-controlled stereo system. Faith was thrilled he exhibited such interest in electronics, but she could have done without the thundering hip-hop at 7:30 in the morning.

She walked over to the answering machine for the umpteenth time to see if Hunter somehow managed to leave a message without her noticing. Nothing. She picked up the receiver and dialed the number to his home yet again. A few moments later a recorded message came on the line.

"Due to technical difficulties, your call cannot be completed as dialed. Please hang up and try again later."

She slammed down the phone. This could not be happening. She needed to get in touch with him. She had his cell phone number at the office, but she feared leaving Jeremy alone even for the short time it would take to run over and get it.

A knock at the front door.

It might be Hunter. She suddenly realized she only had on a

sheer nightgown and felt naked. She hustled into her bedroom and slipped on her robe.

The doorbell rang.

"I'm coming."

She ran to the door then pulled it open. Two female police officers stood on the steps, both wearing mirrored sunglasses.

"Faith McGuire?" the petite blonde asked.

"That's me."

"Ms. McGuire, my name is Lt. Denholm. Do you own a Dodge minivan?"

"Yes."

"License number R-T-L-2-2-5?"

"What's this about?"

"Is that your license plate number, ma'am?"

"It is."

"There was a fire last night on Overlook, and your van was parked on the street in front of the house. It sustained minor cosmetic damage, but we had to tow it last night to make room for the emergency vehicles. You can pick it up at the impound yard on East 120th and Euclid."

"What kind of fire?"

"A house fire, ma'am."

"Whose house? Whose house burned down?"

"We're not at liberty to say, ma'am. The investigation is still ongoing. But would you mind explaining what your van was doing parked on Overlook when you live here in University Heights?"

"A friend borrowed it."

"And your friend's name?"

"Hunter St. James."

The cops looked at each other.

"What's this about?" she asked, her voice slightly shrill. "Is Hunter all right?'

"Was Mr. St. James here last night?"

"I'm not answering another question until somebody tells me what's going on."

The tall officer's pager went off. She picked it up and looked at the display.

"That's the dispatcher. I'll call her from the car phone." She walked off toward the unmarked car parked at the curb.

"Ma'am, Mr. St. James' house burned down last night."

"Oh my God!" She felt her knees give way then stiffen. "Is he all right?"

"The blaze was so intense the fire department is just now entering the debris field."

"This can't be."

"Ma'am we really need to know if Mr. St. James was here last night. Locating and identifying a body is essential in such cases."

"Yes... yes, he was here last night."

"Did he seem distraught?"

"Distraught?"

"You know, depressed."

"I know what distraught means, I'm a clinical psychologist. What's that got to do with his house burning down?"

"Sometimes when people go through a series of setbacks, you know, losing a job, or losing a girlfriend, they sometimes act irrationally. They sometimes take their own lives."

"No, no, Hunter wouldn't kill himself." Her voice quivered; tears glittered on her eyelashes. "If anyone did it, the Gargoyle did."

"A gargoyle burned his house down?"

"Not a real gargoyle. Prescott. Gordon Prescott. They got into an argument last night and... and..."

"Take a deep breath, ma'am. Maybe I should come inside and talk."

She stepped back, and Lt. Denholm walked in. Faith wiped her face on the back of her hand and fought to control her emotions. *Maybe Hunter wasn't home last night. Maybe he went someplace to hide the file. But where would he go without the van?*

"What exactly took place last night between St. James and Prescott?"

240

"They argued."

"Over what?"

What should she say? Hunter told her about the *Templetons'* influence over the local justice system. He feared for his life, and now his house burned down. Maybe she had said too much already? She needed time to think.

"Ma'am?"

"Yes."

"What did they argue about?"

"Oh, they're old friends and lawyers. They argue all the time. I'm sure it was nothing really."

"Do you know this Gordon Prescott?"

"We just met."

"Was there anyone else here last night who may have witnessed the argument?"

"It really wasn't an argument. More of a misunderstanding really."

"Was there anyone else here?"

"No."

"You're sure."

"Of course I'm sure."

The tall officer walked in the front door.

"Sorry to interrupt, but we have to return to the fire scene. They've located the remains."

53

F aith McGuire cleared the dinner plates off the table. She barely touched her food; her stomach flip-flopped all afternoon, and so far, the package of Tums did little to stop the gastric warfare. She felt numb. Just the night before, Hunter St. James embraced her in this very room. Now his charred remains lay lifeless on a mortuary slab somewhere. The thought sent chills racing up and down her spine.

With a trembling hand she pulled the curlicue straw out of the cup on Jeremy's tray; she dropped it into his lap. She picked up the straw and looked into his face. His head lay at an unthinkable angle over his right shoulder, a stream of drool trickled from the corner of his mouth, and concern radiated from his eyes. He pecked away at the computerized talker.

"What - is - wrong - Mom?"

"Nothing, sweetheart. Mommy's just a little tired."

"You - look - scared."

"You're a perceptive little boy."

"I - am - smarter - than - I - look."

"I know sweetheart." She smiled. "One of Mommy's friends died, and she's a little sad."

"I - am - sorry."

"Everything is going to be just fine."

"Do - you - need - a - hug?"

Her bottom lip quivered. She wrapped her arms around her

precious little boy.

"Why don't you go into your room and play with your stereo until I finish cleaning up, then we'll go to the movies and forget about our troubles for a little while. How does that sound?"

"Great."

The motorized wheelchair navigated around the kitchen table, drove through the living room and disappeared into the bedroom. Faith braced herself on the back of the chair and began to cry. Why was God torturing her? Why give her the man of her dreams only to snatch him away at the first flicker of love? How much could one woman take? Her respiration quickened. The muscles in the back of her neck tightened. She felt lightheaded. Hyperventilation. She sat down, cupped her hands over her nose and mouth, and took a deep breath. Her pulse slowed.

The doorbell rang.

She startled. "I'm coming."

She peeked out the kitchen window and made out the profile of a police car through the evening fog. Alarm bells rang in her intuition. She ran over to Jeremy's room.

"Don't make a sound, kiddo, until Mommy says it's okay."

Worry registered on his contorted face.

"It'll be all right." She kissed him on the cheek.

The doorbell rang again.

"I said I'm coming."

She jogged over to the foyer and opened the door. A tall man with thick wavy hair and mustache stood in front of two officers in black uniforms. She read the inscription on one of the brass badges – Cuyahoga County Homicide Division.

"Good evening, Miss. I'm investigator Jimmy Graham. These are deputies Williams and Reed, and we'd like to have a few words with you."

"Concerning what?"

"Hunter St. James."

"I already told the police everything I know."

"I don't think you did." He stepped forward. "May we come in?"

"No."

"I really think it would be in your best interest to let us in the house."

"Do you have a warrant?"

Graham looked over his shoulder and said to the officers, "She wants to know if we have a warrant." He stepped aside. "Show her the warrant boys."

The officers charged at her.

She tried to slam the door. Something wedged in the jamb. A boot. She braced her shoulder against the door. A massive force from the other side launched her onto her back. The men stormed in.

"Where's the file?" Graham demanded.

"What file?"

"Don't play with me. Where's the file?"

"Hunter took it home." She crabbed backwards on all fours toward the living room.

"That's convenient." Graham stalked forward. "He happens to be dead."

"It's the truth."

"Why don't I believe you?"

"Please—"

"Tear the place up, boys."

The officers assailed the kitchen, ripping open cupboards, smashing plates, and dumping drawers on the floor.

"It would be a whole lot easier if you'd just tell me where the file is."

"I told you—"

"Yeah, I know, St. James took it." He smiled a bitter smile that lifted one corner of his mouth. "Not so gentle boys, she wants to play hardball."

One of the officers snatched a chair and smashed it against the china cabinet, the other kicked over the garbage can.

"That's more like it." Graham kept his eyes riveted on her. "Why don't you make yourself comfortable, it looks like this might take a while."

She scooted across the carpet then pulled herself onto the sofa.

"Williams, find her bedroom. Women like to hide things among their unmentionables."

"With pleasure."

The dark-haired officer with the build of a bear lumbered into the living room.

"Which way?"

She pointed toward the door across the hallway from Jeremy. She tried to think of a way to divert attention away from her son's room. The officer took long strides into her bedroom. A moment later something heavy crashed to the floor with a boom that shook the house. She imagined her grandmother's antique chest of drawers dashed to pieces.

"Sounds like the boys are enjoying their work."

"Please, Hunter took the file last night."

"I want to believe you, I really do, but I can't."

The blond officer came in from the kitchen.

"It's not in there."

"Search over there." Graham pointed at Jeremy's room.

"No!" Faith bolted for the door.

Graham caught her around the waist. He nodded to the officer who stormed into the room.

"What's in there?!" Graham shouted.

"A crippled kid in a wheelchair," the muffled voice replied.

"Ask him where the file is."

"He can't talk," Faith said. "Please don't hurt him."

"That's going to be up to you."

A clamorous racket poured from the room, followed by a yelp, then a thud against the wall.

"He's hurting him! Let me go!" her voice vibrated with frenzy and horror.

She clawed the wall towards Jeremy's room. Graham jerked her back. She spun around and drove her knee into his groin. He released his grasp. She darted into her son's room. The wheelchair lay over on its side, Jeremy gnarled on the floor.

"No!"

She jumped on the officer's back. He flung her to the floor, drew his gun, and pointed it at her face.

54

Hunter St. James pried open his eyes to complete darkness. Where was he? Did he go blind? The stench choked him, a combination of hot dust and dead cats. His body trembled with chill. The muscles along his spine throbbed with pain. He couldn't move. *What happened?* His thoughts plowed slowly through his hazy consciousness, trying to sort out this madness. His pulse quickened. Panic set in. He couldn't figure out where he was. Short bits of memories flickered to the forefront of his mind. He remembered crashing his car then getting on a bus. *How long ago did that happen?* He recalled arguing with Prescott about something or other.

Faith's beautiful face flashed before his eyes. The image soothed his frantic mind. The floral scent of her perfume played upon his senses. The kiss. He remembered the amazing kiss. He smiled. His dry lips cracked; he tried to slide his tongue out to moisten them, but it stuck to the roof of his mouth. Incredible thirst ravaged his throat. *What happened?* He strained to retrace his steps. *What happened?*

The file!

He had gone to Faith's house and left with Saul's discovery file. *That's it.* The fog lifted. Prescott knew about the break-in at his house; Prescott knew about the file; Prescott knew Hunter would expose the *Templetons*. It all came back now. He went home to get Jamison's satchel, searched the house for intruders, then sat on his bed for a minute's rest. Then an earsplitting explosion took his breath!

He had flown backwards, crashed through the window, then plunged two stories. His body ripped through overgrown bushes then thumped against the ground, knocking the wind out of him. The blaze radiated intense heat. He tried to get away but couldn't move his legs. He clawed the grass with his hands, slithered under his neighbor's porch, and then everything went black.

Now he wondered if he was paralyzed. He wiggled his toes. It felt like a thousand bees stung his feet. He bent his knees; his calves cramped. His jaw clenched until the spasms passed. He rolled over on his side. He could see past his feet to the yard outside. Darkness. How long had he lain there? An hour? A day? A week?

He crawled out from under the porch. The crisp, clean air washed over his body. He tried to swallow but couldn't. He took feeble steps around the side of the house. A garden hose lay coiled in the grass. He twisted the knob and held the nozzle to his mouth. A rush of air then stale water sprayed his face. The cool stream flowed over his lips and quenched his parched throat. Water never tasted so good.

He then examined his legs for injuries. They were sore but nothing broken. He felt his arms. Something jagged protruded from his left elbow, a shard of glass. He walked into the back yard under the full moon then yanked out the glass with his thumb and forefinger. Blood trickled from the wound. He looked over at the scorched debris that used to be his house. Everything lost. He took a few steps toward the rubble then a thought occurred to him. *They think you're dead, Old Boy. Can't be seen here snooping around.*

He crouched down behind the bushes that broke his fall then pressed the illumination button on his watch – 10:25 p.m. All this couldn't have happened in an hour. Then he noticed the date. He'd been laying under the porch for 24 hours. *Unbelievable.* He needed to get to Faith's house. She was the only one he could trust. He checked his front pocket. Her keys were still there. He crept along the side of the house, squatted down behind the edge of the picket fence, then looked up and down the street. Nobody. He darted around the corner toward the spot where he parked the van.

"What the—"

He ducked back into the shadows.

"No way the van is gone."

He reached into his pocket for his cell phone, and it shattered in his hand.

"Wonderful."

He needed a plan. He couldn't take the bus looking like he did. Some busybody would report him for sure. He could take a taxi. Drivers don't care what you look like as long as your money is green. But he couldn't walk out in the middle of the street and hail a cab. The house could be monitored. He inched his way back along the house, climbed the fence into the next yard, then methodically traipsed from house to house until he came out at the end of Overlook Road near Cedar Hill. Under the streetlight he got a good look at himself. Ribbons of material saturated with dried crimson hung off his pants. Blood dribbled down his forearm. He applied pressure with his thumb.

He walked past Carlton Road with its collection of red-brick fraternity houses. Not many Case Western students out tonight. He managed to reach Cedar Road without being seen. A couple minutes later he hailed a cab.

"Where to?"

"South Green Road, University Heights."

"Hop in."

Thankfully the driver didn't ask any questions, although several times Hunter caught the man examining him in the rearview mirror. Fifteen minutes later Hunter climbed out in front of Faith's house, paid the fare, then jogged up the walkway. *Thank God the living room lights are on. She must be worried sick.* He rang the bell and waited. Nobody answered. He rang the bell again. Nothing. He beat on the door with his fist.

"Faith, it's me, Hunter, open up."

He tried the knob. The door opened.

"Good God."

It looked like a tornado had ripped through the house leaving only the walls intact. The couch flipped on end. The picture screen shattered out of the television. The kitchen totally destroyed.

"Is there anybody home?"

Silence.

He turned to go. A tapping against the wall from Jeremy's room caught his attention. *Who made that noise?* Hunter's imagination ran wild. *Burglars? Templetons? Prescott?* He needed something to defend himself with. He tiptoed over to the kitchen, picked up a foot-long, serrated knife, then headed for the bedroom. He slinked along the wall, praying for courage. He stopped at the edge of the door, gathered his strength, then pounced.

Jeremy McGuire lay crumpled on the floor, his ashen face twisted and cadaverous.

55

Hunter St. James rushed over to Jeremy and felt his neck for a pulse. The boy's eyes popped open and darted around frantically.

"It's okay, it's okay. It's me, Hunter."

The boy moaned.

"Are you all right?"

Another moan.

"Who did this?"

Jeremy fixed his eyes on the toppled wheelchair.

Hunter flipped the chair onto its wheels, gently scooped Jeremy up, then set him into the chair. The boy felt as light as a feather. Hunter tried to check Jeremy for injuries but didn't know how the mangled limbs were supposed to look.

"Can you use your talker?"

Jeremy pecked at the device.

Nothing.

"Is it turned on?"

Hunter fiddled around with the buttons. The red indicator light showed power, but the keypad refused to respond.

"What do I do?"

Jeremy grasped the joystick and drove the wheelchair into a small plastic table, nearly knocking the electronic stereo equipment to the floor. He rocked his head and shifted his eyes so far toward the stereo, Hunter feared a seizure coming on.

"Calm down, are you all right?"

Jeremy's penetrating stare riveted onto Hunter's eyes; frustration draped his contorted face. He returned to rocking his head and shifting his eyes toward the stereo.

"What about the stereo?"

Jeremy banged away at the talker, but it made no sound.

"What are you trying to say?"

Jeremy locked his eyes on the stereo again. In a breathy, almost unintelligible voice he said, "Liisson."

"Oh."

Hunter pushed the play button, and the compact disc port whirled. The distant sound of plates crashing blared through the speakers along with a muffled male voice. Hunter turned up the volume and made out the conversation.

"What's in there?" a man's husky voice said.

"A crippled kid in a wheelchair," a second male voice said.

"Ask him where the file is."

"He can't talk," Faith said. "Please don't hurt him."

"That's going to be up to you."

Something crashed to the floor.

"He's hurting him!" Faith screamed. "Let me go!"

Footsteps pounded into the room.

"No!"

A loud thump.

"Don't shoot her," the first man said. "I've got to deliver her to Saul's house in one piece."

"What do you want me to do with her?"

"Cuff her and help me get her into the car. You two find the file, and I'll send a car after you."

Scuffling.

"Please don't do this," Faith pleaded.

Smack!

"Not in the face, you idiot. Saul wants her unmarked. Stuff something in her mouth, and let's go."

The talking stopped; the background destruction droned on. Hunter pressed the power button.

"You little genius." Hunter kissed him on the forehead. "I've got to think fast here. Let's see, I need a phone."

Jeremy drove his wheelchair across the hall into the disaster area that used to be Faith's bedroom; Hunter followed right behind. Mattress stuffing littered the floor like fresh fallen snow. The nightstand rested atop a pile of clothes. The wheelchair motored to the side of the bed frame, crunching broken glass into the thick pile carpeting. The phone lay on the floor. Hunter picked it up and dialed 4-1-1.

"I need the number for Peter Saul."

"One moment please," a female voice said. "I have multiple listings for that name."

"The one in Ohio, Cuyahoga County Prosecutor."

"I have an attorney Peter Saul listed in Lakewood, Ohio."

"What's the address?"

"206 Clifton Park."

"Thank you very much."

"Don't you want the number?"

"No." Hunter hung up.

He noticed Monica's name on the speed dial. He pressed it. The voicemail picked up. He didn't want to leave a message but couldn't think of anyone else to call.

"Monica, this is Hunter St. James. Faith is in real trouble, and I need you to come watch Jeremy. I'll explain later. Whatever you do, don't tell Gordon I called."

Jeremy's face suddenly darkened. Hunter felt as if a hand of ice gripped his heart.

"Sorry, Sport, but I can't take you with me." He knelt down and looked Jeremy in the eye. "Everything is going to be all right, I promise. Now, where does your mom keep the keys to her car?"

56

Lakewood, Ohio
11:50 P.M.

H unter St. James turned off the headlights before pulling onto the wooded cul-de-sac of Clifton Park. During the drive over from Cleveland he tried to formulate a plan. Obviously, he couldn't just walk up to the front door, ring the bell, and ask Saul to kindly hand over Faith McGuire. If the *Templetons* followed their previous pattern, they planned an elaborate ritual killing made to look like a suicide or a murder that could be pinned on one of their enemies. But the event seemed premature. Halloween wasn't until tomorrow. Maybe they intended to hold her overnight. But that didn't make sense. Hunter checked his watch.

"Wait a minute, Halloween starts at midnight. Ten minutes!"

He drove to the end of the street and examined the two-story brick colonial that matched the address he got from Information. Cars lined the oval drive, but the house was dark. He turned the car around and parked four houses up. He walked casually along the street in the opposite direction from Saul's house then darted behind a row of hedges. He backtracked through the woods behind the houses; twigs snapped under his feet with each step. A jolting thought occurred to him; he had no weapon. Too late to worry about that now; he would have to improvise.

Saul's house stood about 20 yards away. The full moon reflected off the sliding glass door at the rear of the house. If he could get there unseen, he might be able to sneak inside. He sprinted across the manicured grounds and ducked down behind the corner of the house. He tried the door. Locked. He cupped his hands around his eyes and looked inside. Darkness. He tried the windows on the far side of the house. Nobody home. He searched for something to smash the glass door. A metal chair stood underneath a cabana umbrella. He tried to lift it but could not. He rocked it back and forth until it broke loose. He hoisted it over his shoulder - when something caught his attention to the north of the house. Tiny flickering lights reflected off the lake.

"What the—"

He spun around, eyes darting. Over the cliff and across the open beachfront, a single-file line of torches marched toward the woods; he counted 13 flames about 200 yards away. It had to be the *Templetons*. He dropped the chair and raced down over to the edge of the cliff, keeping his eyes on the flickering lights. He stumbled. His feet sank into deep mud that smelled like manure and wet grass clippings. He stood in the middle of a garden. Iron rods stood in three rows with dried tomato vines laced to them with twine. He grabbed one by the base and heaved it out of the ground. It had to weigh 15 pounds. He slung it over his shoulder like a rifle and pressed forward.

He couldn't find any way down the cliff, so he tossed the rod over the edge, dropped to the seat of his pants, and slid down the loose dirt and rock. About halfway down his feet hit a stump, launching him head-over-heels. He landed on his back with a dull thud.

His body cried out for rest. Just a few minutes to catch his breath. That's all he needed. He checked his watch – 11:55 p.m. No time. He sprang to his feet, picked up the rod and ran toward a private boat dock. Rotten pier timbers jutted from the murky water, the waves slapping against the shore. The smell of dead fish soured his face. Clouds obscured the moon, making the night almost pitch black. He struggled to see where the *Templetons* entered the woods. There appeared to be a narrow footpath in the undergrowth. He scouted it out and saw fire ahead in the distance.

Now what to do? He dared not walk the footpath; trudging through the undergrowth would make too much noise.

The lake.

He jogged over to the dock and dipped his foot. Frigid water filled his white Nike and soaked his sock. He withdrew his foot.

Damn that's cold.

No time to play. He clenched his teeth, lowered his body into the miserable cold water, then waded along the shoreline, holding the iron rod over his head. His legs trembled with each step. The sound of the waves along the shore masked his movements. A layer of fog hovered over the water, rendering him practically invisible. He searched the bank for someplace to go ashore. Dense, tangled tree limbs leaned over the waterline. There seemed to be a clearing a few yards ahead.

An air horn blast startled him; he almost dropped the rod. A Coast Guard cutter churned up the water, darting a spotlight along the beach. Whitecaps rolled off the wake and stirred the fog. Gray-crested swells raced toward land. He broke for the clearing, trying to beat the deluge. A few moments later the first rogue wave struck his back. The cold took his breath away. The next ridge covered his shoulders, and down he went. He struggled to the surface. The force of the current washed him aground.

He crawled up the bank on his belly. His teeth chattered in the frigid air. About 30 feet away the torches formed a circle. An inch-wide circle of salt defined the perimeter. He couldn't see Faith from this angle, but he knew she was somewhere in the midst of that deadly ring of black robes. He couldn't take on 13 men. He needed something to separate and distract them. He crept through the darkness, careful to stay inside the cover of the overgrowth. He wondered which robe was Prescott.

Faith lay on a huge rock, hands above her head and tied at the wrist, feet cinched together, a black gag stuffed in her mouth, her blouse ripped open, bra pulled up around her neck, a pentagram in blood drawn on her breasts and abdomen. A man in a red robe staked his torch into the ground, reached inside his garment, and pulled out a jewel-encrusted dagger. He chanted something in Latin. All eyes fixed on him. The voice sounded familiar.

Saul.

Hunter had to do something fast. He sneaked up behind the man closest to him and whacked him on the head with the rod. The man crumbled; his torch fell against the man next to him. The second man shrieked and rolled on the ground, his robe aflame. The others came to help them. Hunter slipped into the thickets then down the bank. He hated going back into the water, but he had no choice. He heard voices and tramping in the woods. He eased back into the waves, enshrouded by the fog. A couple of torches came right down to the lake's edge. He knew the water should feel cold, but strangely it did not. His heart raced, adrenaline surging through his veins.

If he could come ashore 20 yards downstream then work his way behind the gathering, he might be able to recapture the element of surprise. He checked his watch – 12:08 a.m.

Halloween.

He didn't know how long the ceremony would take, but his disruption probably sped things up. He sloshed through the undercurrent then crawled onto the narrow sandy beach. The unholy congregation reassembled at the original location. He stalked through the brush holding the rod out in front of him like a lance. He reemerged behind the group. His previous victims laid on the ground, one holding a blood-saturated handkerchief to the side of his head. Two down; 11 to go.

From this position he saw directly into Saul's face, hellish and demonic in the flickering firelight. Poor Faith lay half naked and exposed to this vile assembly. He had to get her out of there. But how?

"*Hoc Deo offero sacrificium!*" Saul yelled, raising the dagger over his head.

"NOOOO!" Hunter yelled as he charged.

He knocked the figure in front of him to the ground, then cocked the iron rod like a baseball bat. No one in the outer circle moved.

Saul turned.

Thwack! Hunter struck him across the shoulder, driving him to one knee. He scooped Faith in his arms. The circle of black robes collapsed on them. He tried to shield her with his body. A hailstorm of fists and kicks bombarded him.

"Stop!" Saul shouted.

The mob parted.

"He's mine."

Two men pulled Faith from Hunter's embrace; two others twisted his arms behind his back. Saul held the dagger to Hunter's right eye.

"So nice of you to join us, St. James. I found out an hour ago that the body pulled from the ashes wasn't yours. I had no idea where to look for you, and lo and behold here you are. Osiris smiles on me."

"You'll fry for this."

"What a coincidence, that's exactly what your father said before I strangled and hanged him."

Hunter struggled against his captors, to no avail.

"You've got me, let her go. You don't need two sacrifices."

"But two is always better than one."

"You'll burn in Hell."

"You first."

Saul cocked his arm to thrust the dagger into Hunter's heart.

Boom!

The face to Hunter's left exploded. Blood sprayed everywhere.

Boom!

The man to Hunter's right lurched then dropped dead too.

The group scattered, running in all directions, vanishing into the night. Flaming torches strew the ground.

Saul's dagger lunged forward. Hunter caught his wrist and jerked his arm, then drove a knee into his belly. Saul coughed but didn't drop the knife. Hunter reached for the hilt with his right hand. Saul crushed his heel onto the top of Hunter's foot with three sharp blows. Hunter recoiled, not letting go of Saul's wrist. To his right he caught a glimpse of Faith laying on the ground, struggling against her bonds, the brush around her ablaze.

The two men continued fighting in deadly combat.

Boom!

A bullet whizzed past Hunter's head and slammed into a tree. He flinched. Saul kicked him square in the groin. Hunter wheezed and buckled. Saul jumped on top of him, drew back the dagger then plunged it forward. Hunter squirmed. The blade dug into his left shoulder.

Hunter howled!

Saul jerked it free and slashed again. Hunter deflected his forearm. The knife struck the ground inches from his face. He snatched Saul by the wrist and twisted with all his strength.

Snap! The bone broke.

Saul shrieked!

Hunter drew his knees to his chest, dug his feet into Saul's belly, and kicked. Saul flew like a rag doll and bashed his head against the sacrificial rock.

"Faith!"

Fire encircled her. Hunter dashed through the raging flames, snatched her up, and squeezed her tight. He started running toward the lake, then felt a sharp jab in the back. The dagger! He fell to his knees. Faith rolled out of his arms.

"Ego mitto te ad Gehenna!" Saul roared, his voice undulating with rage. "I'm sending you to Hell!"

He grabbed Hunter by the hair and pressed the blade to his throat.

"Are you going to squeal like dear old dad?!"

Blood trickled down his neck as the blade laced open the flesh.

Boom!

Saul's head exploded. Dead!

57

Faith McGuire watched in horror as Hunter rolled out from under Peter Saul's partially decapitated corpse. The crackle of the burning brush, smoldering a few feet from her head, disturbed the eerie silence. *Who was the shooter? Did Hunter bring help?* Tears streamed down her face. It didn't matter; the nightmare was over. She became suddenly aware of her nakedness, her wrists tied and her torso exposed. She didn't want Hunter to see her so compromised.

She tried to free her wrists, but the ropes had long ago strangled the circulation from her hands, leaving them cold and useless. She managed a muffled scream through the gag; Hunter opened his eyes. He looked pale, his face swollen and battered, his back wet with blood. A great pack of muscles shifted under his soaked T-shirt as he crawled to her. He untied her wrists then slumped over. She pulled her bra and blouse over her blood-smeared torso, loosened her feet, then jerked the gag out of her mouth.

"Oh my God, Hunter, are you all right?"

"Never better." His voice sounded labored and weak.

"Are you hurt bad?" She cradled him in her arms.

"I don't think there's a good hurt."

"I'll go get help."

"No, just hold me for awhile."

"You need a doctor."

"In a minute. Just hold me."

Her tears trickled onto his face. She lifted her hand to wipe them away.

"No, leave them."

"I was so scared. I prayed and prayed... I almost..."

"It's all right now, it's over," his voice diminishing with each calming word. "God answered your prayers. And I thank God you're okay."

"I owe you my life."

"I'll settle for a kiss."

She pressed her lips against his. Inexpressible emotion welled up within her. Feelings of love and gratitude and safety washed over her. This man risked his life for her. She wanted to hold him and kiss him forever. The knotty muscles in his neck gradually relaxed, and his head dropped into her lap.

"Now can we go?" he said with a smile.

"Let me help you up." She stood and pulled his left arm. He yelped.

"Try the other arm."

"Sorry."

She got him to his feet; he swayed, leaning heavily on her.

"Which way?"

"That way." He pointed toward the lake.

Something rustled in the woods nearby. Hunter stepped between Faith and the noise. Two young men emerged into the firelight carrying hunting rifles.

"Are you two all right?" the skinny kid with pierced eyebrows asked. Faith recognized him as Jason Saul.

"What are you doing here?" she asked.

"It's a long story."

"I'm sure it is. If you didn't come with Hunter, what are you doing here?"

"I'm here because of the night my stepdad stole my boots."

"Your boots?"

"These." He raised the Nazi jackboots up to the firelight. "I watched him leave the house on foot, so I followed him. He went into the church, you know, where the girl was killed. I stood outside the window to see what was going on."

"You made the shoeprints by the window?" Hunter asked.

"I don't know if I left prints or not, but I saw everything."

"What happened?"

"I looked through the window and this woman comes running out of one of the rooms looking all crazy followed by some fat, bald guy. He no sooner turns the corner out of this office when a pockmarked guy pops up from behind one of the pews and shoots him in the back with some kind of stun gun, and down he goes."

"It sounds like Prescott," Hunter said.

"I don't know his name, but he and my stepfather grabbed the girl, tied her up on the altar, poured blood on her chest out of a glass jar and then... then... well, you know."

"Who did the stabbing?"

"The pockmarked guy stabbed her in the chest then dropped the knife. He must have missed her heart, because she squirmed to the side of the altar. Blood squirted through the hole. My stepfather grabbed the knife and hacked her up... then he... then he cut a chunk of skin from her chest and ate it. The other guy about puked. That's when I ran before I blew chunks."

"So, the bald guy didn't have anything to do with it?"

"Nope."

"Why didn't you go to the police?" Faith asked.

"My stepfather is the county prosecutor. Who are the police going to believe, me or him? Besides, I was afraid he would do something to my mother."

"How did you end up here, right now?" Hunter asked.

"We came here to assassinate my filthy stepfather. I had no idea you guys would be here."

"Thank God you showed up when you did, or we'd both be dead," Faith said.

"I hope the cops see it that way," Jason said. "I'm going to need a lawyer."

"I know one," Faith said, patting Hunter on the back.

Hunter reeled; his eyes rolled back; he collapsed.

58

Cleveland, Ohio
6:35 A.M.

Hunter St. James opened his eyes and saw white ceiling tiles floating above his head. The inhospitable smell of antiseptic lingered in the air. He felt an odd, euphoric sensation.

"Hunter, can you hear me?"

He shifted his eyes toward the sweet voice. Faith McGuire. Her calm, transfixing face eased his soul.

"Where am I?"

"Cleveland Clinic."

"Have you been here all night?"

"I wanted to be the first person you saw when you woke up."

"What a pleasant way to start the day." He tried to sit up, winced, then laid back down. "What did they do to me?"

"The doctor said he put 23 stitches in your shoulder and another 33 in your back. He also said you were severely dehydrated. They've been pumping fluids into your IV by the gallon."

"That explains it."

"Explains what?"

"Why I feel like a million bucks."

"That good?"

"No, all green and wrinkled."

A small, fussy man with glasses and a considerable sense of his own importance walked in wearing a white lab coat, flanked by a half-dozen interns who looked fresh out of high school.

"Good, you're awake. I'm Doctor Rostov."

"Forgive me if I don't get up."

"Are we feeling a little discomfort in our shoulder and back today?"

"I don't know about yours but mine hurt like hell."

"You sustained six main injuries – a deep punctured laceration beginning at the upper trapezius and continuing into the infraspinatus, a second perforated trauma to the anterior deltoid, lacerations to the neck, chest and elbow, a moderate concussion, and various cuts in both legs. You need a week of absolute rest - no exertion, no lifting, no strain of any kind. Is that clear?"

"Yes sir."

"If that will interfere with your job, I can give you a medical excuse."

"I'm a lawyer."

"Good, you don't do much anyway."

Everybody laughed.

"So when can I leave, Doc?"

"As soon as I check the dressings and sign your release."

The doctor scrutinized the chart at the end of the bed, examined Hunter's eyes with a tiny flashlight, then unwrapped the mummy-like bandages encasing his torso. He lifted Hunter's left arm and rotated it through various ranges of motion.

"Everything looks fine. I think you'll live."

"Wonderful."

"Call my office in a week to make an appointment to have the stitches removed. Also, I'm going to have the orderly give you a rubber ball. I want you to squeeze it throughout the day to increase circulation in the shoulders."

"Whatever you say, Doc."

The medical team left.

"I guess you'll be needing a place to stay," Faith said.

"I'll check into a hotel until I find an apartment."

"What about my house?"

"I wouldn't think of it."

"You have nowhere else to go, and besides you're going to need rest and a bit of nursing. I'll turn the guest room into a hospital room."

"If you promise to wear one of those Candy Striper outfits, I'll think about it."

"Sorry, I'm not a teenager anymore."

A beautiful blonde orderly pushed an empty wheelchair into the room.

"Excuse me, Miss, I need to get Mr. St. James ready for discharge."

"I'll be out in the hall." She leaned over and kissed Hunter's forehead.

Fifteen minutes later the orderly wheeled Hunter out into the hall, his arm tucked into a blue sling, green rubber ball in hand. His back radiated with pain. Faith waited by the nurse's station, looking beautiful and tired.

"May I push him from here?" Faith asked.

"Be my guest."

She took the handles and wheeled him toward the elevator. From the other end of the hall, a little corrugated woman with a face the complexion of walnut shells walked beside a man with gigantic eyebrows and his jaw wired shut. Hunter did a double take.

"Unbelievable," he said.

"What?"

"Don't look, but that's the guy I clubbed with his rifle in Pastor Jamison's basement."

"Where?"

"Down there." He nodded in their direction. "And that's the lady."

"What lady?"

"The neighbor lady whose car I wrecked."

"No way."

"Quick, spin me around. I don't want them to see me."

She pushed him toward the elevator at the other end of the

hall.

"First you wrecked her car, then you broke her husband's jaw."

"Small world, huh?"

Faith started chuckling.

"What's so funny?"

"Maybe you could stop over to their house later and see if there's anything else you can do for them."

The elevator doors opened, and they rode down to the lobby. She helped him into the car, and they drove through the streets of Cleveland in a comfortable silence. A cloudless, salmon-pink sky gleamed behind the skyline. They glanced back and forth, their eyes never quite meeting. After everything they had been through, small talk seemed inappropriate. Scenes from last night flashed through Hunter's mind. It didn't seem real. *Thank you God for watching over us.* He felt the overwhelming desire to stop at a church and pray. Twenty minutes later the car pulled into Faith's driveway and parked behind a blue Dodge Intrepid.

"Whose car is that?" he asked.

"Monica's."

"What a sweetie. I left a message and asked her to baby-sit Jeremy."

Faith's eyes misted up.

"No crying," he said. "Today we celebrate being alive."

"Amen to that."

Faith helped him out of the car. Crisp frost lay like salt upon the grass. They walked hand in hand up the sidewalk. The front door was unlocked. Faith stepped in and yelled, "Jeremy! Monica! We're home."

No answer.

"They're probably sleeping," he said.

"Look what they did to my house."

The war zone remained exactly as Hunter remembered it.

"I'm going to check on Jeremy, then we'll try to find something to eat."

She picked her way across the living room. Hunter shuffled through the debris, squeezing the ball and looking for someplace to sit down.

Faith screamed; her face twisted with terror.

"What is it?!"

She didn't move.

He raced to her side and looked over her shoulder. Jeremy sat in his wheelchair, a sock stuffed in his mouth, his arms and legs bound to the chair with silver duct tape. Directly behind him Gordon Prescott sat on the edge of the bed holding a serrated knife to the back of Jeremy's neck - the same knife that Hunter carried into the room the night before.

"It's about time you two came home. Junior and I were starting to worry."

"Put down the knife, Gordon," Hunter said. "This has nothing to do with the boy."

"Do you have any idea how bad you've screwed everything up?" His voice trembled with barely restrained rage. "Do you have any idea at all, with Owens and Marsh shot to death in the woods!"

"Let's talk this out like men." Hunter sidled in front of Faith. "It's not too late for you to do the right thing."

Prescott jabbed the knife.

Jeremy's eyes bulged open.

Faith gasped.

"Gordon, buddy. I know you didn't mean for any of this to happen. You got in over your head. Come on, put down the knife."

Prescott smiled the cool cruel smile that fit his face so well. He poked the knife again. Blood trickled down the shaft of the blade.

"Please don't hurt him," Faith pleaded.

Hunter slowly slipped his left arm out of the sling.

"The *Templetons* were going to give me the world," Prescott said. "Now I'm out. I'm a marked man."

"We can beat them. Just don't hurt the kid."

"Beat them... beat them," he said in a nervous snicker. "We're already dead. You killed us, my friend, you killed us." Prescott let loose a full-throated laugh, showing the inside of his mouth right back to the pillars of his throat.

Hunter grabbed the ball with his right hand and hurled it, beaning Prescott between the eyes. Hunter charged and tackled him, knocking the wheelchair over. The men wrestled and rolled off the bed, thumping to the floor. Hunter maneuvered on top, pinning the hand with the knife to the ground. Prescott reached up with his free hand and clenched a bandaged wound. Hunter groaned and recoiled. Prescott flipped him over and pounced, drawing back the knife to stab him in the back. Hunter turned and head-butted him twice. No effect. His strength ebbed. The end of the knife dug into the wounded shoulder.

Pain exploded!

Hunter howled and shoved with all his might. Prescott flew backwards, crashing into the nightstand. Hunter sprang to his feet, backpedaling to the wheelchair where Faith worked to free Jeremy.

Prescott staggered forward, his face scarlet and bloated, his eyes glassy and inflamed, the knife thrust out in front. He charged.

Boom!

The acrid stench of gunpowder filled the room.

59

Hunter St. James dove in front of Faith, shielding her with his body; they tumbled to the ground.

"Freeze!" Lt. Denholm stalked through the doorway; smoke wafting off the tip of her 9mm pistol. "Drop the knife, or I'll blow your brains all over these walls."

Prescott dropped the weapon and threw his hands in the air.

"Lay face down on the ground and put your hands behind your back."

"You're making a big mistake, officer. You don't know who I am."

"I don't care if you're the Duke of Earl. Lie down on the ground and put your hands behind your back. Do it now."

Prescott complied, scowling at Hunter with a look that could etch glass.

"You two, on your feet. Who are you, sir?"

"Hunter St. James."

"What are you doing here?"

"He saved my life," Faith said.

"You on the floor, what's your name?"

"Gordon Prescott," his voice muffled by the carpet.

"You're under arrest."

"For what?"

"Murder."

"I didn't kill anyone."

"You were seen dropping Monica Frisk off at Mr. St. James'

house on Overlook moments before it exploded. We've since received word you blew up the house by remote control then drove off in the dead woman's car."

"You broke into my house - and blew it up - and tried to kill me?" Hunter asked.

"Monica's dead?" Faith asked.

"You knew the victim?"

"We've been friends since Girl Scouts."

"Her body was identified this morning through forensic testing. An APB went out a few hours ago on her car."

Detective Myles walked in wearing rubber gloves and carrying an electronic device in a plastic bag.

"Look what I found in the passenger seat of Ms. Frisk's car."

"That wasn't in the car."

"I'll bet you dollars to doughnuts your fingerprints are all over this thing."

"I'm being set up."

"Hey, big mouth," Denholm said, you have the right to remain silent. Anything you say can and will be used against you in a court of law."

"I know my rights. I'm an attorney."

"Good, then you're familiar with the concept of cuffs, chains, jail cells and sky-high bail."

Denholm and Myles cuffed Prescott and escorted him through the house. Hunter followed them to the front lawn. As they stuffed Prescott into the back seat of the patrol car, Hunter shouted, "Don't worry about the *Templetons* archive. I'll deliver it personally to the new county prosecutor!"

Hunter watched the car drive away. A couple minutes later Faith joined him.

"How's Jeremy?" he asked

"He's fine, just a scratch really. I bandaged him up and put him to bed."

"Poor kid is probably exhausted. So you know, he saved your life."

"He is so special, so loving."

Hunter studied Faith's exquisite face. The breeze lifted her hair and played with it. Her eyes stared off in the distance, the tip of her tongue showing a little between her teeth.

"What are you thinking about?" he asked.

"I can't believe Monica's dead." She shook her head. "So sudden. So final."

"None of this seems real."

"Strange thing is, I'm too numb to cry."

"There will be time enough later."

Silence.

"How did all this happen?" She grabbed his hand and laced her fingers between his. "All of this death and destruction is so evil."

"For the world it goes back to the fall of man, but for me it started with Peter Saul. If a man like that isn't damned to Hell, he should go straight to the Lake of Fire."

Faith looked pensive. She started to speak, then stopped, then finally said, "A psychologist tells someone that he or she is basically good, but can do bad things. This whole experience has taught me that human beings are basically inclined to do bad things." Faith sighed. "I can diagnose problems, but I can't prescribe solutions. I'm beginning to see that only real repentance and a loving God can change your life."

The wind blew two fallen leaves across the yard. Hunter turned and looked into her eyes.

She smiled. "I like the way you look at me."

"After the nightmare we've been through, I really don't see much sense in playing games with one another." He took her hands in his. "My heart is capable of great love, and over the course of my life it has found few objects to cherish. It chose well when it..." He leaned closer. She didn't move to meet him, but her tender eyes were riveted on his face. "What I'm trying to say is... I... uh..."

"Yeah, I know, I love you too."

She threw her arms around his neck. They kissed and then turned to go inside. Hunter stopped and shook his head.

"What's wrong?" she asked.

"Nothing. Just thinking about Pastor Jamison."

"I know, the poor man. But he is in Heaven. After all, it's impossible to kill a saint. Every true Christian is a saint, looking forward to pain-free eternal life." She smiled. "Just think, right now Howard Jamison is having a conversation with the Savior."

"If it wasn't for him, I'd still be an atheist, the *Templetons* would go on murdering with impunity, and you and I would never have met."

"It's amazing how God can use one man's pain and suffering to bring about such amazing results."

"I guess in the hands of God, one Man's sacrifice can change the world."

The End

Please Enjoy The Following Excerpt From:

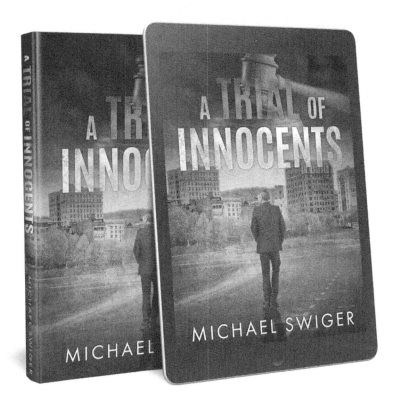

1

Friday, August 4, 2000
Steubenville, Ohio
9:35 P.M.

"You mean to tell me this psycho picks his victims by going through the obituaries?" Sergeant Gates shot a dagger-like glare at the handcuffed perpetrator, bent over and spread-eagled on the hood of the patrol car.

"It sure looks like it, Sarge. I found these crumpled-up papers in his back pocket," Officer Sharps said while holding out his find. "One is from the phone book and the other is the obituary section from today's *Herald-Star.*"

"Lemme see that."

Gates snatched the papers from the rookie's hand and held up his flashlight to get a better look. The page from the phone book had an entry circled in red: *John and Dorothy Bernhart, 303 Lovers Lane, Steubenville.* Gates twisted his neck to look over his left shoulder past the meticulously cut lawn, past the perfectly manicured shrubs, past the six white pillars to the three white numbers affixed to the two-story, brick Colonial.

Gates shuffled the pages and said, "The obituary is for Dr. John Bernhart. It says that he died in a car accident three days ago. Tonight is the last night to view the body; the funeral is first thing in the morning."

Gates paused as the hellish nature of the crime sank in.

"That pregnant woman this sicko just beat unconscious is the newly widowed Dorothy Bernhart."

An awkward silence lingered in the air begging to be filled. The rookie gave in. "He probably didn't expect to find anyone home if he was robbing the place."

Sergeant Gates stared down at the crumpled papers in his trembling hands, completely oblivious to the rookie's comments. His mind replayed the heinous scene. A pregnant woman lays on the floor, clad only in a thin nightgown. A bear of a man straddles her waist, savagely beating on her chest. Blood trickles from her nose and mouth.

Gates looked over at the heartless criminal and shook his head. He wadded the papers and slammed them against the hood of the car. He spewed a stream of obscenities, then in one swift motion spun around and thrust his knee deeply into the perpetrator's groin.

The huge man exhaled and winced in pain.

Gates pounced. He laced his fingers through the back of the degenerate's long, greasy hair and snapped his head back.

"You're a big tough guy beatin' up women, you wanna go a few rounds with me, punk?"

"Let him go, Sarge, let him go! Wait till we get him back to the station."

Gates redoubled his grip and pulled even harder.

"The paramedics are comin' out of the house, Sarge, let him go."

Gates let go of the thug's hair and then stepped back as if nothing happened. The paramedics rushed the unconscious Dorothy Bernhart into the waiting ambulance.

10:03 P.M.

"What's wrong with the court appointing an attorney?" Danial Solomon asked, looking at his watch.

"Danial, you don't know what it's like down here. I've never seen so many people all worked up. You'd better get down here right away." Andy Lewis sounded unusually rattled. "I'm afraid some hotheaded cop may kill this guy if he thinks he can get away with it."

"All right. Meet me in front of the courthouse in 15 minutes."

"Thanks, I owe you one."

"You owe me more than one," Danial said. "Ever since you started volunteering down at the jail I haven't had a minute of rest."

"That may be true but look at all the business I'm bringing you."

"I define business as a paying customer," Danial said in a condescending tone. "I'll see you shortly."

Andy Lewis nervously paced along the sidewalk at the base of the Jefferson County Courthouse steps. A few minutes later the silhouette of a new Dodge Charger pulled into the attorneys parking lot. Andy watched his friend park the car then walk down the street.

Danial Solomon stood about 5 foot 10 with a muscular, athletic build. Prematurely gray shoots speckled his thick brown hair. Danial fought hard to comb his wiry mop to the side in a professional manner, usually with little success. His compassionate, dark blue eyes made people feel comfortable in his presence. An average nose sat on top of wide full lips. A square jaw bordered the bottom of his face. By all accounts, Danial Solomon was a good-looking man.

The two men shook hands, entered the building, and headed for the jail in the courthouse basement.

"So, what's this guy's name?" Danial asked.

"I don't know."

"What's he in for?"

"I don't know."

"Where's he now?"

"I don't know."

"What do you know?" Danial asked.

"All I know is he supposedly beat up a pregnant lady, and he hasn't said a word since being arrested."

"Have you seen him?"

"Only at a distance, they wouldn't let me near him." Andy paused. "To be honest, he didn't look quite right. He was a little off."

"Off? What do you mean a little off?" Danial asked. "Off like crazy?"

"No, off like a little slow... I don't know... it looked like something is wrong with his head. You'll see."

The jail sat in the basement of the courthouse, the oldest part of the building, built after the Civil War and it smelled like it. The two men stepped down the worn marble steps and stopped at the booking desk. Danial put down his briefcase and turned toward the female deputy sheriff wearing a black uniform and sitting behind the old Formica counter.

"I'm attorney Danial Solomon, and I'm here to see... um... um..." He looked over at Andy for help.

Andy leaned forward and said, "The weird-looking guy who beat up the pregnant lady."

Danial rolled his eyes.

"Are you his lawyer?" the deputy asked.

"Not officially," Danial said. "I'll need his consent before it will be official."

"Good luck. He won't even say his name," the deputy said. "Hold on, and I'll call the detective handling the interrogation."

The deputy picked up the phone and a couple minutes later a stocky man turned the corner of the long hallway leading toward the booking desk. He wore an inexpensive, wrinkled brown suit. His bald head and stern face were red and glistening with sweat.

"I'm Detective Demus. What can I do for you?"

"I would like to see the suspect arrested for allegedly assaulting the woman on Lovers Lane."

"Allegedly? That's a good one," Demus said, not trying to hide his agitation. "First of all, we caught him in the act, and Mrs. Bernhart is more than allegedly unconscious. Besides, what's a big-shot lawyer like Danial Solomon interested in a psychotic scumbag like this for anyway?"

In spite of the angry detective's tone, Danial felt flattered to be recognized. "Well, the U.S. Constitution guarantees the right of every psychotic scumbag to be represented by counsel."

"Did I mention he had the obituary section of the paper in his pocket? Yeah, it seems he goes and robs families while they're out burying their dead. He should be a real media darling with that M.O."

"Be that as it may, I would like to see the detainee."

University Hospital
10:30 P.M.

In spite of the Emergency staff's best efforts, Dorothy Bernhart slipped into a coma. The doctors were now faced with a dilemma. The severe head injuries Dorothy sustained left her in critically unstable condition. Meanwhile, the life of her tiny unborn baby ebbed away with each tick of the clock.

"We've got to move now," Dr. Dwight Davies said. "The baby won't survive if we wait any longer. We've got to go in and get it with a C-section."

"It's too risky," Dr. Edward Parks said, "the mother is too unstable. She can't take any more trauma."

"The mother may die no matter what we do. Let's at least give the baby a chance."

"We can't sacrifice one for the other. And we can't be sure they both won't die in surgery."

"They both could die if we do nothing," Dr. Davies said. "It would be a lot easier for the hospital to explain that we lost them in surgery than if they both died while we sat here twiddling our thumbs."

The white-haired, overweight Chief of Staff rubbed his jowls, deep in thought. He nodded his head and said, "All right, do what you've got to do. But if anything goes wrong the blame will fall squarely on your shoulders."

"I can live with that!" Davies shouted over his shoulder as he dashed off to the operating room.

Jefferson County Jail
10:45 P.M.

Demus led Danial Solomon down the dimly lit corridor. The multiple layers of paint chipped off the walls, and a thick, musty smell of rotting timbers lingered in the air. The hallway led to a dead end with two doors on either side of the hall. Demus picked up the phone outside the door on the right and said, "Access Interview Room 1." The latch buzzed and the door swung open.

Dingy blue paint covered the walls, floor and ceiling of the claustrophobic cube. A single light bulb hung from a wire over a small square table. Sergeant Gates stood behind the suspect who sat slumped over the table with his face buried in his folded arms. He looked up when the two men entered the cramped room, his face swollen and a generous stream of blood running from the corner of his mouth.

The suspect flinched as Demus reached near to gather up the paperwork.

"What happened to him?" Danial asked, his anger beginning to burn.

"Our friend here suffers from self-defense injuries inflicted by the victim," Demus said with a smirk on his face. "Looks like she did pretty good for herself, huh?"

Demus flashed a knowing smile over at Gates. Danial snatched Demus by the wrist and glared at the detective's bleeding knuckles.

"What happened here?" Danial asked through barely parted lips. I suppose you cut yourself shaving."

"How'd you guess?"

The two men locked eyes. Demus tugged his arm free. Danial took a step forward and stood nose-to-nose with the man. "If my client said so much as a mumbling word, I'll get the statement thrown out, and I'll have your badge."

"Relax, counselor. We couldn't even get his name out of him."

Demus and Gates stormed out, and Danial sat down alone with the disheveled young man. Danial took a good look at him. He could not be more than 30 years old, probably 6 feet 4 inches or so, maybe 275 pounds.

Danial opened his briefcase and took out a legal pad.

"I guess we'll start from the beginning. In order for me to represent you, I'll need to have your consent. Do you want me to be your attorney?"

No answer.

"If you don't want me to be your attorney, speak now or forever hold your peace."

No answer.

"Well, I'm going to take your silence for consent."

Danial stood to get a closer look at the scar running down his forehead and cutting through his eyebrow. *Looks like a gruesome injury. Andy was right; his head is definitely lopsided.*

"What's your name?"

Still no answer.

MICHAELSWIGER

"No matter. After they plaster your face across every TV station in the area, there will be hundreds of people eager to tell your whole life story."

University Hospital
10:50 P.M.

"We're losing her!" shouted the nurse as the gurney burst through the operating room doors.

"We're not losing anyone!" Dr. Davies shouted as he ran to meet the frantic group. "Get her on the table! Stat!"

Immediately four pairs of hands grabbed the battered, comatose woman and flopped her onto the operating table. The trauma unit scurried out of the way as the awaiting surgery team dashed into action.

A blur of hands sliced away Dorothy's nightgown, strapped down her arms and legs, and scrubbed her bulbous midsection. A ring of purplish discoloration encircled the base of her protruding abdomen.

"She's slipping, doctor. Her pulse is 54 and dropping. Pressure is fading too."

"Damn!" Davies cursed. "It's now or never. Scalpel."

Davies precisely traced the instrument a few inches below Dorothy's belly button.

"Retractors. Get me some suction over here," Davies said. "Dr. Hayes, clamp here and here."

Hayes clamped open the incision.

"How's she doing?" Davies asked.

"She's fading. Pulse is down to 48."

"She'll make it. Man, there's a lot more blood in here than there should be. More suction here... no... here by my little finger."

Davies reached in through the incision and lifted out the limp body of the premature baby girl, her left eye black and blue and swollen shut, her tiny body riddled with

282

bruises.

"Oh my God!" shouted one of the nurses when she got a glimpse of the child.

Davies cleared the baby's airway, his hands moving with intricate precision. He pressed his ear against the baby's chest.

"She's not breathing! No pulse!"

The surgical team divided its attention. Dr. Hayes took half the team and attended to the mother, while Davies and the rest of the team frantically tried to revive the baby.

Don't Miss These Best Sellers By

MICHAEL SWIGER

A LEGAL THRILLER

LETHAL AMBITION

MICHAEL SWIGER

Romance. Revenge. Redemption.

A crusading congressional candidate, Marcus Blanchard, is framed for an election-night murder. Three powerful foes - his entrenched opponent, a drug lord, and a racist political boss – all want him dead. Accused of killing the woman ordered to kill him, Marcus turns to the only man he can trust.

Distinguished Law professor Edward Mead, 77, still brilliant but struggling with the challenges of age, reluctantly takes the sensational case. Clinging to the twilight of a long, illustrious career, while nursing his wife of 52 years through Stage 4 breast cancer, Mead is thrust headlong into the gritty underbelly of the inner city. He collides with drug dealers, thugs, race riots, and an all-pervasive political corruption that enslaves its citizens in poverty while sowing the seeds of division and hatred.

Ripped from today's headlines, this fast-paced murder mystery wrapped in a legal thriller grapples with the complicated urban issues and unrest in African American communities across the country. This book will leave you exhilarated and entertained, breathless and shaken, but most of all it will make you think.

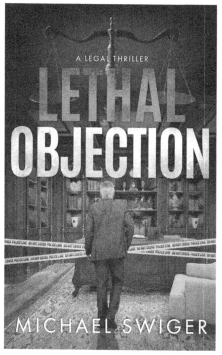

A sensational trial. Dark motives. Deadly secrets.

Arrogant and abusive Judge Samuel Chesterfield is brutally murdered in his chambers during a sensational wrongful death trial against a prominent abortionist. Only the four trial lawyers had access and motive.

Edward Mead, a 77-year-old distinguished law professor, acts as special prosecutor. Still brilliant but struggling with the ravages of age and the recent death of his beloved wife, Mead is thrust headlong into a lethal maelstrom of crime and corruption that threatens to submerge his mind and body, with the slightest misstep costing his life.

Special Agent Sarah Riehl sees the case as her one chance to shatter the glass ceiling that has suffocated her career at the FBI. Her impetuous drive to succeed recklessly propels her on a deadly gambit where the hunter becomes the prey.

This fast-paced legal thriller ripped from today's headlines combines the action and suspense of John Grisham with the classic twists and turns of an Agatha Christie locked room murder mystery, leaving the reader breathlessly guessing until the final page.

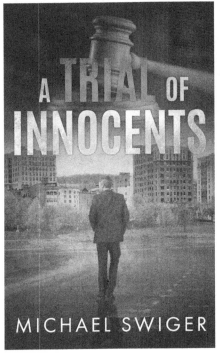

A pregnant woman is savagely beaten, leaving her unborn baby dead, and the would-be mother clinging to life in a coma. A special-needs man, who can't or won't talk, is arrested. The sensational crime draws all national media to a quiet Ohio Valley community crying for vengeance.

Prosecuting Attorney Ms. Lori Franks, beautiful and ruthless, will stop at nothing to advance her career. Having sought an abortion years before, she now seeks the death penalty against a handicapped man accused of killing an unborn baby. When a chance meeting followed by a DNA test confirms her baby was switched at birth, she sues to gain custody of the little girl she once tried to kill.

Defense Attorney Danial Solomon is drawn into both cases. Sparks and attraction fly as he and Franks clash both inside and outside of the courtroom. Solomon's crusade for the truth catapults him headlong into a lethal labyrinth of conspiracy and corruption that may cost him his life.

This fast-paced, faith-based legal thriller races from the life-and-death decisions of the operating room to the tension-packed fireworks of a murder trial with the unique mix of legal intrigue and page-turning suspense that catapulted John Grisham to the Bestseller list.

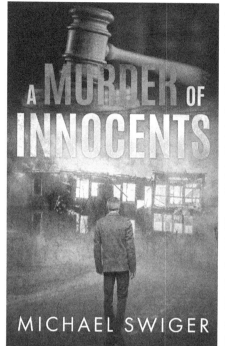

A deadly terrorist explosion rocks a peaceful Ohio Valley community and triggers a massive, relentless nationwide manhunt. A teenage girl is accused of concealing her pregnancy then killing her newborn baby. A ruthless political operative will stop at nothing in his quest for power.

Defense Attorney Danial Solomon must unravel these divergent strands - snatched from today's headlines - before it costs him his life. With one client dead and another client's life hanging in the balance, Solomon's blossoming romance with Lori Franks swirls into a lethal vortex of crime, conspiracy and corruption.

In this masterful sequel to *A Trial of Innocents*, Michael Swiger once again entwines the reader in a tense, twisty legal thriller. It is a penetrating, fast-paced, faith-filled journey until the final page. Swiger proves once again that no reader can outguess a master storyteller.

ACKNOWLEDGEMENT

A special thanks:

... to Dr. James Dobson, whose 20 years of influence on my life has profoundly impacted the contents of these pages;

... to Edward DiGiannantonio, Esquire, for vetting the courtroom scenes;

... to Ann Collett at the Helen Rees Literary Agency, whose thoughtful suggestions have vastly improved this book;

... to my editor, proofreader and copy editor, Mike Jackoboice, whose penetrating insights and impeccable sensibilities have smoothed off some of the rougher edges of my prose, and whose tireless efforts, keen eye, and quest for perfection have resulted in a book that I am very proud of;

... to my wife, Susan, whose collaboration is indispensable to everything I write; and

... to my Lord and Savior Jesus Christ, in whom I live and move and have my being.

Made in the USA
Las Vegas, NV
27 October 2024

10540312R00164